# THE KNIGHT'S TALE

*Also by M.J. Trow*

*The Kit Marlowe series*

DARK ENTRY *
SILENT COURT *
WITCH HAMMER *
SCORPIONS' NEST *
CRIMSON ROSE *
TRAITOR'S STORM *
SECRET WORLD *
ELEVENTH HOUR *
QUEEN'S PROGRESS *
BLACK DEATH *
THE RECKONING *

*The Grand & Batchelor series*

THE BLUE AND THE GREY *
THE CIRCLE *
THE ANGEL *
THE ISLAND *
THE RING *
THE BLACK HILLS *
LAST NOCTURNE *

*The Peter Maxwell series*

MAXWELL'S CROSSING
MAXWELL'S RETURN
MAXWELL'S ACADEMY
MAXWELL'S SUMMER

* *available from Severn House*

# THE KNIGHT'S TALE

M.J. Trow

SEVERN
HOUSE

First world edition published in Great Britain and the USA in 2021
by Severn House, an imprint of Canongate Books Ltd,
14 High Street, Edinburgh EH1 1TE.

Trade paperback edition first published in Great Britain and the USA in 2022
by Severn House, an imprint of Canongate Books Ltd.

severnhouse.com

*British Library Cataloguing-in-Publication Data*
A CIP catalogue record for this title is available from the British Library.

ISBN-13: 978-1-78029-135-2 (cased)
ISBN-13: 978-1-78029-801-6 (trade paper)
ISBN-13: 978-1-4483-0540-7 (e-book)

*All Severn House titles are printed on acid-free paper.*

Typeset by Palimpsest Book Production Ltd.,
Falkirk, Stirlingshire, Scotland.
Printed and bound in Great Britain by
TJ Books, Padstow, Cornwall.

# ONE

He crawled along the alleyway, dragging his useless legs, forcing himself over the cobblestones, inch by painful inch. His lungs burned in his chest and his mouth was bricky dry. All around him was darkness and the evil smells of the gutter. All around him was death. Somebody else's, his own. It hardly mattered now. Ahead he could make out a light, dim, wobbling like a candle in a chantry for the dead; like the light at the edge of the world.

He could hear his own breath like a rasp on iron, like a rusty saw on tough timber. His eyes were streaming, so was his nose, and warm drool hung from his chin in gleaming ribbons. The shivering, the aches, the tender skin, all that was past now, along with the sneezing. Now the pain under his arms and between his legs was like nothing he had felt before. His skin was black, the buboes weeping pus. Ahead of him he was aware of others, like himself; some staggering on swollen feet; some on all fours. Some had stopped, dead in their tracks, the air gone from their lungs, the life drifted from their bodies, just too exhausted to fall down. All of them were making for that light at the end of the alleyway, for that last glimmer of hope.

Then he heard the sad clanging of the bell, tolling for the end of days.

And the light went out.

He sat bolt upright in bed, sweat trickling down his temples into the already greying beard. He blinked away the darkness and the crawling monsters numb with pain. He breathed in, forcing the clean air of the pre-dawn and the new season into his lungs. The creatures of the night had gone and only the solemn bell remained. That was the voice of Old Purgatory, the oldest bell of the Holy Trinity, louder, more commanding than the others. But the others weren't far behind. St Mary and St Francis clanged from beyond the wall, in the godless encampments east of Houndsditch. His own parish of St Katherine Creechurch was next; higher, newer, a peal of friends. St Olave by the Tower cut them up and, to add to the cacophony, the bells of St Peter in the Bailey echoed around the castle walls and drifted south-east along the river.

He kicked off the coverlet and forced himself upright. The memory of his dream had stiffened his limbs and dried his mouth; he stretched his arms and smacked his lips, coming to himself in his tiny room high above the street. He extended his back until he felt it crack and then collapsed in on himself, muscles loose, joints relaxed and waited a moment for his blood to stop pounding in his ears. Then, ready, he crossed the room in three long strides and wrestled with the window catch. Ahead of him, the Essex marshes wobbled in the early morning light through the thick, cheap glass. He threw the window wide and breathed in again. It was April, promising sweet showers and Zephyr, the west wind, was bringing the countryside to his nostrils, high in his eyrie over Aldgate. He put his hand on the wall as he leaned out of the window and knew that spring was come at last – all winter he had felt the clammy sweat of the stone and had sworn, as he had sworn for six winters already, that he would move out of this place as soon as he had the time to arrange an alternative. Then, spring had come, and he fell in love with his little stone-lined nest all over again. He checked the calendar pinned to the crossbeam, carefully positioned so that it didn't poke him in the eye as he passed. Others were not so lucky, but frequent visitors soon learned to duck. He ran his finger along the line; yes, he was right. The Ram had already run half his course. This was the day.

There was a commotion in the street below and he looked down. They were already there, as usual, the carts and wagons bringing food to the city. Draymen in their rough fustian, drovers from the shires with their flocks bound for slaughter at Smithfield, chickens squawking and flapping as though they couldn't wait to feel the poulterers' cleavers on their necks.

The officer of the Watch craned his head up at him, the toothy grin unmistakeable under the kettle-hat.

'Lauds, Master Chaucer,' he called by way of explanation of the cacophony of bells. Every spire in the city, all one hundred and sixteen of them, was calling to each other now, reminding the world, with its thirty-five thousand inhabitants, that the sun was due soon and a brave new world beckoned.

'Yes, thank you, Ludlum,' Chaucer waved to the man. 'I *am* aware.'

And suddenly, Chaucer was aware of something else. Beyond the melee of wagons waiting for entry through the Aldgate, a solitary horseman waited patiently. There were other riders, too, messengers in the king's livery, fluttering with the royal harts, huntsmen in their Lincoln green, the odd abbot on an ambling pad. But this particular horseman was different. The light was still poor and Chaucer had had one of those nights again, when the terrors of his childhood came to haunt him and the victims of the Pestilence crawled to drag him down with them to Hell. He rubbed his eyes. No, he was right. The bay was flecked with foam as though its rider had ridden through the night. His cloak was muddy. So were his boots. Chaucer had not seen this man for nearly twenty years, yet here he was, awaiting entry to the greatest city in the world and about to ride under Chaucer's own home above the gate.

'Ludlum!' Chaucer called to the Watchman. 'The knight on the bay.' He was pointing vaguely into the crowd. 'The bear rampant. Look, there on his jupon.'

Ludlum's view was very different from Chaucer's. He was thirty feet below and he couldn't see any bears at all, rampant or otherwise.

'On the bay, man.' Chaucer sensed Ludlum's confusion. 'Cloak, jupon, all a bit . . . well, a bit besmottered, if I'm honest. It's Richard Glanville, an old friend of mine. Never mind the others. Let him through.

''Ere,' a particularly sharp-eared shepherd had caught the conversation and wasn't having any of it. 'There's a queue down 'ere, mate. That's your French for a line. I'm at the front of it and whoever you're talking about is halfway back, so you can stuff it, all right?'

Ludlum's face darkened under his kettle-hat. He gripped

his quarterstaff in both hands and jammed it hard against the shepherd's chest, forcing him backwards.

'You!' he snapped, looking down at the man from his imposing height. 'Do you know who you're talking to?'

Clearly the shepherd didn't.

'That's Master Geoffrey Chaucer, Comptroller of His Grace's Woollens and poet to the court of the late king. And probably the present one. He's the man who pays your wages in a roundabout sort of way. Now, you will, first and foremost, shut your mouth. Second, you will stand aside and let Master Chaucer's friend pass. Otherwise you'll still be standing there when I lock this bloody gate at the curfew bell tonight. Do we understand each other, thick knarre?'

The shepherd blinked and swallowed hard. The officer of the Watch was not much smaller than the mighty stone towers he guarded. *And* he was bristling with weapons. *And* he had four or five armed men at his back. The shepherd decided in that instant that discretion was the better part of valour and Ludlum marched past him, kicking his sheep in all directions.

Even with the officer of the Watch to expedite things, Chaucer knew that it would be a while before his old friend could get through the Aldgate and find someone to hold his horse – someone who wouldn't have sold it on within the first ten minutes – so he had ample time to prepare. There was a sharp rap at his door and Chaucer opened it. The bells had slowed down now, so that only in distant St Dunstan's in the West was some hapless minion still shredding his hands on the bell ropes.

'Today's the day, Master Chaucer.' A beaming face looked up at him.

'Come in, Alice,' he said, 'although there may have to be a change of plan.'

'Oh?' Alice swept past him, carrying bundles of clothes. 'How do you mean?'

'Well, I saw an old friend of mine in the crowds a moment ago, you know, waiting for the gate to open. Ludlum's expediting things.'

Alice had no idea what that was, but nothing would surprise her about Ludlum.

'I don't suppose for a moment that he's come to see me; he's probably here on some official business. But I can't miss the opportunity.'

'No, sir, of course not.' Alice was busy arranging things on Chaucer's bed. He was still in his voluminous nightshirt, but Alice had been doing for Master Chaucer for six years now and she felt comfortable around him. A proper gentleman was Master Chaucer, not one to take liberties unless such liberties were made available on a wooden plate. 'Now,' she said, standing back with some pride at the array before her. 'The houppelande,' she spread her arms across the three robes that lay there, 'I thought the lime green, you know, spring, little birds singing all night, their little tongues bright with happiness, that sort of thing. I thought that fabric would be lovely. I had to darn it under the armpit there, but you'd never know . . .'

'Yes, indeed, Alice, but—'

'Right, so the lime green it is. Now, the liripipe.' She held up her choice of hats with their sweeping, scalloped tails. 'The dark green complements the lime, of course, though people might mistake you for a walking forest.' She narrowed her eyes at Chaucer, imagining him dressed in his best. 'If you have half an hour, I could run home and get some fur I had set aside. I could trim it a bit, break up the line. Or how about the black?'

'Not too sombre, Alice?' Chaucer wondered aloud.

She held up both hats, one on each side of his face. 'I think you could take the black,' she said. 'Gives you a certain . . .'

'Gravitas?' Chaucer suggested.

She hit him gently with the green liripipe. 'Oh, you scholars,' she said. 'I love it that a man I work for speaks Latin.'

Chaucer smiled.

'Here's your purse.' Alice had laid that out too. 'You're taking the poignard, I s'pose?'

Chaucer looked at the dagger in its silver sheath. 'I wish I didn't need to, Alice,' he said, 'but these are dangerous times. And you can't be too careful in Kent.'

'Doggett has saddled your mare, Master Chaucer,' Alice said, always proud of her husband's harnessing skills, 'and he's done something or other with the bit, too. Apparently, she won't pull so much to the left now.'

Chaucer was glad to hear it. 'That's lovely, Alice,' he said, 'and be sure to thank Doggett for me. But . . .'

There was another rap at the door.

Alice tutted. 'It's like Westcheap and Poultry around 'ere this morning,' she said and swung the door open. Faced with heraldry like the visitor wore, Alice immediately knew her place and curtseyed. It would never have passed muster at the royal court, but in Chaucer's cramped quarters over the Aldgate, it served its purpose.

A tired-looking rider stood there, his cloak thrown back to reveal a stained fustian jupon with a double-stitched bear rampant embroidered on the chest. His gilt-chased belt glinted in the morning sun and his sword-hilt lay awkwardly under his cloak, bunching up the fabric.

'Master Geoffrey Chaucer?' His voice sounded as tired as he looked.

'Who should I say is calling, sir?' Alice was putting on her best Stratford-at-Bowe voice.

'For God's sake, Alice,' Chaucer said, 'I'm standing right here. Master Hugh,' he half bowed.

'Master Hugh!' The visitor's face softened into a smile, the teeth regular and even under the feathery moustache. 'That's plain Hughie to you, Geoffrey. It always will be.'

The two men hugged each other, the squire in his armour, the Comptroller of Woollens in his nightshirt, the years between them falling away.

'I took you for your old father, down there in the crowd. How is the old bastard?' A fear clutched Chaucer's heart and a goose walked over his grave. Surely, a ride such as Hugh had undertaken could only mean bad news. He tried to keep his voice level and not meet trouble halfway. 'When I saw you last, Hughie, dear boy, you were struggling with that quintain at Clare.'

The squire laughed. 'I know,' he said. 'I've still got the scars.'

The quintain was an unforgiving nurse. Little boys of ten would ride at full tilt and strike the hanging shield with their lances. That, in turn, would swing the pivot and the morning star, six pounds of murderous, dangling iron, would whizz through the air and crunch into their backs. What happened next was God's will. But it made men of boys and it was the way Hugh Glanville's world turned, if turn it did, on the backs of elephants riding the Great Turtle through God's universe.

'Where are my manners?' Chaucer threw a pile of parchment scrolls off a chair and let the squire sit down. 'I don't usually eat this early, but I've got some . . . Alice, be a dear and get . . .'

'No, no,' the squire held up his hand. 'Nothing for me.'

'Wine, then? Alice . . .'

'I won't turn that down,' Glanville said.

'Alice. Two bottles of Lepe. Tell Winter to put it on my slate.'

Alice sighed. It was what she had always suspected – Master Chaucer had no idea of the size of his slate and Winter was staring penury in the face. She made for the door at about the same time that Chaucer caught the look of horror and disbelief on Glanville's face.

'Wait a minute, Alice. On second thoughts, something from Gascony . . . er . . . just the one bottle, though.'

Comptroller of the King's Woollens Chaucer may have been, but he wasn't made of money. Alice curtseyed and left.

'She does for me,' Chaucer told the squire, suddenly aware of an unspoken question hovering near the lad's lips.

'I'm sure she does,' Glanville said. 'And how's Philippa?'

'She's fine,' Chaucer said, perhaps a shade too quickly. 'We write regularly.'

'Still in Lincolnshire?'

'Oh, yes,' Chaucer told him. 'Very flat, Lincolnshire, at this time of year. You've ridden straight from Clare, have you?'

'More or less,' the squire sighed and when Chaucer looked more closely, he did seem tired – he had dark shadows under his eyes and there were furrows in his face which didn't belong in a man his age. 'I set off in the early afternoon, oh . . .' he pressed his fingers to his temples as he tried to recall – 'three days ago.' He looked up and it was hard to tell if he was surprised at how quickly the time had gone or how slowly. 'It's good to see you, of course, but . . . well, I came for a reason, a sad one, I'm afraid.'

'Oh?' The goose stepped out again. 'Not your pa?' Chaucer feared the worst.

'The Duke of Clarence.'

'Lionel?'

'Dead.'

'No!' Chaucer crossed himself, muttering a prayer under his breath. The squire did likewise.

'Ague?' Chaucer asked. 'Styche? Ipydyne?' His eyes widened as he remembered his nightmares with a jolt. 'Mother of God, not the Pestilence?' And he crossed himself again, just to be sure.

'No.' The squire didn't sound too sure, even to his own ears. 'No, none of those. Father found him,' he said. 'Dead, in his bed.'

A smile crept unbidden to Chaucer's lips. 'That must have surprised him, Lionel, I mean, as well as presumably your poor father. What with the wars, I expect he expected to meet his end in some muddy French field somewhere.'

'That's more or less what Pa said,' Glanville nodded.

'How's he taking it?' Chaucer asked.

'Well, His Grace was no spring chicken, of course, so, in a way . . .'

'And Violante? How is the duchess?'

Glanville rolled his eyes. 'You know these Italians, Geoff,' he said.

Actually, Chaucer didn't. He kept away from the Italian merchants in the City and the only Italian book he'd ever read was by Dante Alighieri and it had left him rather cold. He shrugged.

'Screams,' Glanville explained. 'Tears. She's a rich woman now, of course.'

'I'm sure she'd rather not be.' Chaucer was always circumspect when it came to the fair sex. And nobility. He'd learned to be wary of both.

'Quite. Anyway, there it is. Pa thinks there's something odd about Lionel's passing. All right, he was nearly seven feet tall, son of a king, brother of the Black Prince' – they both crossed themselves – 'a man of many parts, but a man for all that. I can't give you any more details. All this happened three days ago, we assume in the night sometime. Pa found him early in the morning. His bedroom door was locked as usual, so he had to break in. And there he was, sprawled on the bed, the blankets all thrown back, as if he had been about to get up. Poor old Pa was quite shaken; it was a horrible thing for him, the dog howling, Violante screaming, the maidservants having hysterics. As soon as we got everyone in some sort of semblance of calm, Pa sent me south, for you. As I left, Clement was giving the old boy the last rites, though it seemed a bit late for that.'

'Clement?'

'Lionel's new chaplain. I don't much like him, I must admit, but there it is. Something of the Lollard in him.'

Chaucer tutted and shook his head. Then he crossed himself, just in case.

Glanville took in the array of clothes on the comptroller's bed. 'But, look, I've caught you at a bad time. You're clearly on your way somewhere.'

'Er . . . just my pilgrimage. I go every year if I can, looking for the Holy Blissful Martyr, you know.'

'Becket.' Glanville knew. 'Talking, as we almost were, about dodgy churchmen.'

'Ah,' Chaucer smiled. 'The youth of today. So cynical. No, it's not so much the religious bit, important though that is, of course. It's the company. All day, every day, I deal with merchants and toadies. City men who worship the groat and the angel. On pilgrimage, you get to meet really interesting people. Like . . . um, I don't know, shipmen and pardoners and . . . and . . . people from Bath.'

'Gripping,' said Glanville.

'However,' Chaucer snapped back from the image of the winding Pilgrims' Way that had formed in his head, 'that's off now. From what you tell me – and the speed of your arrival – your dear old pa needs my help.'

Glanville was suddenly serious. 'He does, Geoffrey,' he said. 'Will you come back with me?'

'Of course. And, in many ways, it's helped me out of a dilemma. I couldn't decide which houppelande to wear. Now, it's got to be funeral black.'

The squire smiled. Just as well, he thought to himself; he wouldn't be seen dead riding alongside Chaucer in that lime-green thing.

Geoffrey Chaucer had always liked to think of himself as rather cosmopolitan. He had travelled more than any other man he knew and he sometimes smiled to himself as he made his way through the jostling crowds of the city that he had been further than anyone else he touched. But even so, he had been looking forward to his little jaunt to Kent. Santiago de Compostela was all very fine and good, but the people there were so terribly *foreign*. And even the smallest trinket to take home to show the less well travelled cost a small fortune – a cockle shell cost as much as a silver ring at home and, oddly, wives seemed to prefer the latter. He had often discussed his pilgrimages with his old friend Nicholas Brembre, a City man who, if Chaucer were to be brutally honest, took a bit of watching. He had already been Lord Mayor of London and it was through him and the great John of Gaunt that Chaucer had his lodgings, like hens' teeth after the Pestilence. It was rumoured that Brembre had lent the king money. At the thought of him, a bright idea suddenly came to the comptroller and he did a sharp left turn down an alleyway, upending a woman with two baskets on a yoke as he did so.

When he was shown into Brembre's counting house, his cheeks were still red with embarrassment. Brembre jumped up and showed his friend and sometime adversary to a seat. He looked as if he might be on the verge of an apoplexy at the very least. 'Geoffrey, you are unwell. Sit down and let me have someone bring you a drink. Some water, perhaps. I'll send my man.'

Brembre was not known for his generosity, but with the water in London being the way it was, Chaucer was surprised to find he was also intent on killing his friends. Brembre saw his expression.

'Freshly drawn from my private well only this morning. I drink it all the time and look at me; fit as a flea.'

Chaucer did look at the man and he did seem to be in the peak of health. Which would make his next few remarks if anything, a touch insincere, but he would have to try his best. 'I am perfectly well, Nicholas, thank you for your concern. I merely had an altercation with a market woman and her language would make a sailor blush, let alone a humble Comptroller of the King's Woollens. But you' – he gazed at the wool merchant with a furrow in his brow – 'are *you* well? You look a little peaky.'

As blatant lies went, he had told worse, but the merchant looked sceptical and didn't even glance at the polished mirror to his left. 'I am feeling well, Geoffrey, as a matter of fact. I eat well – as you know – sleep well; in fact, I feel very full of the joys of spring. Business, I don't need to tell you, is also booming.'

Pies and fingers leapt into Chaucer's mind unbidden. He thought he would try once more. 'A holiday would do you good, Nicholas.'

Brembre looked at Chaucer from under his suddenly beetling brows. 'Geoffrey, you are trying to sell me something. I know that look.'

Chaucer spread his hand on his chest and arranged his features in an expression of distressed innocence. 'Sell? Me? What a suggestion!'

Brembre laughed and got up, walking over to the door to open it. A cat, huge and brindled, walked in and jumped up onto the desk, sprawling out to be stroked. Although it looked as though it could bring down a deer single-handed, Brembre proceeded to tickle it under the chin, crooning endearments. There was a solid gold ball dangling from its collar. Eventually, he looked up. 'Yes. Sell. You. I prefer straight talking, Geoffrey, so please, give it to me in simple language.'

Chaucer took a deep breath. 'I find myself . . . unable to go on my yearly pilgrimage due to the . . . illness of an old, dear friend. So I wondered if you would like to go in my stead.'

Brembre thought for a moment, then smiled. 'What are we talking about? Compostela? Rome? God, not *Jerusalem*?'

'Canterbury.'

'Ah. Well, that sounds like something I would consider, Geoffrey. I am assuming there would be a substantial discount?'

'A discount, certainly,' Chaucer replied. 'As to substantial . . . I am not a rich man, Nicholas.'

'We'll talk about that. Now, Canterbury; your usual, in fact.'

'Yes. A lovely journey. Very restful. Very picturesque. Lovely at this time of year.'

Brembre shook his head. 'You don't get out enough, Geoffrey,' he said. 'When does it leave?'

Chaucer glanced out of the window, judging the sun. 'In a couple of hours,' he said, his smile becoming a little anxious.

Brembre crooned a little more to the giant killing machine laid across his papers. 'Oh, I am sorry,' he said to the crest-fallen comptroller. 'That is far too short notice. I am not my own man, you see – for I must consider my cat, Geoffrey.' The animal looked at Chaucer and almost seemed to grin.

'If I said I would look after it?' Chaucer suggested, but he knew the day was lost. With a sigh, he took his leave of Brembre and his obvious familiar – he would save that thought for if he ever needed any leverage against the man – and pressed on to face Harry Bailly, for what *that* was worth.

As he walked across the bridge, he rehearsed through the conversation he would have with the landlord of the Tabard Inn and organizer extraordinaire when it came to pilgrimages short or long. It went surprisingly well, and so the Comptroller of Woollens was smiling as he turned into the stable yard, which was loud with stamping hooves and the cries of grooms, and pungent with that exciting smell compounded of leather harness, warm flanks and horse shit.

'Master Chaucer!' Harry Bailly hated it when his pilgrims turned up early. He hated it, he would have to admit if asked, even more than when they turned up late. Late and they could always catch them up on the road; anywhere the London side of Shooter's Hill would do. Early and they would see all the little shortcuts that made the whole enterprise financially viable; the old nags made to look young again with a spot of soot smeared on the grey hairs in their manes; the wine being watered down or worse before being distributed into the leather bottles; the old bread made passable by a quick soak under the pump. 'Master Chaucer! You're a touch early, if you don't mind my pointing it out?'

The grooms froze. When Master Bailly was this polite, someone was going to get their ears boxed or they were going to lose a lot of money. Once or twice, it had memorably been both.

'I'm sorry, Harry.' Chaucer neatly sidestepped a prancing horse and joined the man on the threshold of his inn. 'I'm afraid I have some bad news. I will not be able to come with you today.'

Bailly's eyes narrowed, but he wasn't dismayed. The pace of the pilgrimage was slow enough that even several days in, a fastish rider could easily catch them up. 'Tomorrow, then,' he said. 'I'll give you a note for . . .'

'No, Harry,' Chaucer clapped him on the shoulder in a comradely fashion. 'I won't be able to come with you at all, in actual fact.'

'Ah.' This was different. This was money. 'I can't fill your place at this short notice, Master Chaucer,' Bailly said, a basilisk smile creeping over his usually amiable features.

'Goodness me, no,' Chaucer cried. 'I hadn't expected you to.' Something deep inside wanted to remark that filling Geoffrey Chaucer's shoes was almost impossible under normal circumstances, the best soft moss apart, but there was something about Bailly's bearing that warned him it would be unwise to employ too much levity.

Bailly's smile became more friendly. 'Oh, well, I am pleased, Master Chaucer,' he said. 'Some people who cancel this late expect to get their money back. Ha. Ha.' The laugh, if laugh it was, had no humour in it.

Chaucer's face fell. He had, indeed, expected his money back. After all, if he didn't *go* on the pilgrimage, how could Bailly reasonably take his money? He would be wearing out no horse, sleeping in no bed, eating no food, drinking no second-rate ale. Not even having to negotiate the extortionate fees of the hermit of Blean. 'But . . .'

'Come now, Master Chaucer,' Bailly said, stepping forward into the stable yard and leading the hapless comptroller. 'Surely you must realize, as a man of business yourself, that certain disbursements have already been made.'

Chaucer tried to look like a man of business but in truth he had people for that. He cocked an eyebrow at Harry Bailly and waited for him to explain.

'I have hired the horses already, as you see. I can't get my money back there. And then there are the beds on the way. The inns won't be able to fill those at such short notice, so I will have to pay for those.'

Chaucer nodded slowly. 'But I won't be eating the food . . .'

'That's *very* true, Master Chaucer,' Bailly said, nodding. 'But I fear that the unscrupulous innkeepers on the way will not give an inch in respect of that. They claim that they fill their pantries and their cellars especially for my pilgrims and, although *I* know and *you* know that that is nonsense, well, you know what a tight-arse that bloke who runs the Chequers of Hope is.' He spread his arms in helplessness. 'I'm afraid my hands are tied on that one.'

The grooms looked at each other and smiled. They had rarely seen it better done and they had seen just this scene a lot.

Chaucer looked at the ground and then the patch of sky above the stable yard, hoping for inspiration, but God had chosen this moment to be about His business elsewhere. 'Money for the priests?' he ventured. 'At the cathedral end, I mean.'

'Job lot,' Bailly said, as quick as a viper. 'Wouldn't matter if only one pilgrim turned up, costs the same.' He looked rueful. 'It's the incense, apparently. Same amount for any number of people. Then there's the tolling. And the wages of the woman what scrubs the stones – can't have you getting grubby knees, now, can we?' He shrugged and smiled. He had won and he knew it.

Chaucer put his hands behind his back and covertly counted on his fingers. 'So, you would be able to give me a refund of . . .?'

'Precisely nothing,' Bailly said. 'Wish it could be otherwise, Master Chaucer, but as I say, my hands are tied.'

Chaucer looked at the man, wishing they could be, and to

a cart's tail as they whipped the rogue around the streets of the Borough. 'If I were to book again for next year?' Chaucer was clutching at straws.

'Ah, now that would be different.' Harry Bailly was in expansive mood and the grooms held their breath. 'I could give you a discount of . . . shall we say, one thirtieth?'

'A thirtieth?' Chaucer couldn't even do the sum. Pieces of silver swirled in his brain. 'Could I have that now as a refund?' Anything would be better than nothing.

Bailly smiled and backed into the inn again, closing the door as he did so. 'Ah, that would be wonderful,' he said, 'and I wish it could be done. But prices are going up everywhere. You know how it's been since the Pestilence. Not just the labourers in short supply, you know. Come to think of it, it's high time there was a Statute of Innkeepers. By next year, the pilgrimage as you have booked it will be more expensive. But a small deposit will secure. Let me know if you want to come along and I'll put you on the list. Good day, Master Chaucer. See you in the Year of Our Lord 1381.' And the door closed in his face and the bolt was shot.

The grooms watched him trail dejectedly out of the yard. Chaucer shook his head as he made his way back to the bridge. That wasn't how it was supposed to go at all. Not at all.

# TWO

Chaucer had to admit that his old nag, the grey with the hard mouth, was not spoken of highly when men met to discuss horseflesh; innumerable times over the next three days, he found the animal trailing in the wake of the squire's spirited courser. Touch of Syrian blood, he shouldn't wonder, but then, what Geoffrey Chaucer knew about horses could be written on a pinhead.

He was wearing funereal black as he trotted out along the old Roman road to Stratford. The legions had made it to get to Camulodunum, as they called Colchester. They would have got their feet wet wading through the Lea (hardy lot, the Romans), but some queen or other, and for the life of him, Chaucer could not remember which, had had the bow bridge built in 1110 so that any future Comptroller of Woollens would not have to paddle. What he *did* have to do was rummage in his purse for the toll, the squire having no spare coinage at that moment in time. As he pointed out to Chaucer, completely unnecessarily, jupons had no plackets.

They rode on, the monks at the abbey on the Channelea toiling in the spring fields, sowing before they reaped the whirlwind. There were peasants in the manorial fields at Theydon Bois too, yoked to the oxen that swayed and bellowed in the furrows. Dogs ran at their heels, snapping and yelping, and little children fell over each other, throwing up showers of the warm, dark earth. The poet in Geoffrey Chaucer could not help being moved by it, but he was moved rather more by the huge shadows in Epping Forest, as night fell on their first day.

The pair gave thanks at the little wayside chantry of John the Baptist, then collapsed gratefully into the hard testers of the Three Tuns. It had been a while since Chaucer had been in the saddle for this long and his arse let him know it; so did his thighs. His feet he couldn't feel and, as soon as decency served, he bade his young friend goodnight and retired to bed, peeling off the hose and storing the moss carefully – it would do for another day. Supper did not impress. It was Lent, of course, so meat was out of the question; even eggs were off. The barley bread had seen better days, but the ale was surprisingly acceptable.

There had been little chance during the ride for Chaucer to find out more about the Duke of Clarence's death. The boy was full of tales of his own father, however, the knight who had fought with His Grace in France all those years ago. Hugh's eyes positively sparkled when he spoke of the man's exploits in Prussia and Latvia, where men had faces in the middle of their chests and women peed standing up. Against that, the mere death of a son of the king of England paled into insignificance.

They were up before the sun, Chaucer reliving the agony of the day before as soon as he mounted his nag, as blister met saddle like the old friends they were becoming. They trotted ever north-east through the beeches and the oaks that crowded the rutted road like gathering demons, bright with green shoots though they were.

'You know this place is a thieves' kitchen, Geoffrey, don't you?' Hugh asked, remembering to rein in his bay so that the comptroller could keep up.

'It is?' Chaucer hadn't heard that, but then, he didn't get out of London much, apart from the pilgrimages, so it was hardly surprising.

'Robber gangs here in the old king's day,' the squire nodded. 'Merchants, priests; nobody was safe on the road.'

Chaucer's frozen grin said it all. He carried his poignard at his hip, as all men did in King Richard II's England, but he wouldn't say he was a dab hand with it. He glanced at Hugh's broadsword slung from his saddle. Three feet of finest Toledo steel. But how useful was the lad with that? He certainly *looked* the part, like a crusader coming home from the wars, but he was so *young*. He'd barely finished shitting yellow.

'Over there,' the squire pointed, 'is Dead Man's Bottom.'

Chaucer acted nonchalant; didn't *everywhere* have one of those?

'Two children were found there only last year,' Hugh said. 'Michaelmas time. They'd been horribly mutilated.'

Chaucer tutted and shook his head. Not for nothing did men call this the hurling time; God himself was surely out of his Heaven.

'Naturally, in other countries – Father's Prussia or Latvia for instance – everybody would assume the Jews were responsible, of course.'

'Of course,' Chaucer nodded.

'But as they're rather thin on the ground here . . . it was probably the pig.'

'A pig?'

Hugh chuckled. 'Sorry, Geoffrey,' he said. 'Not just any pig. *The* pig. A boar the size of a horse. Epping's teeming with them. Normally, of course, they're shy woodland creatures, but every now and then, one turns rogue – and then, look out.'

Chaucer's eyes swivelled wildly in all directions before focusing on the squire again.

'I know of two knarres who broke their spears trying to kill him, but he got away. So, keep alert, eh? Eyes and ears. He'll bring that horse of yours down in three shakes of a porker's tail. And once you're on foot . . . well, I don't have to paint you a picture.'

The squire did not. And Chaucer was glad he was wearing funereal black.

Great Dunmow was already looking forward to its summer fayre, when the great and good of Essex and half the thieves of London would wend their way to the bustling town, giving thanks to God and dear old Henry III who had granted the place its charter all those years ago.

Cattle filled the High Street and an entire gaggle of geese took exception to Chaucer – or perhaps the grey legs of his horse – as he rode by them. The last time he had been hissed at like that was a particularly nasty Friday in the company of a large number of Merchant Adventurers. He didn't want to go through that again.

'I'd like to be here for the flitch trials,' he called to the squire. 'Six bachelors and six maidens – could they find that many, do you think? – competing for half a pig. Nice to see these old traditions still being observed, isn't it?'

But Hugh Glanville wasn't listening. He was following an older tradition still, tilting his bascinet at a pair of ladies of the town who were lolling on a balcony near the town hall. He was not to know they were for the exclusive use of the mayor, but from the low cut of their bodices, he must have realized that they were not nuns of the Augustinian persuasion. Chaucer rolled his eyes. What was it about a certain type of woman and men in armour?

The great castle of Clare stood on its motte over the Stour. The two horsemen cantered through the orchards, the pear blossom bright in the afternoon sun. Tenants, some wearing the bull livery of the Duke of Clarence, waved at Hugh. Others looked askance at Chaucer. Even those with long enough memories would not recognize the chubby horseman with the greying hair and beard now. Could that *really* be the ruddy-cheeked lad with the auburn thatch who had once ridden at the quintain with the squire's father? Followed the dogs through the forest looking for stags? Crashing through the undergrowth with a hawk on his wrist and the bells ringing in the morning? They were different days. But they were the days of Chaucer's youth. And that, in a way, was why he had come back.

They rode under the Nethergate and the memories came flooding back. Chaucer half-expected to feel the cold water hit him on the head and shoulders from the murder-holes above as Richard Glanville ambushed him again. The pair of them had had a running joke for years – how many windows at Clare castle? As boys, they'd hung flags and kerchiefs from every lintel, arrow slit and even, dicing with death on the slippery slopes, the garderobes. They'd done this dozens of times, but they'd always been foiled. That old bastard Griswold, the duke's seneschal, had got wise to them and told the servants to take the cloths away. Surely, the old shit was dead by now? Even so, this was not the time to indulge in schoolboy pranks; the castle was in mourning.

'Welcome, Master Chaucer.' A solid-looking man in the

duke's livery was holding the grey's bridle. 'Butterfield, the duke's seneschal. I am sorry to meet you in these circumstances.'

'And I you, Master Butterfield,' the Comptroller of Woollens was glad to leave the saddle again.

'I've put you in the Auditor's Tower, sir. I hope that meets with your approval.'

Chaucer smiled. He had lost his virginity in the Auditor's Tower; he wondered briefly if little Joyce still led her ducks to water in the swannery. But then, the years had passed. Little Joyce probably wasn't so little any more; she'd probably be a grandmother with several chins and hips like a drayhorse.

'If I may pay my respects first?' Chaucer said.

'Of course. You remember your way to the chapel?'

Chaucer did but he let the seneschal take him, across the inner bailey, up the spiral staircase, worn with a thousand feet, Chaucer's among them, up to the light, airy solar where the sun burst through the oriel window and lit the warm stone with spring. Then, they turned sharp left, Chaucer remembering just in time to duck. It had been years before the bruises had healed from his boyhood collisions with the unforgiving stones here.

The chapel of St John was peace itself, exactly as Chaucer had remembered it. Well, perhaps not quite. A dead man lay on a table in the nave, the flesh equivalent of the marble effigies around him. He was covered from head to toe in a shroud, bound above the head and below the feet. Even so, there was no mistaking Lionel of Antwerp, taller than two cloth yards and broad with it.

'He is clean shriven,' a voice said at Chaucer's elbow, 'cleansed of his sins by contrition of heart and by absolution.'

Chaucer turned. The man was his height, perhaps ten years younger, with the alb and tonsure of a cleric. 'Father Clement, I assume.' Chaucer extended a hand.

'You are well informed, Master . . .'

'Chaucer,' the comptroller said. 'I was once a ward of His Grace.'

The priest took Chaucer's hand. 'I understood from Sir

Richard that you had been sent for. Though why, I cannot fathom. The wardship was a long time ago, wasn't it?' The priest looked the comptroller up and down, with a look that could etch stone. He was clearly less than impressed with what he saw.

'It was,' Chaucer conceded, 'but I owe this man my life.'

'Indeed?' Clement gave Chaucer the air of a man who wanted to know too much. But the comptroller had nothing to hide – well, not much, anyway.

'In the wars against France,' he said, as the priest relit one of the candles which had gone out, 'Richard and I were in the duke's company at Rheims. The king was there too. It was all rather awkward, but I managed to get myself captured. The duke arranged my release – paid for it himself.'

'Oh? How much?'

Chaucer's eyes narrowed. Hardly an appropriate question for a churchman to ask. But no one fazed the king's Comptroller of Woollens. 'Sixteen pounds, as it happens. How did he die?' One awkward question deserves another, Chaucer thought.

'God called him,' Clement said.

Glib bastard, Chaucer thought. 'Of course,' he nodded, 'but that doesn't give me the how and why, does it?'

'And why should you want to know that, Master Chaucer?' Clement turned to face the man.

'Because I asked him to.' Another voice made both men turn. Richard Glanville stood half in the shadows, the candlelight glowing on the gilt embroidery of his houppelande. 'Geoffrey Chaucer!' The knight crossed the chapel in three strides and clasped his arms around the man.

'Sir Richard,' Chaucer tried to bow, but it was difficult in the grip of a man who had once unhorsed the Chevalier Melanges, the biggest bastard in the French army.

'Sir Richard, my arse,' the knight laughed. 'Oh, begging your pardon, Father,' and he crossed himself. 'It's Rich, Geoff.' He took in Chaucer's expression. 'Oh, I know – the years have been less than kind. The moustache is fuller, as is the waist, but it's me, all the same.'

'It is,' Chaucer smiled, and for a while the two old friends just stood there, arms locked, grinning at each other. Then, the moment vanished, and they both remembered where they were, and why.

'What price this?' Chaucer asked. He was looking down at the shrouded man.

'We needn't keep you, Father,' Glanville said. For a moment, the priest hesitated, then he bowed curtly and left, gliding over the flagstones like a ghost. 'I don't like that man,' the knight said when he had gone.

'Your son doesn't either,' Chaucer said.

'What do you think of him, Geoff?' the knight asked.

'A fine boy,' the comptroller said. 'A man, I should say.'

Glanville slapped him on the shoulder. 'You won't say that tomorrow,' he chuckled.

'Oh? Why?'

'I sent him to you in his armour – nothing like a bit of heraldry to clear the crowds, eh? Tomorrow you'll see him in all his finery – the rings, the hair. Don't get me started on the perfumes – musk, ambergris, cardamom – I can't keep up.'

'A ladies' man, eh?' Chaucer winked.

'You could say that. Now,' he sighed, 'shall we?' He untied the shroud knot and pulled the cloth back. Chaucer was mildly astonished. The years had fallen away from Lionel of Antwerp – he looked half the age of the men still standing. His long hair was combed out over his broad shoulders and his beard was neatly trimmed. In the week since death had called him, time had taken its toll and the nose, forehead and lips were taking on the waxy sheen of death. But otherwise, in the cool of the chapel, he could still be taken as only sleeping. Glanville pulled the shroud back and the Duke of Clarence lay as naked as the day he was born.

Chaucer crossed himself. 'What am I doing here, Rich?' he asked. 'The man looks as if he'd just fallen asleep.'

The knight looked at the Comptroller of Woollens. 'You are a wise man, Geoffrey Chaucer,' he said, 'the wisest man I know. And you once said something to me that I've never forgotten.'

'Really?' Chaucer couldn't imagine what that might be.

'You said "beware the smiler with the knife".'

Chaucer chuckled. In that silent, death-canopied chamber,

it sounded stark, disrespectful and he crossed himself again. 'I was probably pissed when I said that,' he said. 'And anyway, how . . .?'

'How does it fit the passing of Lionel of Antwerp? I don't know. *That's* why you're here. This place,' he waved his hand, 'this castle of Clare is full of smilers. We just need to find the hand that held the knife – albeit a metaphorical one. Who have you met so far?'

'Apart from you and Hugh, er . . . the seneschal. What's his name? I confess I was half dreading it might still be Griswold.'

The knight laughed. 'Butterfield, you mean,' he said.

Chaucer nodded. 'And the priest, Lionel's confessor.'

'There's two to watch for a start. Smilers both, but I wouldn't turn my back on either of them. And you're right, by the way, to include me and Hugh.'

'Rich,' Chaucer was shaking his head, frowning.

'No, no, I'm serious. I was first finder – I smashed Lionel's lock and found him dead. That means men can point a finger at me. As for Hugh, he's a good boy; he'd follow his old pa through the fire and into Hellmouth. If I said, "Kill Lionel", he'd do it, no questions asked.'

Chaucer looked down at the dead man's face. 'But he looks so peaceful,' he said.

'Death does that,' Glanville nodded. 'Smooths the wrinkles. But you and I have seen death, Geoff, up close and personal. I know "unnatural causes" when I see them. So do you, or you wouldn't be here.'

Chaucer sighed. If Richard Glanville said something did not sit right, that was good enough for him.

'All right,' he said, 'Tell me everything.'

'I will, of course. But not here. It's cold, for one thing, and I don't trust that priest . . . let's get His Grace back in his shroud and we'll talk in my chambers. There'll be comfortable seats, some wine and no ears that shouldn't be there.' The knight looked round, his eyes heavy with too many sleepless nights, and with sorrow. He bunched the linen shroud together and tied it at the head. Chaucer went to the foot and tied it there. With gentle hands they smoothed the fabric down and soon Lionel of Antwerp slept again, inside his chrysalis, a butterfly who would never fly again. The two men stood for a moment with bowed heads, each alone with their thoughts. They differed in the detail, where the Devil lurks, but one thing they had in common; they would find who had killed this man to whom they both owed so much. And then, woe betide.

Chaucer sat back on a cushioned settle in Sir Richard's solar high in the Confessor's Tower and looked around. His own little garret in Aldgate would have fitted comfortably in one corner and left room to swing any number of cats, even ones as giant as Nicholas Brembre's familiar. He warmed the wine between his hands and inhaled the bouquet. Richard Glanville lived high off the hog; Chaucer hoped that it wasn't simply self-interest which had called him to Clare. What would happen to the household, now that Lionel of Antwerp was dead?

A small fire was burning in the enormous fireplace and Glanville threw on a couple of small logs, which spat and hissed as the flames took them. The knight turned to Chaucer and spoke over his shoulder, as men will when they are not sure of the response they will get.

'I suppose you're wondering whether I called you because I don't want to lose all this,' he said, and Chaucer shuddered, as if a goose had walked over his grave.

'No, no, of course not,' he said, he hoped sounding sincere. 'I know you are above such things, Rich.'

Glanville threw himself down on a couch on the opposite side of the fire and reached for his goblet from the small table between them. 'Lionel was good to me, Geoff, both in life and death. His widow will keep the castle, unless she remarries, in which case he has made other arrangements; a distant cousin, I believe. But I, whether the Lady Violante or others are mistress or master here, can keep these rooms until I die, with a modest income.'

Chaucer was surprised. That was unusually generous, he knew.

'I gave up everything for him, you see,' the knight said, simply. 'Hugh's mother lived with her parents for almost the whole of our marriage. I barely knew the woman, but even so, it would have been good to have a home instead of traipsing about this country and any other you care to name in Lionel's wake. I am blessed that Hugh has come to live with me, follow in my footsteps, you might say. It could have been so different – and Lionel knew that. He was not an ungrateful man.'

'You sound as if he may have had other failings, though.' In his work as comptroller, Chaucer had developed a keen ear for the word unsaid, which so often meant more than a dozen spoken,

'Not *failings* as such, no.' The knight sipped his wine, giving himself time to think. 'He was . . .' he looked up and smiled, the years dropping away. 'Well, you must remember. He was a bit of a one for the ladies.'

Chaucer raised an eyebrow. That was an incredibly polite way of putting it. It was a well-known fact that when Lionel of Antwerp rode to town, the womenfolk would hide. They'd hide – but then come out in twos and threes, to be snared in his net. He never had to pay for a woman and there was no coercion. His immense height, his flowing hair and roving eye did all that for him, and no one with delicate sensibilities would approach his tent when the flap was down. 'An understatement,' he chuckled. 'But not lately, surely?'

The knight laughed, silent tears pouring down his cheeks. 'Yes, lately. That's why no one thought to break the door down sooner. We all assumed he was . . . busy.' He brushed away the tears and looked solemn. 'Although Lady Violante is a hard one to love, sometimes, we did feel for her. It wasn't like Lionel to be quite so . . . shall we say, blatant. He had imported a girl from the town, young enough to be his daughter, granddaughter, even, at a pinch. And he flaunted her at feasts, took her to his bed, kissed her – and more – in full view of everyone.'

Chaucer was shocked. He knew the reputation of Lionel of Antwerp back in the day was of a louche and rapacious lover, but he had never thought him to be ungentlemanly. 'Did no one . . . remonstrate?' he asked.

'I would imagine that the Lady Violante did. In fact, no, I *know* that the Lady Violante did. We could hear her remonstrating all over the castle, often with the music of breaking glass in the background. She has always been a tricky woman to serve. Her maids come and are gone in days, often, because of her tantrums. But she isn't old. She is still beautiful. And why should Lionel take a common townswoman to his bosom when he had such beauty at home?'

'Love is a funny thing,' Chaucer remarked. There seemed little else to say.

'Talking of which,' Glanville said. 'I have been more than uncivil. How is Pippa these days? I didn't ask.'

Chaucer smiled and spread his arms, with a chuckle. 'Well, you know Pippa. Always busy. I hear regularly from her – still serving her mistress out in Lincolnshire.'

'She's still there? Well, that's wonderful. Why don't we, when all this bother is over, go and visit her? It would be . . . oh, a week, would you say? We could take it steady. Why don't we make it into a pilgrimage? The shrine of St Hugh . . .'

'Oh, I don't know,' Chaucer shook his head. 'I've already had to leave a lot of work on my table. I don't know if I can manage another month or so away. Wool doesn't comptrol itself, you know.'

'I've often wondered what it was you did,' Glanville said. 'Is the work hard?'

Chaucer let his head fall back. 'You really couldn't imagine such work,' he said. 'It's never-ending.'

'Oh dear.' Glanville was genuinely sorry. He had always rather liked Mistress Chaucer. 'Some other time, perhaps.'

'Yes,' Chaucer smiled. 'Some other time. Now, this girl from the town. Was she, in fact, with His Grace on the night he died?'

'No one knows. She wasn't there when I broke the lock, but she could have been and gone.'

'Was the key still in the lock on the inside?' Chaucer asked.

'Well, I broke the lock, Geoff.'

'All right, be pedantic if you must. Was the key somewhere inside the room?'

'Yes. It was on the floor, just over by the window.'

'So it could have flown there, when you battered the lock?'

'Easily.'

'The point I am getting to, Rich, is that if the door was locked, and the key was on the inside, then the lady in question – what is her name, by the way? – if she had been there, had gone when Lionel was still alive.'

'Blanche. Her name is Blanche Vickers. Hugh carried a bit of a torch at one time . . . but that's another story. Yes, as far as the lock is concerned, Blanche is obviously blameless. But' – Glanville looked at Chaucer with a piercing eye – 'do you believe it is possible to die of a broken heart, Geoff?'

Chaucer thought for a moment. There were currents beneath this seemingly simple death that he wasn't sure he wanted to plumb. 'I think you can, yes,' he said. 'I had my share of broken hearts when I was young and a couple of times asked death to take me, if I couldn't have the love of my life by my side. But I was young and foolish and after half a day of pining, I was myself again. The other kind of broken heart, a heart which gives up beating because it is old and tired, that kind of heartbreak can kill, and quickly, too. I've seen it at the Bourse and in other places, where tempers run high. Did Lionel show signs of that?'

'He was as strong as an ox,' Glanville said, shaking his head. 'He put most of the young men to shame. He came back from Italy a little peaky, but was soon well again, with good, hearty English food and good Suffolk air.'

'Was there any food or drink in his room?'

'Nothing.'

Chaucer leaned his chin on his chest and twirled his wine goblet between his fingers, letting the glint of the fire on the chased metal clear and calm his mind. The room was silent except for the settling logs and the faint calls of tradesmen in the streets beyond the castle walls, shouting their wares. After a while, he looked up. 'The dog? Did you say that there was a dog howling?'

'Yes. Ankarette, the wolfhound. Enormous damned great thing. Lionel let it sleep in his room; if he didn't, it would howl all night.'

'Didn't it . . . you know . . . howl when Lionel had company?'

Glanville chuckled. 'It was used to that.'

'I see. When did it start to howl?'

'I suppose we should say "she". Lionel was very particular about that. He used to say she was the only female he could rely on. She had been howling for about half an hour when I broke the lock, which was mid-morning.'

'So, she wouldn't howl just because she was shut in. She would only howl when – not to put too fine a point on it – Lionel was dead.'

Glanville looked puzzled for a moment, then understood. 'I see what you're getting at. So, taking Ankarette's howl as the point in time, we know when he died.'

'To within half an hour or so. The dog might not have been aware at first; if he was lying still, she might have thought he was sleeping. Then, she wanted to go out, tried to rouse him and found he was dead. So we can put his time of death at around . . . what . . . an hour or so after dawn.'

'*Now* we're getting somewhere!' Glanville was sitting bolt upright, eyes gleaming. 'I *knew* it was a good idea to bring you here, Geoff!'

'Well, I'm glad you think so,' Chaucer said. 'But time of death doesn't help us much, not with that locked door. And no food or drink, you say.'

'Nothing. He sometimes took wine to his room, to give him . . . you know . . . strength.'

'I see. So Blanche – if she had visited his room that night – might have taken the bottle away?'

'That doesn't sound like her,' Glanville said, doubtfully. 'She's not a girl who does little odd jobs for no reason. And since Lionel took her to his bed, well, she does nothing but give orders.'

'What will happen to her now?' Chaucer asked.

Glanville shrugged. 'It may have happened already, for all I know. Out in the street, bag and baggage, I would imagine. Except that Lady Violante will make sure that it is just the bag and baggage she arrived with, if I know anything.'

'I see. She had received gifts, had she?'

Glanville rolled his eyes. '*Gifts!* That's an understatement. She had been showered with gifts, from clothes to jewels and money. Lionel gave many pieces of plate to the church in her name. She had servants of her own – more than Lady Violante, as a matter of fact. That rankled, especially with the servants. They didn't think she was worthy of their servitude, but what choice had they? Lionel was besotted and would hear of no argument.'

Chaucer was an observer of men and he could often see beyond subterfuge to find the man beneath the mantle, but he didn't need those skills now. Glanville's face was set in a mask of disapproval. Chaucer thought he would check, though, nevertheless. 'You don't like Blanche?' he hazarded.

'No, I don't like Blanche,' Glanville replied. 'She and Hugh had an understanding. More, they were betrothed. I can't say I was delighted – her father is a corn merchant. He has premises in the town and a manor at Borley; he has plenty of money, but no breeding – but she is a beautiful girl and Hugh was head over heels in love. In lust, perhaps, but he thought of little else. Then, he brought her to the castle, to meet Lionel before their wedding and . . . well, the rest is history.'

'It sounds to me as if Hugh had a lucky escape,' Chaucer offered. 'No one likes a gold-digger.'

'True. It was better that it happened before the wedding, but a betrothal is bad enough. Her father is saying now that Hugh must honour his pledge. Her father says that because he doesn't want Blanche back in his house, with sin on her head. Well, we don't want her either. I suppose I will have to petition the Pope or something. It's not as if it's something a father has to sort out every day of the week. Do you know the drill, Geoff?'

'I can't say that I do,' Chaucer said.

'But you did study law?' Glanville made it a question, but he knew he was right.

'I *studied* it,' Chaucer said. 'But I never practised. I never had a single person ask me to represent them. Except that pig, that time, but I really couldn't see my way clear to helping some mad village clear out the skeletons in its belfry, if I have that right. No, I have no idea – but I'm sure Father Clement can help you.'

'The less said about that, the better,' Glanville said, darkly. 'But we've got off the subject, Geoff. It's time we had something to eat. I'll point everyone out to you while we dine and then I'll leave you to it. Lady Violante likes to go for a ride in the late afternoon now the days are getting longer and she needs me to go along, for protection.'

Chaucer opened his eyes wide. He had heard about the giant pigs, true, but surely not in the streets of Clare.

'I know,' Glanville chuckled. 'It's all for show, really, but I don't mind it. She's a clever woman and makes me laugh.' He blushed a little. 'I'm not too old to appreciate a pretty woman, I hope.' He sounded a little defensive and Chaucer made a mental note of it.

Chaucer drained the dregs of his goblet and put it down on the table. Standing, he realized just how stiff riding had made him and he had to straighten up in stages. 'I'm out of practice, Rich. That boy of yours sets a cracking pace on that courser of his.'

'I know. He doesn't always think of us older folks.' It was the first thing close to a criticism of his lad that Chaucer had heard him utter.

'He's a good boy, Rich,' Chaucer said. 'You should be proud.'

'Oh, I am,' Glanville said, ushering his friend out onto the top of the spiralling staircase. 'I am. And you'll see him in all his finery in a minute, at table.'

# THREE

'Finery' was an understatement. The squire was wearing what Chaucer had heard described as the Devil's clothes. His doublet was glowing with cloth of gold in twirling tendrils, his shoulders, elbows and wrists dripping with tippets laced crimson and his arse was encased in satin, the silver ties bound to the doublet, front and back. His collar was up to his earlobes and his cuffs were massive, dangling almost to the ground. Chaucer couldn't see how the lad could walk in his pointed shoes, but he minced along, negotiating chairs, tables, dogs and servants adroitly. His hair was curled over his ears, shorter at the back so that his collar was on permanent display. Nicholas Brembre was the best-dressed man Chaucer knew; he'd have to rethink that now.

Hugh took his place at the next-to-highest table. He had not won his spurs yet and, what with the duke's passing, all that was on hold. The ladies fluttered around him and one hapless maidservant poured wine all over herself, lost in adoration of his curls.

The women sitting near to Hugh Glanville were at a clear disadvantage, but the only one in the room who mattered was the Lady Violante. She sat at the head of the table and was dressed in deep black, with just a thread of white linen edging her ramshorn wimple, worn in the Italian fashion. Her hair was as black as a raven's wing, shot through with blue lights from the sunlight filtering through the window to one side. The panes of coloured glass lit the table linen spread in front of her, which stopped two places down. No use wasting good linen, she always said, on oafs who would only besmotter it with gravy. Her platter was silver, her knife handle chased ivory. Her horn goblet was as thin as a promise and held a wine whose ruby hints shone through its translucency and gave another splash of colour to the white linen. She sat so still she could have been a painting, her eyes downcast and her mouth thoughtful. Chaucer thought she was the loveliest thing he had ever seen; if he had been surprised to hear the ring of love in Glanville's voice, he was no longer. Chaucer had been very fond of the duke's first wife, Elizabeth, but she had been a dowdy frump by comparison, and he crossed himself at the indecency of that comparison, the lady in question being a long time dead.

Glanville led Chaucer to the head of the table and touched his lady's arm. She started and flinched as if his touch had been red hot, then relaxed when she saw who it was. She bowed prettily in greeting and touched Chaucer's hand briefly, with a hand as cold as ice.

'Sir Richard has told us of your impending arrival, Master Chaucer,' she said, in a low voice laced with a slight accent. 'It was good of you to come, though I fear it is for no reason. My poor husband died of a surfeit.'

'A surfeit, madam?' Chaucer had to ask. He knew there was no such thing, but he feared the reply, nonetheless.

'Yes,' she said, with a smile. 'A surfeit of flesh, young and unschooled. At his age, it is important to be temperate and he would overindulge. As Sir Richard has doubtless told you.'

Chaucer was covered in confusion. Had Richard been given permission? Had he spoken out of turn? He was framing a suitable answer when she helped him out of his quandary.

'Don't mind me, Master Chaucer. Sir Richard will explain everything and with my blessing. Meanwhile, if you will excuse me . . .' and she rose from the table, waving down the lesser folk further down the board who rose with her. 'Please,' she said, louder so the least page at the far end would hear, 'go on with your food.' And with another bow, she had gone, the black fur trim of her court piece shimmering out of sight.

Chaucer looked after her as she made her way across the room, stepping around and over the dogs lounging everywhere. Once the door was closed behind her, he turned to Glanville. 'You didn't say . . .' he said.

Glanville looked down. 'She's hard to describe,' he said. 'It sounds like hyperbole.'

Chaucer felt behind him for his seat and sat down heavily,

immediately regretting it as his saddle sores sent daggers of pain up his spine.

Glanville took the recently vacated seat at the top of the table. 'It's easier for me to direct your eyes from here,' he said. 'There are some at this board who you need to know.' He looked around and nodded discreetly in the direction of some rather portly gentlemen sitting about halfway down and looking as if they expected to be further up the board. 'Those four . . . no, five . . . are from the Guilds. Corpus Christi, St Augustine, St Peter, the Blessed Virgin and John the Baptist.'

'Ah, the usual suspects,' Chaucer smiled. 'Quite.'

'I'll introduce you all later. The one furthest from you is Blanche's uncle.'

Chaucer followed the knight's gaze and saw five men so alike as to be indistinguishable to a stranger. They all had bald or balding heads, paunches which almost stopped them reaching the table and rich but completely hideous clothes that no one in London had worn since the Flood. 'Self-made man' might as well have been stitched in gilt letters across each of their chests.

'Nearer to us,' Glanville said, out of the corner of his mouth, 'are various members of Her Grace's household, who came with her on her marriage and have managed to embed themselves here, much to their own benefit. Nearest of all is Niccolò Ferrante, her seneschal. Needless to say, he and Butterfield are at loggerheads most of the time, though as yet, no blows have been struck. Just as well; he looks the kind who can handle a poignard like you and I handle a spoon.'

Chaucer looked at the rather effete Italian sitting three seats down and on the opposite side of the table. If it came to a straight fight, his money was going on Butterfield, no question, poignard or no poignard; English oak against Italian cedar any time.

'The boy he is talking to is Giovanni Visconti. He is Lady Violante's brother and I suppose of all her entourage has most right to be here. He is considerably younger than her, as you can see, and was her ward when their parents died. If you can believe it, he was another suitor for Blanche; I think you will be expecting her to be more beautiful than the day, but to be honest, she seems a bit ordinary to me.' He flashed a smile at Chaucer and the years fell away. 'Perhaps she just isn't my type.'

Chaucer grinned. 'Perhaps not. Where can we find this girl? I feel I need to speak to her as possibly the last person to see Lionel alive.'

'She is back at her father's house near Sudbury, but I understand under sufferance. If I were a gambling man – and as you know, I am – I would say that that young lady has a convent in her very near future. And not the Priory of Clare, believe me.'

'From what you tell me,' Chaucer said, 'that sounds like an extremely good idea.'

'It sounds good in principle, I agree,' the knight said. 'Though from what I hear, there are more nuns giving birth in any one week than almost any other group of women one could name. However, let us not descend to scurrilous gossip. To leave the guests for a moment, let us look at the servants. Ummm . . .' He raised his head to look around the room and found a face he thought Chaucer might remember. 'Look, there, Geoff. Do you remember her?'

Chaucer followed his finger, no discretion now; a man could point at servants as much as he liked. In the crowd of women scurrying around the trestle at the end of the room, dirty platters were being returned at one end as fresh food was being distributed at the other. The lower sort at the end of the table were still chewing on their bread trenchers while the middling sort were mopping the gravy up with white, wheaten bread. But Chaucer wasn't looking for differences such as those, if he even noticed them. He was scanning the faces for the raddled grandmother of his imagination. He didn't see her there. 'I was expecting to see Joyce,' he said. 'But I don't seem to be able to spot her. Who are you pointing to?'

The knight laughed. 'I'm pointing at Joyce,' he said, poking Chaucer in the ribs. 'She's there, look.'

Chaucer looked, set his mouth and shook his head. 'No. Sorry, Rich. No idea which is her.'

'She hasn't changed a scrap,' Glanville said. 'Look – there, with the ewer. Tall, dark hair. *Look*, for the love of God.'

Chaucer looked and his eyes nearly fell out of his head. 'That's little Joyce?' he said, amazed. 'I thought she'd be . . .' He puffed out his cheeks and crossed his eyes. 'Old. Fat.'

Glanville laughed again. 'Just because you are, Geoff, doesn't mean everyone is. She is a fine figure of a woman, I will give her that. She could be a grandmother, as a matter of fact. Besides, she's not yet forty.'

'Nor am I,' Chaucer lied by two months. 'But I don't look like that!'

'Granted,' Glanville agreed. 'But a green kirtle and a plait down your back isn't really your look, Geoff, is it? And she'd look *ridiculous* in a beard. Shall I call her over? I could do with some more Romonye, anyway.' He waved his empty goblet in the air.

Chaucer scrunched down in his seat, trying to be inconspicuous, in doing so, making several guests at the top end of the table assume he was a cripple. 'No, don't do that. I will need to speak to her, if, as you say, she was one of the first into the room after you broke the lock. But . . . I think I would rather make it in private.'

'You can't lose your virginity twice, Geoff,' the knight pointed out, gesturing as he did so to a lad bearing a dish of carved boar. 'Let's eat. We've done enough talking for one afternoon and we must keep our strength up.' He speared a hunk of meat the size of his head and dumped it on his platter. 'You?' he stared at Chaucer, his eyebrow raised in query.

Chaucer looked down at his paunch and glanced up at Joyce, undulating like a Naiad amongst the pots and pans. He looked around. 'Just some fruit, Rich, I think,' he said. 'An apple, perhaps. Ample for this time of day.'

'The apples are a bit musty by now,' Glanville said. 'And one day's abstinence won't make you sixteen again, Geoff.' He dumped a lump of pork on the comptroller's platter. 'Eat up. It'll put hairs on your chest. Here.' He called over another lad, carrying a charger full of some shapeless green stuff. 'Have some cabbage. Coney food, I call it, but if it will make you feel better.'

Some green slime slid from the platter alongside the pork.

'Come on,' the knight said, round a mouthful of crackling.

'After this, I'll take you round the park. Help you get your bearings. New tilt yard since your day.'

Chaucer had nursed fond memories of Clare to him for many years. He had never lived in such a place since the day he took leave of it, though it was true he had rubbed shoulders with the great and good, and often at that. But Clare was his home, whenever he thought of 'home' at all, and it was a strange walk he took with his friend through corridors and rooms half remembered, and yet in many ways so changed.

After many twists and turns, he was still almost sure he knew where they were. Glanville opened a door that led to the kitchens and, to his surprise, Chaucer found himself in an enclosed courtyard, complete with a well.

'Where . . . I thought that was the kitchen door,' he said, looking lost.

Glanville looked puzzled, then his brow cleared. 'I see where you went wrong,' he said. 'When we took the left turn out of the solar and went down the spiral stairs and then across the hall, *you* thought we were three rooms along from where we were. Lady Elizabeth had the other rooms added years ago – I've got so used to it I had forgotten how it used to be.'

They walked across the courtyard and went into the building again, by a small studded door in a corner. Along a dark passage, the sun could be seen shining in on worn flags through an open door. Beyond, the marble of a terrace shimmered in the spring heat.

'I don't remember a marble terrace,' Chaucer said, as Glanville led the way.

The knight smiled. 'Lady Violante has brought a taste of her homeland with her. In her first summer, she tried to persuade Lionel to brick up the fireplaces. Then she had a Suffolk winter and she ended up putting in more.'

Chaucer laughed. He remembered those mornings, snow sweeping in from the east, unimpeded, it seemed, by so much as a tree as Muscovy exhaled its frosty breath. Sleeping in your clothes, with a hat on the worst days. Breathing on the glass in a usually vain attempt to melt the frost enough to see how many more feet of snow lay outside. Happy days. Snow in London just wasn't the same. For a start, it wasn't half as cold! 'But a marble terrace, though. That must have cost Lionel dear.'

'It did,' Glanville agreed. 'But don't forget, the Lady Elizabeth was no slouch. The lion house? The goldsmith's workshop?'

'True. True.' By now, Chaucer was outside on the terrace, feeling the warmth from the sun-kissed marble seeping welcome into his soles. He leaned on the balustrade and looked out over the woods and parks of Clare. Turning to look back at the castle, rising grey and dour at his back, he had to share his thoughts. 'This is lovely, Rich but . . . is it me, or does it look a bit . . . odd? As if . . .' Chaucer sought for an analogy and, unusually for him, failed.

'It is as if,' a soft, lightly accented voice said behind him, 'an old woman had suddenly thrown off her wimple and let her golden hair cascade down. The hair is no less beautiful for being on an old head, merely a surprise. Don't judge my terrace, Master Chaucer, simply enjoy it. Lionel didn't like me spending the money at first, but when it was finished, he loved to sit out here in the sun, and he didn't like change, did he, Sir Richard? In some things, I should say. In other parts of his life, he embraced change, quite literally embraced.'

Chaucer bowed and blushed simultaneously. 'I do like your terrace, Lady Violante,' he stammered. 'It is just that . . . the years . . . I don't recognize . . .'

She smiled and waved aside his apology. 'Don't worry yourself, Master Chaucer,' she said. 'I do understand. But not all change is bad. Perhaps in a thousand years, when this castle is dust, my terrace will remain. People will walk along it and wonder who we were, who thought we could build for ever. Do you think that, Master Chaucer? How long will London stand, do you think?'

Chaucer knew better than most that London wasn't built to stand. Almost every day, a house fell down, burned down or otherwise disappeared, to be swiftly replaced by another. London was built on sand and, if it outlived him, he would be amazed. Cities were ten a penny and went where the people went. And London was not to be compared with Clare, with its wide eastern skies and air full of the scent of new leaves and the sound of birds. 'For as long as we need it, madam,' he said.

Lady Violante blinked and smiled. 'A very pretty answer, Master Chaucer,' she said, then turned her attention to Glanville. 'Are we to ride this afternoon, Sir Richard?' she asked.

Glanville glanced at the sun. 'I had no idea it was so late, my lady,' he said. 'Today has run away with me. I will go and make sure the horses are saddled and ready.'

'Already done,' she said. 'I sent Niccolò and, as you know, what I send him to do, gets done.'

Glanville bowed. He didn't trust himself with a spoken answer.

Violante inclined her head to Chaucer. 'You will excuse us, Master Chaucer.' It could have been a question, but in her mouth, it was an order.

'Ummm . . . of course,' he said, a little knocked off kilter. 'I believe Sir Richard was going to take me—'

Glanville cut him off. 'You'll find what you need in the laundry, Geoff,' he said. 'I'm sure you'll know it when you see it.'

Violante looked from one to the other. 'The laundry?' she said, puzzled. 'Do you do your own laundry in London, Master Chaucer? No need for that here.'

'Indeed, my lady,' Chaucer agreed. 'I simply need to ask . . . I have a houppelande of a delicate shade of green and I want to ask . . .' He had rather boxed himself into a corner and rolled his eyes at Glanville.

'. . . how to prevent it fading,' Glanville continued, as smooth as silk. 'He thought Hugh might know, but alas – no help. In fact,' and Glanville laughed extravagantly, 'he said he wouldn't be seen dead in that colour. Didn't he, Geoff?'

Chaucer was puzzled now, then realized what was going on. 'Oh, ha, yes, indeed. Saucy young pup!' And he too laughed, even less convincingly than the knight.

'Well,' Violante looked from one to the other, her eyes hooded. 'If Hugh doesn't know something about clothes, it isn't there to know, Master Chaucer. But, if you will, please

do ask my washerwomen. I understand they are friendly.' She
smiled at the two men. 'At least, I don't believe they have
eaten anyone alive as yet.' And with that, she turned on her
heel and walked off, Glanville in hot pursuit. He grimaced
over his shoulder at Chaucer and pointed to the other end of
the terrace, then waved his arms this way and that. After the
mime for 'turn left, down the stairs and through the door to
the right,' Chaucer was hopelessly confused, so just set off
hopefully, knowing he could always ask the way.

'Will you hawk alone, sir?' the Lady Violante nudged her
chestnut forward towards the Nethergate.

Richard Glanville reined in his black, steadying the saker
tied to his wrist. The falconers hovered at the horse's haunches.

'Send these men away, Richard. I need a word.'

The knight clicked his fingers and the falconers bobbed
away, although they looked at the lady with apprehension; the
peregrine on her gloved wrist flapped at the end of its lanyard,
checking his head to make the jess-bells ring. That was His
Grace's hawk. It wasn't right . . .

As if Violante had read their minds, she smiled at them.
'Don't worry, boys,' she said. 'I'll look after Guesclin; he'll
come to no harm.'

'You won't be calling him that tomorrow, will you, my
lady?' Glanville smiled at her.

'Why not?' she asked, wheeling her mare round. 'I think
it's a charming name.'

'It's a French name,' Glanville reminded her. 'Worse, it was
named after Bertrand du Guesclin, your late husband's sworn
enemy.'

Violante laughed. 'My husband had many enemies, Richard,'
she said.

'Not many ran rings around him like Bertrand.'

'The man's a freebooter,' she snorted, 'a commander of
*jacquerie*. He's not even a gentleman. I'll race you to the river.'

The woman was using the new side-saddle the Italians had
introduced. Glanville knew it would never catch on, but he
had to admire the way Violante handled it, cantering over the
cropped grass that led to the Stour. He kicked his courser's

flanks with his spurs and followed her, the saker flapping and squawking on his wrist.

At the Stour's bank, Violante reined in and Glanville drew up alongside, giving her a gentlemanly lead of a few seconds. When a lady says 'race' she really means 'let me win' and he was nothing if not chivalrous.

'You needed a word, my lady?' he asked her, as they let their horses amble alongside the river. The sky was a cloudless blue, a perfect hawking day, without a breath of wind. The peregrine certainly could hear a mouse move at three hundred paces and the saker wouldn't be far behind. But Violante had other things on her mind.

'Who was my husband, Richard?' she asked suddenly, her voice small and alone in a big, friendless world.

Glanville checked his horse in surprise, jerking back on the reins. 'My lady, I . . .'

She held up her free hand. 'I know,' she said. 'He was the companion of my bed and board, my lord, my lover. But who *was* he? I can't say I ever really knew him.'

'He was the son of a king,' the knight said, 'the wisest king in all Christendom. He was the brother of its greatest knight, Edward, the Black Prince,' and he crossed himself. He caught the look in her eye. 'He was your husband, madam,' he said softly, 'and he loved you deeply.'

She nodded. Was it a trick of the light glancing up from the speeding waters of the river, or was that a tear that trickled from the darkness of her lashes? 'And who would want him dead?'

Glanville leaned in closer, his arm on the pommel of his saddle. He didn't think he was going deaf, but she was speaking so quietly and the river was loud just at this point in its journey. Besides, he needed time to think. 'My lady?'

She urged her chestnut up a step or two, until they were almost knee to knee. She stroked the peregrine's hood, making the bells tinkle again. 'Isn't that what your Master Chaucer is doing here?' she asked.

'He's not *my* Master Chaucer,' Glanville told her.

She smiled. 'I rather suspect he's not anybody's Master Chaucer,' she said. 'Hugh tells me he's a comptroller . . . what's that? Some sort of glorified clerk? A book-keeper?'

'Something like that,' Glanville said.

'But he's something more, isn't he?' she asked, searching his face.

'A lot more,' he said.

'He's here to find out how Lionel died.'

'God called him.' The knight knew the platitudes well enough.

'Don't give me that priestly claptrap,' she snapped. 'Death helps those who invite him in. That's why Chaucer is here, isn't it? To find out who let Death in?'

'Geoffrey Chaucer was His Grace's ward, my lady,' he told her. 'I explained all that. He has come to pay his respects, that's all.'

She suddenly reached out and gripped Glanville's wrist. 'Richard. You and I know that Lionel was an old man, but he was as strong as the lion after which he was named. There is something . . . unnatural . . . about his death. I am from Pavia – we know these things. You are from Suffolk, but you know these things too. Will you and this Chaucer find the truth? For me? Tomorrow, we will lay Lionel to rest, but I will never rest until I know what happened. You will tell me,' she moved her chestnut closer still and leaned across and kissed him on the cheek. 'You will tell me what you find out?'

'Count on it,' Glanville said.

'I think it only fair to tell you,' she said, lowering her eyes, 'that in my opinion and that of my seneschal and brother, that it was that little witch Blanche.'

'Witch is a hard word, madam,' the knight said, alarmed. The last thing they needed was that kind of name-calling, which could end so horribly, if not watched.

'Bitch, then,' she said, looking him straight in the eye. 'It's not for me to tell you and Master Chaucer where to look, but, mark my words, she is the killer. She ensnared my husband with her unnatural ways and then she killed him.'

As Richard Glanville sat there, dumbstruck, Violante hauled on the rein and turned to ride for the ford and the woods beyond. 'Come on, then' she called over her shoulder. 'It's a good day for the hunt.'

Glanville watched her go, the peregrine squeaking and

champing at its tether. 'Tomorrow,' he said, almost to himself, '*please* don't mention the Guesclin name. Because tomorrow, the most powerful man in England will be here. And, just like he did your husband, Bertrand du Guesclin made a fool of him as well.' And he drove his spurs home.

Chaucer was feeling quite exhausted by the time he pushed open the heavy door, pointed out to him by what seemed like the thousandth servant whose help he had sought. In some ways, he was grateful to be on foot rather than riding, so that another part of his body got a pounding it was woefully unused to. But enough was almost enough, and he promised himself that if the next door didn't have a whole lot of boiling water and red-faced women behind it, he was going to give up.

He offered up a small prayer to St Christopher when he stepped into what to some might look like a circle of Hell. Huge fires were burning under cauldrons of seething water and the air was thick with a cloying steam. Here and there, a brawny arm broke through the miasma as it hefted a bleached stick, festooned with sodden cloth. Above the slapping of wet linen and crackling of fire came a sweet voice, singing. It wasn't a tune he knew; he had no ear for a tune, a great sadness to him as he loved a cadence in the spoken word as well as the next man, but he could tell that it was a pretty thing and the words were clear and simple. They told of a lost love, of a maiden left forlorn, the usual thing, but without the graphic detail that he had often heard in the London inns. As soon as the singing ended, the women's voices were raised in conversation again, shouting for the lye, the soap, the tongs. In this chaos, somewhere, was Joyce. But where?

Out of the firelit fog, a shape loomed, with arms like hams and a head swathed in a cloth. The face ran with sweat, but it was smiling and the eyes were kind.

'I think you must be lost, master,' the woman said. 'Gentlemen have no place here. We deal in dirty linen here and nobody wants that washed in front of prying eyes.'

Invisible in the steam, women laughed, as women who work in Hell will on hearing a familiar joke.

'I'm looking for someone,' Chaucer said, adding, hurriedly,

before another bawdy joke was offered, 'I'm looking for Joyce, if she's here.'

'Joyce doesn't work in here, sir,' the washerwoman said. 'She's kitchens, she is. But you might find her out the back, there. Butterfield won't trust us with Her Ladyship's table linen, so Joyce does it.' The woman looked over her beefy shoulder into the cloud. 'Is Joyce here, does anyone know? Anyone seen Joyce today?'

A head stuck out from the steam, which was clearing slightly in the draught from the still-open door. 'She's out back, with the slickstones on the linen. Or she was just now.'

Chaucer stood, undecided. Was this an invitation to step into the clouds of hot and soapy steam, or would someone fetch her? He looked expectantly at the woman who had come to his rescue and she smiled back, but they seemed to be at an impasse. Eventually, the washerwoman realized that he was waiting for her to make a move.

'I wouldn't like to disturb her, master,' she said. 'That Butterfield, he's a masterpiece when it comes to being strict. He comes in here once every week, he weighs the lye, he does, makes sure we're not using too much. He takes the linen to the window, checks how white it is by a cloth he keeps in his pocket. Not white enough and . . . back it goes. No, I wouldn't want to annoy Master Butterfield, and that's a fact.'

'I'll not stop her work, mistress, I promise,' Chaucer said, taking a small coin from his purse and looking at it ruminatively. 'If someone could take me to Joyce, I would be more than grateful.'

The washerwoman's eyes gleamed. The coin looked small, but who would pass up even a small coin for the sake of not annoying the seneschal, who in her opinion was getting above his station. 'I shouldn't, but I will,' she said, coming to a decision. Turning, she raised her voice. 'Gentleman coming through, souls. Dress according.' She turned to Chaucer and explained in softer tones. 'Some of the women get a bit hot in all this steam, master. They like to' – she nudged him and nearly knocked him over – 'get a bit comfy, if you know what I mean?' She gestured vaguely at her own ample upper regions, mercifully swathed in an apron and a cambric shift. 'We'll give them a moment to cover up, then I'll take you through. You might want to hang on to my apron strings and step careful – the floor's slippery and you can't see far ahead.' She called, 'Ready?'

'Ready.' Voices from the gloom told them it was safe for a man to walk through.

'Come with me, then,' the woman said, 'but, like I said, step careful. Step careful, now.'

Chaucer could feel the floor like glass under his feet. The woman, though as close as an apron string, was almost swallowed up by the steam and women, but made it to the other end without undue incident. His guide pushed open a door and yelled, 'Joyce. Gentleman to see you.' As she turned to go, she laughed and nudged Chaucer again, nearly bowling him over. 'I thought she'd give all that up, at her age, I must say. But to each his own, that's my motto.' With a final glance at Chaucer and his fairly ample charms, she went back to her copper and the shouts and laughing of her washerwomen.

Joyce was passing a glass slickstone over a length of linen stretched over a frame, outlined by the sun coming through the high window behind her. The room was mercifully free from steam and, for that alone, Chaucer was very grateful. He stood silently for a moment, waiting for his first love to look up from her work. She carefully placed her slickstone in its cradle and gave the handle of the frame a half-turn, to stretch the linen to its furthest extent. She leaned sideways, looking along the surface, and flicked an almost invisible speck away with a practised finger. She looked up, finally.

'Her Grace is very particular,' she said, checking once more and then stepping back. She looked Chaucer up and down, but not with disdain. 'Hello, Geoffrey. I don't believe you've changed a scrap. Not like me. Grey hair, look.' She flicked her plait over her shoulder and held it out for his perusal.

Chaucer was dumbstruck. That he had changed, there was no doubt. He could have been carrying that youthful Chaucer she had deflowered in the stable loft curled up in the front of his gown. His hair was grey and scrubby. His beard was long and greyer than his hair. For all that life had not been unkind to him, he looked years older than his age. And yet, standing there in the warmth of Joyce's smile, he could have been sixteen again. 'Joyce . . . I . . .'

'Still the old tongue-tied Geoff,' she laughed. She took his arm and tucked her hand into the crook of his elbow. 'Come and sit in the sun with me for a while. Tell me what you've been doing with yourself. Married? Children?'

Chaucer allowed himself to be led, like a milk-fed calf to slaughter. 'Umm Yes. And yes.'

She laughed and sat down on a sun-warmed wall on the edge of an old orchard, full of gnarled apple trees. Blossom was breaking over her head and a light breeze skipping down the valley ruffled her hair where it had come loose from the plait. She patted the wall and he sat beside her. 'That's no answer. What's her name? How many?'

'Ummm . . .' Chaucer was known for his way with words, and yet this serving woman seemed to have robbed him of every one. 'Philippa. Pippa, everyone calls her. Three children.' He counted on his fingers. 'Yes, three. Two girls, one boy, Thomas.'

'You don't seem too sure.' She looked at him askance. 'How can you not be sure how many children you have?'

'Well, they're lodged in fine houses, you see. For their education. We don't see each other much. The youngest, that's Agnes, she's with her mother.'

'And where's *that*?' Joyce had never taken much notice of the people around her, the ones above her station. Now she came to think of it, though, there did seem to be children with no parents among the household. Poor little things. She would have to bear that in mind the next time one of the brats spat at her or called her wench. Poor, motherless mites.

'Lincolnshire.'

'And where do *you* live?' Now she was beginning to regret all those dreams, all those longings for a life with young Geoff Chaucer, all that time ago. She would rather live the way she did, all hugger-mugger with her children and the man of the moment, than in splendid isolation, without husband or children.

'London. Aldgate, to be precise.' Chaucer was beginning to regain the power of speech. 'I have a room. I . . .' He realized that to describe the way he lived would only incite this woman's sympathy. There was no way on God's earth that he could make her understand how he loved his little room, his books, his meals sent up from the inn that he rarely paid for. 'I'm very comfortable. I am' – he smiled and sketched a quick bow – 'Comptroller of the King's Woollens.'

'That sounds nice. He has a lot of woollens, does he, the king?'

'All woollens belong to His Grace, I suppose, but . . . I suppose you could say, I work for the customs.'

'Oh. Well, that sounds nice, as I said.' She grabbed his hand. 'It's just so good to see you, Geoff.' What she didn't tell him was that she was now certain her eldest wasn't his. She had often wondered, but now she saw the nose, the eyes, the mouth, she could see that what her mother had always told her was right – the lad was the living spit of the blacksmith's apprentice, Matty, who had come along very soon after Geoff had gone. In some cases, within the hour. She didn't know whether to be glad or sorry. She looked again at the comptroller. No, on balance, probably glad.

'Tell me about yourself.' Chaucer's innate good breeding reasserted itself. He hadn't been brought up by Lionel of Antwerp to behave like a knarre.

'Oh, I haven't done anything, Geoff. Not like you, moving to London, three children in great houses, no, nothing like that.'

'Oh.' Chaucer was horror-struck. 'Four children. I forgot Lewis. Sorry.' He saw the look on her face and realized he was a knarre after all.

'I have nine children living, four dead. I don't live in the castle, not with all that brood. I have a house down in the town, only small, but it's mine. My father built it and I live there with him. He's a bit infirm these days, so he needs some looking after. But the children help me, they keep him happy.' She smiled and she really did look happy; Chaucer was envious, suddenly.

'Who did you marry, in the end?' Chaucer knew that when he was a lad, disporting himself in the hay with Joyce, he wasn't the only apple in her barrel. He was intrigued to know who she had chosen. His money was on the blacksmith's eldest.

She laughed and clouted him on the back, almost knocking him off the wall. 'I never got *married*, Geoff! Who'd have me? Three fine boys by the time I was eighteen, none of them with a father I could name for sure. I never hid what I am. I just like . . .' she knew the words she would use among her friends, but she didn't know if Chaucer would even know what they meant. She lowered her eyes and blushed. 'I have a bit of a reputation, Geoff. I'm where the men go when their wives aren't the friendly sort.'

Chaucer was shocked and yet somehow not surprised. She had brought experience to the hayloft which he hadn't encountered often since in women twice her age, and never in Pippa's bed. 'Well . . .' he was somewhat stuck for words, then he smiled at her. It was hard not to smile when Joyce was near, as many men in the castle could attest. 'You're happy, and that's the main thing.'

'It is, Geoff. I'm not as busy as I was, to tell the truth. The duke took up a lot of my time, o' course. But then he went abroad and met the duchess, so that slowed him down for a bit. Then there was Blanche . . .' She looked at Chaucer and, for the first time, her brow was furrowed. 'To tell you the truth, Geoff, that did irk me, did that. I was carrying my youngest when he brought the duchess home, so that was fair enough. But this Blanche . . . well, she's no better nor she should be, and I was ready for getting back on the horse, as you might say, by then. But no, he moves the hussy into his bed . . .' Her brow cleared again and the smile was back. 'Still, she's got her comeuppance, hasn't she, Geoff? Back at home and bound for a nunnery, so they say.'

'So they say,' Chaucer echoed. If his list got much longer of people who wanted to kill Lionel of Antwerp, it would be easier to list those who *didn't* want to kill him.

'He didn't love her, though,' Joyce mused. 'He couldn't love nobody what Ankarette didn't like.'

Chaucer searched his brain. 'Ankarette?' He'd heard that name before.

'His wolfhound. Great thing. Size of a donkey, near enough.

Slept on his bed and all sorts. She wouldn't mind me, nor the duchess. But she kicked up hell when that Blanche was there. He had to tie her up outside he did, while he did his doings.'

The final sentence gave Chaucer pause, but he worked it out slowly, using his fingers. 'I see. But Ankarette was in the room when they found the duke dead?'

'Yes. I took her down to the kitchen and fed her, calmed her down. She was howling fit to wake the dead. That's how we knew there was summat wrong, see.'

'Yes, I see. I didn't know she didn't like Blanche.'

Joyce sniffed. 'She's a hunting dog. She knows a gold-digger when she sees one.'

Chaucer hadn't been aware that that was one of the quarries of the hunt but was always ready to learn.

'She's a lovely old thing.' Joyce was presumably back on the subject of the dog. 'Shared His Grace's food and everything. Treated her almost like a child, he did. Fed her from his dish. Even gave her a drop of wine sometimes.'

Chaucer was not a pet lover. He had had enough of Nicholas Brembre's cat to last him a lifetime. But he was polite. 'Where is the dog now?'

'She's living in the kitchen. They give her scraps, but I take her for a walk when I can.' She jumped up. 'I ought to be there now. They'll be wondering where I've got to.'

Chaucer had become so embroiled in Joyce and her life he had almost forgotten the question he had for her. 'Was there any food or drink in His Grace's room?' he asked.

Joyce shook her head and her plait swung from side to side. 'Oh, no, Geoff. Not a morsel. Now, I must run.' And run she did, with the grace of a girl, leaving Chaucer feeling strangely lonely without her.

# FOUR

Peasants toiling in the fields below the castle saw them first, a small army coming from the south-west. At their head fluttered a banner they all knew, the leopards and lilies of England. They were less sure of the differencing that marked the flag as that of the Duke of Lancaster.

Giovanni Visconti saw it too, standing, as he was, on the battlements of the keep. 'Who is this, Signor Chaucer?' the lad asked. Beyond the heraldry of Milan, the Italian was lost.

Chaucer had not been looking forward to this moment. 'That is John of Gaunt,' he said, 'the late duke's brother. Your own brother-in-law, if you keep track of that kind of thing.' He turned to Giovanni. 'And he's the most hated man in England.'

There must have been two hundred men in Gaunt's entourage, all armed to the teeth, with the duke's badge stitched to their jupons. Giovanni swore he could feel the earth tremble under the thunder of the trotting hoofs, but it might have been the wind on the battlements. He turned to say something, but Chaucer had gone, his brain whirling as he hurried down the spiral of the stairs. Halfway down, he stopped to look out of the arrow-slit. No, he hadn't imagined it. That was Gaunt all right. Back in the day, he had written a poem in honour of the Lady Blanche, Gaunt's wife, and now, he regretted it. It wasn't his best work, but as a young man he had stood open-mouthed at Blanche's beauty. A lovely face and a lovely soul. Like most men, Gaunt included, Chaucer loved her in his own, distanced way. But *The Book of the Duchess* would lie closed for ever now; the great lady had been called to God twelve years ago and Gaunt had married some Spanish tart as part of his latest political adventure. If there was some awkward position to take, an attitude to strike, Gaunt would do it. If there was a flow to mankind, a direction in which the world turned, Gaunt would be travelling in the opposite direction, pushing against the tide. So many metaphors swirled in Chaucer's head; he had composed a dozen different greetings before he reached ground level.

At the Nethergate, Gaunt's column halted, all snorting horses and the creak of leather. Butterfield and his people were all there, paraded in their Clarence finery for the most powerful man in the land. Gaunt did not wear the crown, but he who did was a twelve-year-old boy and everyone knew it was the Duke of Lancaster who actually called the bow-shots.

'You are?' Gaunt threw back the weepers of his liripipe so that his bearded face was in evidence.

'Butterfield, my lord.' The seneschal rose from his deep bow. 'His late Grace's . . .'

'Yes, yes,' Gaunt snapped. 'Where will I find the duchess?'

'If you will follow me, my lord?' Butterfield clicked his fingers and a lackey dashed to hold Gaunt's bridle. The Duke of Lancaster dismounted. He followed no one, but there were certain practical considerations he could not avoid and he let Butterfield take him across the bailey, staff bowing and curtseying in all directions.

'Good God!' Gaunt stopped in his tracks, unbuckling his sword and throwing it to a minion. He didn't look where it was going; in Gaunt's world, where he threw something, there would be someone to catch it, and he had never been wrong yet. 'Geoffrey Chaucer, as I live and breathe.'

The Comptroller of Woollens had thought he had better get this over with. He bowed at the foot of the stairs. 'My lord,' he said, and was a *little* surprised when Gaunt whipped off his glove and held out his hand. For a moment, Chaucer wasn't sure how to respond.

Gaunt sensed his dilemma. 'Well, shake it, man. This isn't Spain. We don't kiss rings here except in the case of the king. Or, God forbid, the Pope – and we're not likely to get a visit from him in the next six hundred years – whichever one we're talking about.'

Chaucer shook Gaunt's hand.

'What are you doing here?' the duke asked him.

'You may remember, my lord, that I was ward to His Grace back in the day. I owe him a great deal.'

'Oh, yes,' Gaunt said. 'Paid your ransom, didn't he – that Rheims business?'

'Indeed, my lord. Were it not for His Grace, I'd still be mouldering in some French oubliette.'

'Hmm,' Gaunt mumbled. 'Well, Chaucer, I'll be here for a few days, see my brother laid to rest. We must talk. Relive old times.'

'I'd be delighted, my lord.' Chaucer could gush for England when he had to. 'But first, please accept my condolences.'

'Yes,' Gaunt sighed. 'Well, to be frank, Lionel and I were never close, especially recently. He was drifting towards the Italian states, I to Spain. By the way,' he nudged Chaucer closer to him, 'I don't want to chance my arm at all, but come Michaelmas, you might be talking to the new king of Castile.'

Chaucer looked gobsmacked. 'My lord,' he managed. 'I mean, Your Grace.'

'Yes, well,' Gaunt tapped the side of his nose. 'That's strictly entre nous, as we used to say during the war. Butterwick,' he spun to the seneschal, 'don't just hover there, man, where's that sister-in-law of mine?'

Chaucer bowed as the duke made for the stairs and, suddenly, Giovanni Visconti was at his elbow. 'My God,' the lad's whisper was barely audible, 'that's him!'

Chaucer tried to follow the pointing finger but all he could see was a mass of men, some dismounting, others still in the saddle, and a wall of noise as they gabbled among themselves.

'Who?' he asked. 'Where?'

'There, on the black. Giovanni Acuto.'

Chaucer, ever the scholar, translated in his head. Giovanni Acuto was Italian for that civilized language, Latin, Johannes Acutus. That, in turn, in English, was John the Sharp. And that meant that Chaucer was none the wiser. The duchess's little brother looked at the comptroller; was the man some kind of idiot?

'John Hakvod,' he explained.

'Hak . . .' Chaucer frowned. 'Oh, *Hawkwood!*' Realization dawned; the groat had dropped.

'I saw him in Milano once,' the boy burbled. 'Oh, I cannot have been more than twelve.'

Chaucer looked at him; was that yesterday?

'He was there with his White Company,' the lad went on, 'offering his services to Uncle Bernabo. They say he earns eighty thousand florins a year.'

Chaucer's jaw dropped. That was twice the money that passed through his hands at the Wool Exchange and he had never seen so much in one place in his life. Clearly, he was in the wrong job. But he knew more about John Hawkwood than the boy at his elbow. His White Company were free-booters, men the French called *jacquerie*, who sold their souls to the highest bidder. They raped and plundered, sacked monas-teries and cut men's legs off for laughs. He might never have seen the man before, but he knew his reputation.

And as he watched, John Hawkwood dismounted. He hauled his bastard sword from the saddlebow and hung it over his shoulder so that the blade hung down his back. Then he made for the archway where Chaucer and Giovanni stood.

'Giovanni Acuto!' the boy said excitedly, remembering just in time to bow.

Hawkwood was a head taller than the Italian and broad with it. In an age when the moustache bristled supreme, he was clean-shaven, his hair close-cropped and tawny, his eyes hard grey.

'Do I know you, boy?' he asked.

'No, sir,' Giovanni said. 'Well, in a way. We are family, you and I.'

'Mother of God,' Hawkwood muttered. 'How so?'

'I am Giovanni Visconti.'

Hawkwood blinked at him.

'Bernabo, the Lord of Milano, is my uncle. Once removed, of course.'

Of course. As Hawkwood knew well; it was the Italian way.

But Giovanni Not The Sharp was well into his family tree by now. 'Your wife, Donina, she is Bernabo's daughter, if a little the wrong side of the highway. So we are . . . cousins, sort of.'

Hawkwood winked at him. 'Stay with the "sort of",' he said and walked on. He was on the first step when he all but collided with Butterfield, having left Gaunt with his brother's widow. 'Sir John,' the seneschal said and the mercenary cut him dead.

'Do you know that man?' Chaucer asked Butterfield as he passed.

The seneschal looked a little discomfited. 'Doesn't everybody?' he asked. 'He's—'

'John the Sharp,' Chaucer chimed in, 'of the White Company.' He flashed a glance at Giovanni. 'Yes, I know.'

It was raining the day they buried Lionel of Antwerp, as if Heaven itself wept and the angels bowed their heads. Monks from the priory of Clare carried the coffin, adorned with the duke's arms and a funeral helm hung with black. Behind walked John of Gaunt, a black cloak over his heraldic jupon, the one he had worn not long before when he had buried first his big brother, the Black Prince, and then his father. The Plantagenets were wilting fast. Behind him walked John Hawkwood, unusually unarmed, although he carried a slim Italian dagger in his sleeve as was his wont; even in peaceful Suffolk, you couldn't be too careful.

The chanted *Te Deum* echoed in the cloisters where the rain ran down the stone tracery and splashed onto the flagstones. Behind Hawkwood, a knight bearing Clarence's arms rode the dead man's horse. The embroidered bard, of velvet and gold, dragged on the ground, and the animal snickered and whinnied, unused to the chanting and unsure of a different man on his back. Chaucer walked with the Glanvilles behind the animal, glancing up every now and then to stare at the great helm with its bull crest and its mantling fluttering in the breeze. It was as though the ghost of Clarence rode behind that sad retinue, watching with envy the souls who still lived. Beneath the clatter of hoofs, the creaking of leather and the hum of the crowd, he thought he could almost hear the spirit sigh.

Chaucer looked behind him. The Lady Violante walked alone, her brother and her seneschal a few dutiful paces back. A black veil hid her face, but her head was held high and her bearing was, as ever, superb. She looked straight ahead, though Chaucer got the feeling that, beneath her veil, her dark eyes missed nothing.

At the priory door, circled with its Norman arch, the column halted and the prior himself, in his robes edged with black for the occasion, held up his seal. Butterfield came out of nowhere and bowed before the man, before taking it and smashing it to pieces on the step. Then he bowed to the prior again and stood aside as the monks continued into the dark chill of the church. At the end of the nave, the columns rising to God on either side, what seemed like a thousand candles blazed, their flames dazzling on the gold and silver and the many-coloured glass.

From the walls, the painted figures looked down at the procession. The Virgin herself, highest and best, smiling at another soul due to join her in Heaven. Her Son was everywhere, lecturing to the scholars in the Temple, curing the lame and the sick, lifting Lazarus from his grave. And the older icons were there – Moses, Isaiah, Job; all the great and good of the ancients bearing silent witness to the laying of Lionel of Antwerp in his grave.

That grave had been dug in the south aisle, where, on a good day, the sun hit the floor with the blues, reds and greens of the glass, the holy colours of Mary herself. Father Clement, crossing himself, lifted the funeral helm from the coffin and held it up to the altar, intoning in Latin the dirge for the dead. The monks laid their burden down and the prior took charge of the Mass. There was a murmur as the poor were allowed in, men, women and children in rags and filth, kneeling before the altar in something akin to terror as the prior blessed them. Then he pressed a silver coin into the hands of each one.

'Nice to see *somebody* getting what's due to them,' Chaucer heard someone mutter, and turned to see the party of guildsmen he had noticed at dinner in the castle, in their various liveries, standing together and scowling at Lionel of Antwerp's largesse. Of such, Chaucer noted, and not for the first time, are the Kingdom of Heaven.

The rain did not stop until darkness fell. By that time, the living had left the priory church, leaving the dead behind with a solitary monk whose knees were soon numbed by the hard cold of the flagstones. When he saw the last mourners leave, he walked around the nave, solemnly extinguishing all the candles – the breath of God – until only one remained, the one that glowed dimly on the coffin lid, deep in the still-open grave.

Up at the castle, the Lady Violante had put on a spread scarcely seen in Suffolk and the wine flowed freely. Cry for a dead man in church as his body is laid in the cold ground. Then laugh with him as you remember all the good things in his life, but most of all, because he is dead and you are not; that thought was written clearly on every face in the warm, crowded room. She looked around the hall at Clare, seeing, just briefly, her late husband wandering between the tables, shaking hands, kissing cheeks. Everyone would remember this day for the rest of their lives.

'Well, Chaucer.' John of Gaunt was still wearing his funeral black, but he had lost the uncomfortable armour and nobody was further from his mind than Lionel of Antwerp. 'Still in the Aldgate?'

'Indeed, my lord,' the comptroller told him. 'Many thanks to you, as always.'

Gaunt shook his head. 'Think nothing of it,' he said, between mouthfuls of blancmange. 'I know lodgings are like hens' teeth. I, for instance, can't build the extension I'd like to at the Savoy because of the bloody river.'

'Dreadful,' Chaucer sympathized.

'I thought I could divert the Thames, build some sort of weir, perhaps, but the engineer chappies say it can't be done. I'll just have to expand to the north a bit, along the Strand, you know, towards Charing Cross.'

Chaucer knew.

'By the way,' he leaned back in his high-backed chair at the top table, gesturing to the man on the other side of him. 'You know Johnny Hawkwood, of course.'

'Er . . . no,' Chaucer said, apologizing for reaching across His Lordship to shake the mercenary's hand. Suddenly, the comptroller realized that he had no idea how to address the man. Some said he had been knighted by the Black Prince himself after Poitiers; others that he had no title at all. To John of Gaunt, of course, he was just another Johnny.

'Sir,' was the best Chaucer could manage.

'Chaucer,' Hawkwood grunted. He was not the most civil of men and funerals brought out the worst in him.

'I'm surprised you two didn't meet up on that mission I sent you on. Milan. Two years ago now, wasn't it?'

'Oh, you know how it is, my lord,' Chaucer gushed. 'In a busy life . . .'

'Hmm. You don't remember Chaucer, Johnny?'

'Never seen him before in my life,' Hawkwood growled, 'before yesterday. I thought he was some sort of vintner; has that look about him.'

Chaucer's moustache bristled. He had once been the king's squire, for God's sake; his wife was minor aristocracy – oh, all right, gentry. But major gentry, mind you. But he found himself looking into Hawkwood's cold, grey eyes and felt it would be unwise to ruffle this hawk's feathers.

'How is that, Chaucer?' Gaunt wanted to know. 'Both of you were on the same mission, I haven't got that wrong, I know. Milan's not *that* big a place, is it?'

'Well, my lord,' Chaucer was having to think quickly. 'Bernabo Visconti was a difficult man to pin down. I seem to have spent weeks loitering outside his palazzo.'

'Is that where you met Violante?' Gaunt asked, clicking his fingers for more wine.

'Er . . . no, I didn't have that pleasure until the other day. She was away when I was in Milan; good works, I understand, with the sisters of Saint Eulalia.' Chaucer had no idea whether they even existed, but it sounded plausible and John of Gaunt was a Hispanophile to his rerebrace, so he *should* be none the wiser.

'Well, there it is,' Gaunt sighed. 'Funny things, missions.'

'Aren't they, though?' Chaucer beamed.

'Look,' Gaunt leaned across to him, 'I'd better make small talk with the sister-in-law, although, technically, I suppose she isn't that any more,' and he left.

Chaucer sat back down again and found himself with John Hawkwood as a table companion, which was a little like striking up a conversation with a gargoyle; it was more of a one-versation, if Chaucer had been forced to describe it. On his left was young Hugh Glanville, all pomade and peacock beauty, but since there was a particularly gorgeous lady on *his* left, the comptroller was suddenly alone. Then he noticed the guildsmen at a lower table and remembered the intriguing comment he had heard whispered in the church. Excusing himself to Hawkwood, who barely noticed, he scuttled over to them.

'Gentlemen,' he said with a smile, 'Geoffrey Chaucer, Comptroller of Woollens.'

All five of them struggled to their feet. 'Charmed, sir,' said the first. 'Simon Fawcett, tapicer – of the Corpus Christi Guild.' Chaucer knew that from the man's livery, the elegant badge embroidered on the shoulder of his houppelande. 'This is David Ifaywer, of the Carpenters' fraternity.'

'Guild of St Anne.' Ifaywer shook Chaucer's hand.

'Robert Whitlow, haberdasher.'

'St John the Baptist Guild,' Whitlow explained.

'Nicholas Straits, the dyer.'

Straits half-bowed. If Chaucer was a woollens man, these textile people must stay together. 'Guild of St Augustine,' he said, indistinctly to his own knee.

'And last, but certainly not least, Andrew Trumpington, cordwainer.'

'Guild of St Peter,' the leatherman explained.

Chaucer, who was very good at grips, weighed each man's handshake in turn. Judging by the softness of them, none of them had done a hand's turn in their chosen craft for years.

'This might not be a very appropriate time, Master Chaucer,' Ifaywer said, 'but are you a queck man?'

'A what?' Chaucer asked.

'Give it a rest, David,' Fawcett scolded the man good-naturedly. 'Now is *not* the time, what with His Grace fresh in his grave. And, anyway, queck is a Suffolk game, Master Chaucer's from London – he won't know of such nonsense.'

'I heard you lived here as a lad,' Ifaywer said, taking in Chaucer's greying hair. 'Before my time, of course.'

'I'm sorry,' the comptroller smiled, 'but I've never heard of the game.'

'Another time, then,' Ifaywer said. 'We'll introduce you to it. And, believe me, once you've savoured the delights of the queck board, you'll never be the same.'

'Indeed,' Chaucer beamed. 'I was very touched, gentlemen, that you approved of the late duke's bounty in giving alms to the poor at the Mass.'

The guildsmen looked at each other.

'That's what the guilds are all about, Master Chaucer,' Fawcett said, 'looking after the poor. We provide for six widows and orphans, pay for burial services, hire chantry priests to keep souls from Purgatory.'

'A worthy cause,' Chaucer nodded, but the phrase he had heard in church sounded nothing like that. 'It's good of you to come and pay your respects to His Grace.'

'Oh, it's the least we could do,' Straits said. 'We all owe the duke such a lot.'

And Chaucer didn't fail to notice the smirk that passed between them.

Across the hall, as the wine flowed and the solemnity of the occasion gave way to something approaching mirth, Lady Violante's seneschal, Niccolò Ferrante, helped himself to Chaucer's chair and sat sideways, staring at John Hawkwood.

'Was there something?' the mercenary asked, without turning his head.

'The stiletto up your left sleeve,' the Italian said. 'Is that just habit, or are you expecting trouble?'

Hawkwood still didn't turn. 'Only perpetually,' he murmured.

'I thought you'd made your peace with—' but Ferrante didn't get far with that sentence.

'I did,' Hawkwood cut in. 'That's over with.'

'Lady Violante!' There was a shout from the hall's entrance and a huge man in a houppelande strode in, roughs at his back armed with staves. A dozen men were on their feet, Ferrante and the Glanvilles among them. Chaucer was already standing but he noticed the guildsmen remained firmly in their seats.

Butterfield crossed the floor in what seemed like a single stride and confronted the man.

'Have you come to pay your respects, sir?' he asked. 'If you have, I would ask your men to lay their weapons at the door. This is not a fairground.'

'I have come to talk to the Lady Violante,' the man said, 'and it's private and personal.'

Chaucer wondered what the approach would be if it were public and generic. He bent to the nearest guildsman. 'Who's he?' he said.

'That's Peter Vickers,' Fawcett told him. 'Has lands over Sudbury way.'

Chaucer thought the man looked vaguely familiar, but he had seen so many new faces in the last few days. 'He wouldn't have a daughter called Blanche by any chance?'

All five guildsmen looked at him. 'How do you know Blanche?' Whitlow asked, his face oddly crimson all of a sudden.

'I don't,' Chaucer said, looking closely at Whitlow. 'Although I believe several people do.'

Richard Glanville had joined Butterfield. He stared Vickers in the face. 'I believe the seneschal has made our views clear, Vickers,' he said. 'He speaks for us all.'

'I only want what's right.' Vickers stood his ground, obviously hoping that the thugs at his back would carry more weight than this solitary knight. The arrival of an overdressed fop of a squire didn't shift his views at all.

'Hoo!' There was a shout from the corner. 'I am John of Gaunt,' he announced, as if that were necessary. 'Duke of Lancaster. As the highest ranked in the room, may I take over, Sir Richard?'

'Be my guest, my lord.' Glanville bowed and stepped to one side.

'Hawkwood,' Gaunt clicked his fingers.

The mercenary had barely left his seat when the poignard hissed through the air to thud into the chest of the oaf at Vickers' elbow. The knarre grunted and staggered back with the sudden impact before collapsing in a heap, his blood pumping from his chest.

There were gasps and screams all over the hall.

'I am sorry the ladies had to see that,' Gaunt said. 'My Lady Violante, sister, please accept my deepest apologies.' His face, however, showed no apology whatever. Neither did John Hawkwood's; the man had already sat back down and was finishing his drink.

Speechless with shock and fury, Vickers spun on his heel and helped his men carry his dead tenant out of the hall.

'Butterfield.' Richard Glanville tapped the man's arm. 'Bring your people. Let's see those bastards off the premises.'

Although John Hawkwood's display of knife-throwing was not intended as entertainment, it did change the tenor of the gathering and, one by one, people began to gather up cloaks, dogs and wives and make their way to the great double doors which led out of the hall and into the inner bailey. Soon, the click of hoof on cobble told those still within that the horses were being brought to the door; the crowd had thinned considerably. Chaucer looked around and noticed that the guildsmen had all gone; he was surprised, they had struck him as men who would stay at any table while a crumb was uneaten or a mouthful of wine unswallowed.

As the guests began to leave, so the servants began to clear the debris on the tables. They were all but invisible as they quietly went about their work; Butterfield ran a tight ship in the castle at Clare. Chaucer looked about him for the one face he knew; Joyce would be bound to be about her work, elegant, slender, her plait swinging down her back. He found himself wanting to see her very much; although she had perhaps not been the innocent girl he had thought her all those years ago, a first time is a first time and she would always hold that place in his heart. Finally, he saw her, in her apron and simple gown, walking away from him, a basket on her hip, collecting the half-chewed crusts that guests had left in their wake, like flotsam on a shore. She reached the bottom of the table and hitched the basket up, then raised her eyes to look straight into his.

In what seemed to be only a few strides, but what in fact was a stumbling struggle through people all heading the other way, he was by her side.

'Joyce. You're crying. Whatever is it?'

She turned her tear-stained face to him, so trusting it made his heart turn over. 'It's Ankarette. She's dead.'

He knew the name. He just couldn't remember who it was. Not one of her nine children, surely? Not even Butterfield could be *that* strict. He set his face in an expression of general sympathy, to be adjusted accordingly, depending on who the dead Ankarette was.

'His Grace's dog. The wolfhound I told you about.'

Chaucer sighed with relief. A dead child would have been a hard thing to commiserate with in this setting. 'I do remember, yes. Poor animal. Grief, do you think?' He pushed his head forward, slightly turned, the classic pose of the person who sympathizes without caring one jot for the other's loss. A dog, for the love of God. When the whole castle was overrun with the curs.

The woman wiped her cheeks with the heel of her hand and sniffed. 'I would have said that, Geoff,' she looked quickly from side to side to make sure her discourtesy to a guest had gone unremarked, 'but she seemed to be cheering up. The scullions spoiled her, she had the best food and as much attention as she could want. Yes, she missed her master; any animal will do that. But even dogs are fickle – when there is fowl and warm milk on offer, they'll soon have a new master. But,' she shrugged and hitched her basket again, 'she's dead, so I must have been wrong.'

'Was she old?' Chaucer had no idea how old dogs lived to be. Five years? Twenty? Seventy? He'd never been interested enough in one to know. When he had lived in fine houses, there were hounds of every kind everywhere you stood, but they were all just one entity of Dog, not individuals. Though he remembered Lionel often had a favourite.

'No, not old at all. Well, not *young*, but not old enough to die of age.' She looked around again; it wouldn't do to be seen talking too long. 'I felt sorry for her. When she'd lived in His Grace's room with him, sitting under his table for meals, that kind of thing, he would pass her titbits and he would pour a little wine into her bowl. She liked a nice fruity Gascony best, but she wasn't fussy, bless her. There was a drop or two left in a bottle in His Grace's room, so I saved it for her. I hid it in my smoothing room and gave some to Ankarette today. It seemed only right, with her master being taken to his grave.'

Chaucer became aware that his mouth was hanging open

and he shut it with a snap. 'There was wine? You said there was no food or drink in the room.'

'Did I?' Joyce appeared to think back. 'Yes, I suppose I did. What I meant was that there was no meal, no plate of food, no goblet with drink in it. All there was was a crust on the table by the window and the bottle of wine with a dry goblet. Ankarette's dish was empty.'

Chaucer was not angry. No, that was wrong. He *was* angry. But he knew it wouldn't do any good if he showed it. He smiled as best he could. 'Do you have the bottle still, Joyce? Did you give all the wine to Ankarette?'

'Yes. There was only a drop. About half a cup full, if that. I put it in her water. Why?' The tears started to flow again. 'Was there something the matter with the wine? Had it gone bad? I don't know about wine. I thought it would keep.' She dropped her basket and held her apron to her eyes. 'I killed her,' she wailed. 'I killed Ankarette!'

Butterfield was suddenly at their side. Chaucer had never known a man walk so silently. 'Is there trouble here, Master Chaucer? Joyce?' He had known Joyce have propositions made – God above knew, he had made some himself – but she usually took them with more equanimity than this. He glanced at Chaucer. He wasn't in peak condition, but Joyce had known worse, he was sure.

'Ankarette's dead, Master Butterfield,' Joyce sobbed. 'The wine was bad.'

Butterfield put his arm around her and hoisted the basket onto his own hip. 'Let's get you to the kitchen,' he said. People were beginning to stare. 'Master Chaucer, my apologies.'

'Nothing to apologize for,' Chaucer said, hurriedly. 'I do want to ask Joyce some . . .'

Butterfield looked him up and down. Had the man no shame? 'Perhaps another time, Master Chaucer,' he said. 'For now, I'll just get Joyce back to the kitchen for a rest. She's over-wrought.' The mention of wine had worried him. Joyce had her habits, he knew; he just didn't know one of them was drink.

As Butterfield made his way to the kitchen stair, Chaucer looked around for Richard Glanville. He was marshalling guests out of the main door but turned at Chaucer's whistle. Chaucer motioned him over and the knight bent to speak to an underling who stepped into his place, beaming with pride at his elevation.

'How can I help you, Geoff?' the knight said, affably. Apart from the fatal knifing, the day had not gone too badly at all.

'I need to find a bottle,' Chaucer told him. 'Lionel of Antwerp, Duke of Clarence, was poisoned.'

# FIVE

Sir Richard Glanville didn't really want to dampen his friend's enthusiasm. But looking for a bottle at Clare Castle was like looking for a needle in a pack of needles. The kitchen was full of them. As was the buttery. The cellar was packed to the gunwales. And that didn't allow for all the bottles secretly removed by servants who didn't mind dregs if they were of the best. A plan was what they needed.

'What we need is a plan, Geoff,' he hissed as they met that night in the shadow of the Maiden Tower.

'What good is a plan?' Chaucer asked, quite reasonably. 'Butterfield carted Joyce off for a lie-down before I could find out any details. She obviously didn't give the dog her fatal treat in the middle of the hubbub of the kitchen or anywhere else like that. She would have done it somewhere quiet, probably on the pretext of taking her for a walk. And she wouldn't have left the bottle in plain sight. Someone would have asked where it came from and who took it, and then she would have been in the potage up to her knees. No, what we need as a plan, if it is a plan at all, which I doubt, is to have no plan at all.'

Glanville looked at him, eyebrow invisibly raised in the gloom. Some said this man had one of the finest minds in the country. He, Sir Richard Glanville, at that moment would beg to differ. 'No plan at all is the best plan?'

'Yes, you have it in a nutshell. With no logic behind Joyce's actions, the bottle could be anywhere. So we will search anywhere. Do you see?'

Glanville shook his head.

'Excellent.' Chaucer had been unable to see which way the head had moved and chose to believe it was a nod. 'I knew you would see my logic. So,' he gestured up to the bulk of stone looming between them and the moon. 'We may as well start here.'

\*     \*     \*

Chaucer couldn't remember quite why they called this the Maiden Tower. And, as a boy here, struggling with his Tacitus and Juvenal, scurrying around Lionel of Antwerp's table trying to carve his meat and serve his wine, he barely gave the names of the parts of the castle a second thought. It was just like all the others, octagonal, arrow-slitted, spiral-staircased. Chaucer understood the need for spiral stairs, tucked into the cylinder of towers. He understood the curve so that a man on the attack could present his shield to his opponent. What he did not understand was how such a man was supposed to cope with the damned things when they reached middle age and when, yes, it must be faced, such a man had put on a few pounds. As a naughty and nimble page, he had bounded up and down spirals two steps at a time; now, he climbed slowly, watching the patterns of the brazier-flames dapple the rough stone.

He entered the solar where a solitary candle glowed near the hearth. A dragon curled around one side of the mantel shelf; St George guarded the other. It was officially spring now, so Butterfield had closed the fireplaces down, told his people to sweep the soot and scrape away the dog shit. There was a long table at one end of the room, set with wooden trenchers and a many-branched candlestick that somebody in Clarence's household had brought back from the Holy Land as a memento years ago.

Glanville signalled that he was going to search the cupboards at the far end. Chaucer opted for the coffer-chest, bound with cold iron. Then, they both heard a sound. It was a thud, followed by a hissed curse, on the stairway they had just come up. Instinctively, Glanville blew out the candle to his right, not thinking that the newcomer would see the light vanish. Chaucer moved as silently as his shoes would let him on the rushes, stepping over them and praying he wouldn't slip. He tucked himself away as best he could behind the arras, that expensive one that Clarence had haggled for in . . . well, Arras, actually. To his horror, he realized that his feet were sticking out from the bottom, but it couldn't be helped. He held his breath.

A black figure glided into the room, looking this way and that. A man, certainly, and in a cloak. He crept past the long table and reached the hearth. Briefly, he paused, bent forward and thrust an arm up the broad flue. Chaucer and Glanville heard the patter of soot hit the stonework; clearly, Butterfield's people had been less than thorough. Then the figure turned, silhouetted briefly against the oriel window, the full moon forming an unlikely halo around his hood. Shit! Chaucer realized that the man was making for the chest, only feet from him. There was no need to look down to check; the comptroller knew he had left his poignard in his room. He tried to remember the wrestling moves he had learned in this very castle all those years before and remembered anew that wrestling had not been his strongest suit. He only won one bout because he'd cracked an earthenware pot over his opponent's head. He winced as he remembered the whipping he had got for that.

The figure bent almost double over the chest, fumbling for the locks. He found them and braced himself to lift the domed lid. Now was Chaucer's time; the rogue had both hands full and there would be no chance like it. Chaucer leapt out from the curtain and threw his arms around the man who let out a squawk. Richard Glanville had come better prepared. In an instant, he was at Chaucer's elbow, spinning the man around and holding his poignard point against his throat.

'Geoff,' he said quietly. 'The candle.'

Chaucer let his quarry go and stumbled across to the flint, striking a spark and holding it to the wick, blowing gently to make it catch. He held it up to the man's face, Glanville's blade glinting wickedly below the ties of his hood.

'Would you do the honours, Geoff?' the knight asked.

Chaucer flicked back the hood and a rather sheepish guildsman stood there.

'Master Fawcett!' Chaucer blinked.

The tapicer looked ever more shamefaced. Then he did his best to look Richard Glanville in the eye. 'If you please, Sir Richard,' he swallowed hard, 'could you remove the knife?'

'I can remove the windpipe just as fast,' Glanville said. 'I'd thank you to remember that.' And he let the blade fall. 'Now, explain yourself. What are you doing here at this hour?'

Freed from the threat of instant and agonizing death, Fawcett relaxed a little. He even became a little indignant. 'I just came for what's rightfully mine,' he said. He sounded like Peter Vickers.

'And what's that?' Chaucer asked, keeping the flame burning uncomfortably near Fawcett's beard.

The tapicer sighed. He'd been caught out and couldn't see how to brazen his way out of this. 'We're all in on it,' he confessed, blaming the mob mentality.

'All of you?' Chaucer frowned. 'Who are you talking of?'

'My fellow guildsmen and I,' Fawcett said. 'Ifaywer, Straits and the rest. We were all duped by His Grace.'

'You'd better explain that,' Glanville demanded. He still had his dagger in his hand.

'The duke owed us money,' the guildsman explained. 'We didn't ask why he wanted it – it wasn't our place. But between you and me' – and all three of them leaned closer as it became confidential – 'the Lady Violante was spending it like water. Yes, I know there are various feudal dues and the odd escheat, but not even Lionel of Antwerp can manufacture his own coin. So, for whatever reason, His Grace was in need. He turned to us, as – and I blush to say it – men of some standing in this community. We were happy to oblige, of course, with the usual interest rates . . .'

'Usury, you mean?' Glanville snapped.

Fawcett looked outraged. 'Please, Sir Richard,' he pulled himself up to his full height. 'We are not Jews.'

'Understood,' Chaucer nodded. 'And I assume the duke reneged.'

Glanville shot the man a disapproving glance.

'He did. This arrangement was made four years ago and, to date, we haven't seen so much as a groat. I was looking for paperwork, a will, a codicil, *something* that could prove the deal we struck.'

'Don't *you* have such paperwork?' Glanville asked.

'Of course,' Fawcett said, 'but without His Grace's indenture, it's meaningless.'

'He's right,' Chaucer said. 'Tell me, Fawcett, are the others here too?'

'Yes,' the tapicer said. 'We're all here. What with the castle being so big and so full of people at the moment, we thought we'd take a tower each; Straits has got the great hall. We're due to meet up at the Corpus Christi headquarters.'

'Callis Street?' Glanville checked.

'The same,' Fawcett nodded.

'Well, then.' The knight spun the dagger in his hand and slid it away into its sheath. 'Let's not keep them waiting, then.'

Callis Street was shrouded in darkness and silence except for the soft pad of footsteps of the three men walking along it. The merchant's houses here were large, respectable and solid, like the men who owned them, tall chimneys probing the night sky. Here and there, a stork's nest in its springtime rudimentary stages gave the look of mad hair sticking out willy-nilly around a stack, and a questioning beak leaned over the side to watch the men pass.

A single candle burned in the leaded window of the guild-house of Corpus Christi. Fawcett had been dreading this moment, but it was here and now and it had to be faced. He rapped the brass knocker, the one with the devil's face leering in the moonlight, and the door creaked open.

'Simon,' a voice said. 'Thank God. We thought . . .' and the voice tailed away as Glanville virtually threw the tapicer into the hall. There were other lights suddenly, coming from the rooms that led off beyond the shadows.

'Sir Richard . . .' somebody said and, after that, there didn't seem much else to say.

'What is the meaning of this?'

'Shut up, Whitlow,' Fawcett snapped. 'It's all up for us. They caught me.'

'I suggest, gentlemen,' Chaucer said, 'that we all sit down calmly and place our cards on the table. Unless, Master Ifaywer, you'd prefer a game of queck?' The carpenter's face lit up in the candle flame.

'Well . . .' The man was clearly interested. Cards were new and foreign; only Londoners played with them.

'Give it a rest, David,' the other guildsmen chorused. Fawcett led the way into a parlour and all candles were placed on the oak table in the centre.

'Well?' Chaucer chaired the proceedings. 'Did anybody find anything?'

The guildsmen looked at each other. And silence reigned.

It was broken by Fawcett. 'God's teeth, they *know*!' He slammed the flat of his hand down on the table. 'They caught me, bang to rights in the Maiden Tower.'

'And you told them?' Straits couldn't believe his ears.

'It's amazing the effect a knife point to the throat has on some people,' Glanville said, straight-faced. He let his hand drop to his poignard-hilt, in case anyone was at all confused over the matter.

'I repeat,' Chaucer said. 'Did anybody find anything?'

'I was interrupted,' Trumpington admitted, 'in the Constable Tower, by that foreigner, the seneschal.'

'Ferrante?' Chaucer checked.

'That's him,' Trumpington nodded. 'Creeps about the place like a cat.'

'Nicholas?' Fawcett half-turned to Straits.

'Nothing,' he said. 'No documents at all in Oxenford. I couldn't break into one chest, however, so it's possible . . .'

'Master Whitlow?' Chaucer looked the man in the eye.

'Deeds,' he muttered. 'Inspeximi. Nothing about the debt.'

'We'll have to go to law,' Ifaywer said.

'Go to law?' Glanville snapped. 'Tell them, Geoffrey.'

The comptroller leaned back in his chair. 'Before you can do that, gentlemen,' he said, 'there is the little matter of trespass in the castle of Clare – with intent to steal. And no doubt, a *certain* amount of damage to property.'

'We only want what's ours,' Fawcett said. He had been saying that, on and off, for the last hour.

Chaucer shrugged. 'Paperwork, gentlemen,' he said. 'Like it or not, this is the fourteenth century. We're drowning in the stuff and I predict it will only get worse. Without the Duke of Clarence's half of the indentures, your pieces of paper are worthless.'

There were rumblings all round, if only because the collective guildsmen knew that Chaucer was right.

'I think a word with the sheriff is in order,' Glanville said. 'Old Gower is not only a stickler for punishment – as painful and prolonged as he can make it – he owes me a favour or two. It'll be the stocks at least.' He made his fingers into scissors and snipped the air. 'And a bit of clipping too, if I know my Master Gower.'

'You wouldn't dare!' Fawcett snarled, feeling the power of the corporations at his back.

'Oh, but I would, rug-maker,' Glanville said. 'If I had my way, all of you would be dangling from Clare's battlements come morning.' He scraped his chair back. 'Don't imagine you've heard the last of this,' he said. 'Geoffrey?'

Chaucer got up too. He paused at the door. 'Another time, Master Ifaywer,' he said, 'for a round of queck. I'll wait until the feeling comes back to your feet after a day and a night in the stocks.'

And they left.

'We let them off too lightly, Geoff,' Glanville said as they padded back along Callis Street.

'Perhaps,' Chaucer said, 'but two things occurred to me as a result of our little chat with them.'

'Oh?'

'First, how is it that five tradesmen are so familiar with the internal arrangements of Clare? And second . . . and you'll have to help me here, Rich . . . where are Ferrante's quarters?'

'Um . . . the Auditor's Tower, floor below you. Why?'

'That's what I thought,' Chaucer nodded. 'So what, in the early hours of the morning, was he doing on the other side of the building, in the Constable Tower?'

Glanville put his hands behind his back and walked on, looking down at the ground in front of his feet. It was a habit he had had from boyhood and Chaucer knew it well. It was pointless trying to interrupt his train of thought now, so all he could do was wait.

They were nearly at the wicket gate in the great door of Clare before Glanville spoke. They slipped in past the sleeping guard and Glanville made himself a mental note to speak to the captain in the morning.

'I have no idea,' he said, in answer to Chaucer's question of at least ten minutes ago. 'I think we'll have to ask around a bit to find that out. One of the servants will know. They know everything.' A thought occurred to him. 'Ask Joyce. You seem to have . . . rekindled a little something there, am I right?'

The knight nudged the comptroller painfully in the ribs and Chaucer staggered, catching himself a nasty one on a low sconce on the wall.

'No,' he snapped. 'And even if we had, if you keep injuring me, I won't be able to do anything about it. Joyce was taken off to the kitchens, if you recall, in a bad way after the death of the dog. And that is, after all, why we're here.'

Glanville looked contrite. 'I'm sorry, Geoff. Thrill of the chase, all that kind of thing. I quite miss being on campaign, days and nights in the saddle. Sleeping under the stars. You know.'

Chaucer had been on campaign, it was true. But he had no memory of days and nights in the saddle and had never slept under a star in his life. His memory was of lavish food, tents with full-size beds in and every possible convenience. True, he had been briefly kidnapped, but in the most gentlemanly of circumstances, and he had been kept in the lap of luxury until Lionel of Antwerp had bailed him out. Also true, but something he preferred not to dwell on, was that it could have ended with his head flying through the air from a swipe of a razor-sharp blade, but it hadn't come to that, so why worry? For now, he wanted to find the bottle and, with a sudden flash, he knew where it was likely to be.

'Richard,' he said, slapping himself on the forehead. 'I know where the bottle is.'

'You do?' Glanville looked around. 'You mean, it's here? You've found it?'

'No,' Chaucer hissed. 'I mean I know where it is . . . except, I don't, really. Because I can't work out where the door is.'

Glanville looked at his old friend kindly. The years spent poring over ledgers had softened his brain. He pointed to the door, as if explaining to an idiot.

'Not *that* door!' Did the man have no brain at all? Why couldn't he follow the simplest train of thought? 'The back door to the room behind the laundry.'

'There's a room behind the laundry?' Glanville was learning a lot this night. He was still chewing over the word inspeximi.

Chaucer sighed. He had hoped this might be easier. 'Yes. The laundry leads into a little room where they stretch and smooth the linen for the Lady Violante's table. She is very particular, apparently.'

Glanville nodded. He had been present many a time when a wrinkle on the table linen had sent the woman into a rage.

'Joyce is particularly good at smoothing. She has a stretching table and a glass thing,' he mimed the size and shape with his hands, 'about yay long and . . . but that doesn't matter. What *does* matter is that she is really the only one who uses that room and if she wanted to have some time with the dog and perhaps give her a draught of her master's wine to try and cheer her up, it would be there. But we just need to find it.'

'Can you give me any more clues,' Glanville said. 'I don't walk the walls as often as I should. What's outside the room?'

Chaucer closed his eyes. 'There's a low wall. And . . . some trees.'

Glanville rolled his eyes. 'That could describe the curtain walls of almost the entire castle. Anything else?'

'The trees are old. They're' – again, Chaucer's hands came up to mime in the air – 'really old. Gnarled.' He smiled and held up a finger. 'They're *fruit* trees. It's an old orchard.'

Glanville smiled and clapped the man on the back. 'I know where that is,' he said. 'We used to scrump there when we were lads, remember?'

Chaucer had no recollection, but it would be rude to say so. 'Of course,' he said. 'I don't know why I didn't recall at once.'

'It's down here,' Glanville said, setting off at a steady pace down a dark passageway, with Chaucer in hot pursuit. The passages seemed endless and occasionally Chaucer lost the knight in his headlong flight, but eventually, a door was thrown open and silver moonlight flooded in. The knight stepped outside and round to the left, skirting a tower looming overhead. To the east, the faintest touch of dawn was brightening the sky and both men knew they must hurry.

The trees were gilded with the moonlight, their blossoms

almost glowing in the unearthly light. The sweet smell of last year's meagre crop, rotting to oblivion in the neglected grass, came to them on a faint morning breeze. It was overlaid with a hot, dry smell of lye and soap. This was the place.

The little door was in the shade of a deep lintel and the latch clicked up with nothing to stop it. No one bothered to lock this door; there was nothing beyond it of any value and, in any case, there was someone in the laundry day and night, making sure the fires never went out.

Chaucer could hardly believe his eyes. On the now-empty stretching table, outlined by a shaft of moonlight as if posing deliberately, was a bottle which had once contained the duke's favourite Gascony. The men looked at each other, each unwilling to be the one to step forward and take it from its place.

Chaucer broke the spell first and took the bottle by the neck. It still carried strands of sticky web around the bottom, gathered in the wine cellar deep below the castle. Otherwise, many hands had wiped the dust away and no one would think now that the wine within had cost the pay of several foot soldiers putting their lives at risk for God in a faraway land.

Chaucer sniffed the neck and wrinkled his nose. Holding the bottle low against his flank, he turned his head and sniffed the air.

'What do you smell here?' he asked his companion.

The knight inhaled extravagantly. 'Lye.' He inhaled again and his moustache positively rippled. 'Soap. Clean linen . . . that's it, I think.'

'Not mice?'

'Mice?' The man was puzzled, 'What in the name of all that's holy do mice smell of?' Sir Richard Glanville knew, of course, that there were such things as mice. He had heard servants speak of them as somewhat of a nuisance. He had seen mice, usually in the jaws of a cat. But as for getting close enough to smell one – why would anyone want to do that?

'Well . . .' Chaucer wafted the bottle towards him. It was at that moment that he knew that a gulf had grown between him and his childhood friend that could never really be bridged. He lived in the midst of a permanent state of war with mice.

There were mice in his clothes press. If he were not careful, there were mice among his papers and his books. He could blush to this day when remembering the time he had unfurled a complex document which had taken him months to prepare and have properly sealed and accredited, only to have a mother mouse and her eight babies fall at the king's feet. All he could do was shrug and, luckily, Edward III had become just a threat gaga by that time, so he probably didn't notice. 'Mice. A kind of . . . acidy, dampy, old leafy . . . *mousey* smell.' He held out the bottle. 'Sniff that.'

Glanville advanced his nose, cautiously, to the bottle and gave a delicate sniff. He recoiled, his hand over his nose. 'What in the name of God is that?' he said, screwing up his face. 'Oh, God, oh, God, it's in my moustache.' He rubbed his hand over his face, desperately trying to dissipate the smell. 'It's . . .' He was lost for words.

'Mouse,' said Chaucer, complacently. 'Or, in the absence of the actual *rodentia* themselves, it's something else.'

'What?' Glanville was spitting discreetly and still wiping his moustache.

'Hemlock. Sneaky plant in that it looks like others that are totally harmless. Do you remember, when we were lads, making pea-shooters from the cow parsley in the lane?'

Glanville smiled. 'I do. Keck, we used to call it.'

'That's right. Well, from what I have learned since, we were lucky. If we had accidentally come across hemlock, we wouldn't be sitting here now. It can kill even by touching it. Or, as seems to be the case here, drinking it in your favourite wine.'

'If I may say so,' Chaucer looked at Richard Glanville as he came into the hall for breakfast the next day, 'you look like shit.'

'Thank you,' Geoffrey,' the knight said. 'That would be because I spent half the night chasing my tail around sneaking guildsmen and poisoned bottles.'

That may have been too loud and he and Chaucer both looked up as servants came and went. Chaucer caught the eye of John Hawkwood a few places along the table; mercenaries never missed a free meal if one was on offer.

'The rest of the night,' Glanville was whispering now, 'I spent compiling this.' He pulled a piece of parchment from his doublet and unrolled it on his lap, under the table and away from Hawkwood's glare.

'What is it?' Chaucer asked.

'Well, I can't pretend it's complete, but it's a list of people who might have wanted to see Lionel of Antwerp dead.'

'Mother of God,' Chaucer muttered. 'This is nearly as long as the book of Leviticus.' He suddenly caught the eye of Father Clement who was making his way to Hawkwood's side. 'Charming custom this,' the comptroller said loudly, 'breaking fast.'

'Italian custom,' Glanville said, equally loudly. 'Lady Violante insists on it, although she takes hers in her chambers.'

Hawkwood belched.

'Very wise,' Chaucer said, helping himself to the bread and cheese, being careful to cut some from an already started piece – a man could not be too careful. And although sharing food with the rest of the table was not a certain way to be safe by any means, at least they could all die in agony together, a small but real comfort. 'Is this in any order of priority?' He was whispering again.

'No. That's a step too far for me, Geoff. That's why you're here. Er . . . pass me that flagon, would you?'

Chaucer reached across to the flagon of ale and sniffed it before passing it to the knight. A few scandalized faces turned to him; what a knarre, going around sniffing his food and drink.

Glanville was a little startled too, and then remembered. 'Mice?' he asked.

'No. Just ale, if a little' – he sniffed again – 'yeasty.'

'Too young, that's the trouble. Hard to keep up with demand in a place this size.' Butterfield's voice from just above their heads made both men jump. 'I do apologize, gentlemen. Shall I call for another?'

'No, no.' Chaucer was quick to reassure him. 'I just have . . . I just have this habit of sniffing my food and drink.' He gave a nervous laugh. 'I've done it since childhood. Do you remember, Rich,' and he gave the knight a savage dig in the ribs with his elbow, 'how His Grace used to take me to task?'

Glanville nodded, laughing loudly. 'Do I?' he said, hoping that was the right thing to say.

'I try not to do it but, sometimes, it all comes flooding back. So, no, Butterfield, thank you. This ale will suffice.'

The seneschal bowed over their heads and slid away, to find a servant to berate.

'Was he looking at the list, do you think?' Chaucer asked.

'No. He's just . . . well, he's just a very good seneschal. He watches every part of the castle's life and you had criticized his ale, that was all. I'm sure he wasn't . . .' but even so, the knight leaned back and scanned the servants for the seneschal's groomed and busy head. He was nowhere to be seen.

Chaucer looked down at the list in his lap and pointed to a name. 'Who's this?'

'Oh, scratch him out. He was Bishop of Ely, but he died the other day, before Lionel, I mean. Just heard now, as I came through the yard.'

'This one?'

'Norfolk, Duke of,' Glanville said. Clearly Chaucer's eyes were not what they had been. 'Tricky lot, the Norfolks.'

'He's six,' Chaucer reminded him.

'Oh, is he?' Glanville had been wrongfooted. 'Well, never mind. He's got people. You can't be too careful.'

Chaucer scratched the precocious lad out in his mind.

'Whitlow?' he hissed.

'Quite.' Glanville was sipping his ale, yeasty or not.

'The haberdasher?'

'Well, I was going to put all the guildsmen in, but then I remembered; Whitlow's Blanche's uncle, Peter Vickers' brother-in-law.'

'We'll need to talk to both of them,' Chaucer said.

There was a sudden guffaw from Hawkwood's table as the freebooter and the chaplain rocked at some bon mot.

'I didn't know Hawkwood could laugh,' Chaucer muttered.

'Nor I,' Glanville agreed. 'I don't think I've ever seen him smile. You know he's staying on, don't you?'

'Really?'

Glanville nodded. 'John of Gaunt's off today, so we won't be stumbling over his heavies filling the baileys, but Hawkwood's staying to recruit, apparently. Wants a few more for his White Company. There's another campaign in the wind, Geoff, for sure.'

Chaucer looked at his old friend. 'Will you go?'

'France?' The knight stroked his luxuriant moustache, dislodging crumbs as he did so. 'I don't know. Du Guesclin's a tricky bastard – and I'm not talking about Violante's falcon. Maybe it's time to hang up my sword. Ah, Hugh, my boy.'

The squire half-bowed to his father and Chaucer. 'Masters,' he beamed. 'I could eat a horse.' He sat himself down, pointing to Glanville's plate. 'Are you going to eat that, Pa?'

# SIX

'Out towards Sudbury way' was all very well. Actually finding the manor house of Peter Vickers was something else entirely. Chaucer set off at first light, declining the company of Richard Glanville, who had spent much of the previous day seeing John of Gaunt off the premises at Clare. He had stood in the castle's outer bailey with Butterfield, the seneschal close to tears at the mess that Gaunt's rabble had left behind. Then, it had been all clash and carry, rubbish to be collected, horseshit to add to the marling, cesspits to be dug and filled. That was no job for a knight of the shire, but Richard Glanville was ever a man of duty and he stayed behind to supervise.

'Even so, Geoff,' the knight had held out his sword, still in its scabbard, 'I fancy Peter Vickers will still be nursing a sore head after what Hawkwood did to that crony of his. Better go prepared.'

Chaucer smiled, laying the flat of his hand on the hilt as he reached down from the saddle. 'All that was a long time ago, Rich,' he said. 'I'd only drop the damned thing on my foot,' and he wheeled the grey away.

The comptroller took the low road that wound its way through Belchamp St Paul and Belchamp Otten. The villages were aptly named; the fields, green with spring shoots, were indeed beautiful. Smocked peasants pruned the fruit trees and bent their backs in the rich earth to plant the peas and the beans. One or two of them looked up at the horseman plodding by. Vintner, thought one. Tapicer, another reckoned. On the other hand, he could be a prelate without his robes; he was plump enough.

Then, Chaucer followed the winding road to the north-east, to Borley. The comptroller had stopped at a wayside inn at midday and had broken bread with the landlord, who, at the drop of several groats, was a mine of information, some of it useful. Yes, the Vickers family lived at Borley Manor. It had been the home of the Waldegraves for years, but old Robert Waldegrave had gone on a pilgrimage to the shrine of Our Lady at Walsingham and had never come back. As he was the last of a long line, the estate was broken up and Peter Vickers had acquired it. The landlord didn't have much time for Peter Vickers. The landlord didn't have much time for anybody, unless that anybody had coin in his purse. And that fact alone made Master Chaucer *most* welcome.

The comptroller rode on, mellower now in the afternoon sun with some good Suffolk ale inside him. He saw the buttresses of the still-new Benedictine abbey away across the fields and heard the bells tolling for None. He spurred his horse, which ignored him; the journey had been long and hot enough without breaking into anything resembling a trot. He had taken the journey at too leisurely a pace and he still had much to do.

The manor itself, tucked away in a valley, was pleasant enough. The Waldegraves had clearly had taste. There was a moat, dark waters dabbled with ducks and geese, and the bright new green of bulrushes in the shallower points carved out by time and weather along the edge. The gatehouse, like the rest of the building, was made of warm Suffolk stone. The walls were crenellated and the battlements looked new; perhaps Peter Vickers was expecting a siege. Chaucer reined in on the little drawbridge and waited, scanning the walls and windows for any sign of movement.

Something in the orchard caught his eye. There. There it was again. A flash of black in the dappled sunlight under the trees. Chaucer's horse snorted and snickered and he calmed it with a pat to the neck and whispered words.

'Hoo, traveller!' A voice from the gateway brought his attention to the front.

'Hoo,' Chaucer called back, giving the universal cry of the tournament. 'Is the squire at home?'

A solid-looking steward walked into the sunshine. He *might* have been one of the oafs at Vickers' back at Clare when John Hawkwood scattered them, but Chaucer couldn't be sure.

'What business do you have?' the steward wanted to know.

'My own,' Chaucer said, and nudged the horse forward. He tugged a seal from his purse. 'You know the king's device,' he said. It was a statement, not a question. *Everybody* knew the king's device. The steward scowled. His job was to keep out strangers, not let them pry into Vickers' business. On the other hand, looking up at him from the rubbed red wax was the king's badge; this was *way* above his pay scale.

'Sir Peter is not at home,' he said.

*Sir* Peter; that was new to Chaucer. The man was a guildsman, albeit with ideas above his station. 'Then I shall wait,' he said. 'Have you accommodation for a servant of the king?'

The comptroller had used this ploy before and it had never let him down yet. The steward hesitated, then social divisions got the better of him and he ushered Chaucer in under the gateway into a small courtyard. He clicked his fingers and a lackey bobbed into view, rather old, rather infirm. 'A room for this gentleman, Ratcliffe,' the steward said. 'Jackie boy, take the horse.' A spotty groom who stank of horse liniment scrabbled up to catch Chaucer's bridle and he led the animal away.

'When do you expect Sir Peter?' Chaucer asked the steward.

'Tomorrow, sir,' the man said. 'Soon after cockcrow. Shall I send some minnow pie for your supper? Or lampreys?'

'Minnows will be excellent,' Chaucer said. 'Thank you.' And he followed the shambling minion, who creaked and puffed and groaned on every stair. It was now that he saw through the steward's little game. He was not going to stay in the main house, but a tiny annexe along a high walkway. He could make out the abbey's tracery tops from here, high above the trees, and he had rarely seen a room so small; it made his premises over Aldgate look palatial.

'I hope as how you'll be comfortable, sir,' the old man said. 'Fresh straw on the floor and the pisspot's empty.' He kicked it to prove that it was so and was rewarded with a dull clang.

'Joy,' Chaucer said. He held the man's sleeve as he made to leave. 'Tell me, er . . . Ratcliffe, is it?'

'It is, sir,' the old man wheezed. 'Man and boy. I used to do for Sir Robert Waldegrave back in the day. Now I do for Sir Peter Vickers . . .' It may have been coincidence, or a sign of contempt, but Ratcliffe suddenly coughed so that his whole body shook and his phlegm spattered onto the fresh straw.

Chaucer already had half an angel in his hand. 'Is Mistress Blanche about?' he asked quietly.

An evil look came over the old man's face. 'She be about five Suffolk feet,' he said, knowingly. Then he tapped the side of his substantial nose. 'Mind you, ask me, they're all the same length laying down.' He already had the silver in his hand when loyalty to his current master got the better of him. 'Why would you want to know about Mistress Blanche?' He peered up into Chaucer's face.

'To pay my respects,' the comptroller lied. 'My wife is an old friend of Mistress Blanche's second cousin.'

'What, that Agatha Tickhill? She's no better nor she should be, though perhaps I shouldn't say, your wife being a friend of hers.'

Bugger, Chaucer thought, but he was in this up to his liripipe now and to back down might seem cowardly. 'That's her,' he beamed cheerily, with a wink to show Ratcliffe that they were all men of the world here.

Ratcliffe looked down at the coin in his hand. 'I dunno,' he said, ruminating on the state of the nation. 'Money don't go nowhere nowadays, do it?'

Chaucer *had* heard heavier hints, but not for some time. He passed the old man another coin. Ratcliffe bit this and instantly regretted it as a partial molar joined the phlegm on the floor. He winked back at Chaucer. 'I'll send her to you,' he said. 'Around twelve of the clock. No promises, mind.' And he was gone.

Chaucer tried to stay awake. The bed was excruciating and the feather pillows felt as if the goose itself was still under the linen. Even so, the minnow pie had been excellent and the wine was not bad in a Suffolk sort of way. So, as midnight approached, he found his eyelids drooping and the candle's glow getting ever fainter as the wick sank into the tallow and sputtered and flickered as it drowned.

'Marie?'

Chaucer sat bolt upright. All right, so he'd been asleep. But he hadn't had his usual terrifying dream, of the damned souls of the Pestilence crawling towards him, ready to drag him down to Hell. But, surely, he had heard a voice; sometimes, in the night, he heard Pippa calling him, but she never called him, what was it?

'Marie?'

Yes, that was it.

'Marie? Is that you?'

Chaucer blew out the remains of the candle. He reached out for the poignard hidden under the coverlet and tightened his grip on the hilt.

'Marie, for God's sake,' the voice hissed, exasperated.

'Yes,' Chaucer whispered back, hoping in his sibilance to pass for the female of the species.

'Let me in. It'll be Matins shortly.'

Chaucer heard the bed creak as he left it. He crossed the floor, the rushes rustling under his feet, and he lifted the door latch, tucking himself behind the oak as he did so. A black-robed figure stepped in. Chaucer had seen Richard Glanville in action; he knew exactly what to do. He grabbed the cowl and swung the man sideways onto the bed. In an instant, he was astride him, the dagger-blade at the man's throat.

Whoever was lying between his legs gave a little squeak, then lay still.

'Marie?' he was still whispering.

'Don't be so bloody silly,' Chaucer said. 'Do I *look* like Marie?'

The man on the bed couldn't see anything. All he knew was that Marie had never pulled a knife on him before. He reached up towards Chaucer's face, feeling the beard, the moustache.

'Do you *mind*!' Chaucer knocked his hand away. Then he got off the night visitor and wrenched back the curtains. The man on the bed was a Benedictine monk, to judge by his habit, and his head was newly tonsured. He had sandals on his feet and a terrified look on his face.

'There's been some mistake,' he said.

'Tell me about it,' Chaucer growled. In the face of a man of God, he would normally have put his dagger away, but the last few moments had been peculiar and he wasn't taking any chances. 'Who's Marie?'

The monk half sat up, crossing himself in the half-light. 'Marie Lairre,' he blurted out. 'That's not her real name, of course. It's just what I call her.'

'Of course it's not,' Chaucer said, and waited for an explanation. When clearly none was forthcoming, he prompted the man. 'So what is?'

'Blanche,' the monk said. 'Blanche Vickers.'

'And you?'

'Sunex Amures.'

'Do what?'

'Father Innocent.'

Chaucer snorted. 'Pull the other one,' he said. 'How old are you, boy?'

'Twenty,' Innocent told him.

'And you hoped to be a monk, eh?'

'I *am* a monk,' Innocent retorted.

'Not after tonight, you're not. Tell me, is this the usual place you and Blanche meet?'

'Yes,' the monk confessed, his subterfuge uncovered, his world collapsed.

'For Bible studies, no doubt,' Chaucer shook his head.

'I have sinned.' The boy's lip quivered.

'Save that for the abbot,' the comptroller said, 'and don't feel too badly about it. I get the impression that Mistress Blanche spreads her favours in more directions than yours. What's all this Marie Lairre, Sunex Amures stuff?'

The monk was blushing in the half-light, but Chaucer couldn't see it. 'Just a little game we had,' Innocent said. 'Sir . . . whoever you are. I know I have broken my vows and that I will burn in Hellfire for eternity.'

'Pretty much,' Chaucer nodded.

'But . . . Blanche and I, we're in love, you see.'

Sweet, thought Chaucer, but he'd probably been cynical enough for one night and said nothing.

'The names we made up, I suppose, disguised my appalling lapse from God's grace.'

Chaucer slipped the poignard away. 'Whatever happens now,

lad,' he said, 'is between you and your God. Mistress Blanche doesn't know I've found you out and neither does the abbot. Neither of them will know from me.'

The monk burst into tears and Chaucer, not for the first time and probably not for the last, found himself gently patting a sobbing Benedictine.

Chaucer's life seemed to be controlled by bells. Nothing was as irritating as Aldgate in the morning, but the bells of the abbey near Borley woke him early. He smiled to himself as he thought of the frustrated – and probably now terrified – Innocent Sunex Amures, going about his ecclesiastical business with Chaucer's face imprinted on his memory and Chaucer's dagger-point tickling his chin.

But the smile on Chaucer's face did not last long. There was a thud on the walkway beyond the wall and the door crashed back. Armed men stood there in a cluster, blocking out the early morning light. The comptroller rolled sideways to grab the poignard but he was far too slow and a quarterstaff smashed into his shoulder and against his hand and then he was pinned against the rough stone wall, sitting up in bed with his nightshirt around his neck.

'I should put that away, Master Chaucer,' the first man said, glancing down. 'Not very seemly for a man who carries the king's cypher.'

Chaucer hauled at the shirt to give himself what dignity he could. 'What is the meaning of this?' sounded an official and outraged enough tone to take.

The man clicked his fingers and the quarterstaffs were pulled back. Chaucer had more room now to see to his dress and took the opportunity to straighten his beard at the same time.

'Perhaps you could tell me,' the man said, 'Why, for instance, would you want to meet my daughter at midnight?'

Chaucer peered up into the man's face more closely. 'Ah,' he said with the air of a man with his fingers in a mousetrap, 'You're Peter Vickers.'

'Nearly,' the man said. 'I am *Sir* Peter Vickers.'

'Really?' Chaucer had recovered his sang-froid. 'I must

have a word with my old friend the Garter King of Arms; he seems to have left you off his list.'

Vickers spat onto the now less-than-fresh straw. 'About Blanche,' he said, levelly.

'Yes.' Chaucer tried to get up but was prodded back with a quarterstaff. 'I did not suggest the hour – your man Ratcliffe did. I want to talk to her about the death of His Grace Lionel of Antwerp.'

'Foreign bloody place, Antwerp,' Vickers said, 'I shouldn't wonder. What do you imagine my Blanche knows about Lionel of Antwerp's death?'

'She was with him the night he died,' Chaucer said. Vickers slapped him across the face with his right hand. 'That's a damned lie!' he growled.

'Is it?' Chaucer licked the trickle of blood from his lower lip. 'Let's let Blanche be the judge of that, shall we?'

Vickers raised his hand again, but Chaucer's brain was faster than any hand in Suffolk, except perhaps one and his was the name he invoked now. 'I wouldn't do that, Master Vickers,' he said. 'Not with John Hawkwood on his way.'

'Hawkwood?' Vickers narrowed his eyes. 'On his way? What, here?'

'The same,' Chaucer nodded. He was lying through his rattled teeth of course, but he'd square it all with his confessor the next time he saw him. 'He's made a fool of you once. And this time, he'll have his White Company with him.'

Like everybody in England, not to mention France, Peter Vickers had heard of the White Company. They hung men in chains from the walls of manors like his, ripped out tongues with red-hot pincers, hung heads from their horse-harnesses as trophies. And he himself had seen what he could do with a knife; old Tom's body in the hayloft awaiting burial was testimony to that.

Vickers grabbed Chaucer by the lapels of his nightshirt and hauled him upright. 'You'll never even attempt to come near my daughter again,' he said, and drove his knee hard into Chaucer's groin. 'Throw this bastard out of here,' he snapped, spinning on his heel as he left.

Vickers' people were used to seeing men who had somehow upset their lord and master being given the bum's rush. Chaucer was half carried, struggling and kicking, to the main gate. Here he was dropped on the grass, quietly grateful that it wasn't in the moat, and his clothes, bag and dagger were thrown at him. The laughter died down from the manor walls and people went about their business again, happy with the day's free entertainment.

It was only now that Chaucer began to feel his aches and pains. His lip throbbed and he could see part of it, an ugly purple through his moustache if he looked down. At least one tooth was loose and his ribs and forearms were dark with the bruising of the quarterstaffs. The knuckles of his right hand were huge and painful. So it was slowly and deliberately that he laced up his houppelande and looked about him for new moss for his shoes.

'Psst!' A sibilance came from under the gateway's arch. Chaucer looked up. There was his mare, saddled and bridled and a spotty lad holding it close to him. He was beckoning Chaucer over. The comptroller creaked into an upright position and wandered over. The animal's nose felt warm, soft and comforting and her eyes were kind and gentle. He pressed his forehead against her warm cheek and drew a deep breath. Almost safe.

'Beg pardon, sir,' the lad bumbled.

'Yes, boy?' Chaucer kept his head against the horse's cheek and his eyes closed. He did his best to speak through the swelling lip.

'Ratcliffe's compliments, sir. He says he's sorry about last night, giving you what you probably take to be false and misleading statements about Mistress Blanche. And to make up for it,' the lad glanced in all directions before continuing, 'he says you'll find her at the Dominican Priory at Bures. Yonder,' he pointed to the south-east. 'An hour's ride.'

'Thank you,' Chaucer said, though why he should believe old Ratcliffe after the fiasco of last night, he had no idea. He took the animal's reins and let the boy ease him up into the saddle. He looked down at him. 'I don't suppose old Ratcliffe was sorry enough to return my angel?' he asked.

The lad shrugged.

'No,' said Chaucer. 'I didn't think so.'

\*     \*     \*

Chaucer was not a natural horseman at the very best of times. An ambling pad was just about acceptable, anything with any life in it at all was something he looked at with trepidation. Riding a horse with somewhat of a mind of its own when nursing more bruises than he had ever had before was almost insupportable. But he had set out from Clare with the intention of seeing Blanche Vickers and – possibly – solving the puzzle of the death of Lionel of Antwerp and, by all that was holy, that was what he was going to do.

In truth, he felt a little sorry for the girl; if the convent was to be her life from now on it seemed a little harsh. Yes, she had crept into the bed of a man old enough to be her grand-father with nothing but gain on her mind. Yes, she had led on a young man of whom Chaucer was very fond, only to break his heart. Yes, she had midnight trysts with young and vigorous monks in hidden rooms in her father's house. Chaucer paused in his musings and had to admit that – even taking just the things he knew about her into account, and he suspected there was probably far more – a convent was almost certainly the right place for her. As long as the walls were high and the locks strong.

The comptroller glanced at the sky. The lad at the gate had said that the priory was an hour away but, somehow, it seemed much further. His bruises had settled into a dull ache now, from their screaming agony of earlier. His lip, though still swollen, was no longer visible when he glanced down. But his buttocks had taken the path of least resistance and were now totally numb. He knew when he eventually reached his destination, he would need some very serious help were he to be able to dismount from his horse.

He and his mount had settled into a friendly amble along an undeniably pretty path. The green shoots over his head were letting through some dappled sun. The birds were singing their heads off, a starling above the rest running through its repertoire of their calls, including a very fair representation of distant bells. Chaucer smiled. Starlings were so often looked down upon – except as a fine dinner, wrapped in pastry – but they were the clowns and entertainers of the bird world, with their spangled feathers and jaunty air. He wished he spent more time in the country. Aldgate was all very well, but you could spend a week there and not see so much as a blade of grass, nor hear a bird except the wheeling gulls from the river.

The horse slowed and then stopped. Chaucer looked up suddenly and realized he may well have been asleep, he hoped for not too long. If he had passed the priory, he would have wept; he didn't want to spend another minute in the saddle if he could help it.

A grey wall was to his left, unbroken by windows and with just a single door, set towards one end. He looked up and saw soaring towers, cut with fine tracery, through which bells could be seen, swaying gently to and fro. He had time to consider the fact that he had never seen that before when the air was filled with the sound of pealing brass. He covered his ears and the mare jinked, making every bone in Chaucer's body shout for mercy. If it hadn't made him and his mount jump, the sound would have struck him as very beautiful, but here, just above his head, it was a cacophony. It was also a nuisance; he knew that it meant the beginning of Sext, and so no one would answer the door or speak to him for a good while.

He was in a quandary. He couldn't get off his mare unaided but, then again, he couldn't bear to stay in the saddle either. The horse dropped her head to crop the short grass and he nearly shot over her neck. The thought of putting up with this for the best part of an hour just couldn't be countenanced and he shook the stirrup leathers and urged the animal on. He had worked out that if he could tether her to a tree, then he might be able to swing one leg over and make a controlled fall to the ground.

The mare, for once, seemed to understand what was wanted of her and strolled amiably enough across the grass to a tree on the far side of the door. Now he was nearer, Chaucer could see the little wicket in the gate and the barred window in the wicket. His heart fell. This meant a strict house; although the rules were laid down in all priories up and down the land, for some prioresses, especially the ones in retirement from the world after a husband or three, rules were made to be, if not broken, at least bent. Such women made sure that the door stood open at all times and visitors were welcomed. The strict ones made their premises as hard to broach as the Tun. This one seemed to be one of those, damnation to it.

The grey stood patiently by the tree until Chaucer had wrapped the bridle around a low branch. If he had been able to read the animal's mind, he would have found that she was as keen to get rid of her rider as Chaucer was to dismount. Once he was sure that the mare was not going to be able to bolt, Chaucer tried raising a leg to swing it out of the saddle, but it didn't seem keen to comply. Shifting his weight to the other buttock, stifling a yelp of pain, he tried again and this time managed to end up with one foot in the stirrup and one knee on the saddle, unable to go either forward or back. The horse shifted her feet petulantly. With most of Chaucer's weight on one side, the girth was digging in cruelly and she wasn't planning to stand this much longer. She shook her head, trying to free the bridle from the tree and that was enough to dislodge Chaucer, who fell like a sack of flour to the ground.

The animal looked down and wondered for a moment whether it might be her fault that the fat rider who had been such a burden for so long was flailing on the ground with a rather strange purple hue around his lips, but decided that, as a beast of burden, it was never her fault. And anyway, the horse reasoned, those flapping black things running towards him would probably see him all right. The mare snipped off a new leaf with her teeth and chewed thoughtfully. It would all work out, she was sure.

'Mother! Mother! Is he dead?'

Chaucer had been unconscious briefly but now wondered, as he came to, whether it might be worse. Was he dead? He hadn't called for his mother in years. Then, he became aware that it wasn't his voice. So why were these women calling his mother? He opened his eyes.

'Of course he's not dead,' a voice said behind his head. 'Look, his eyes are opening.' A face swung into view. 'Are you all right, my good man? We saw you fall. You are dreadfully bruised. How did that happen in a simple fall from a horse?'

'Perhaps he falls off a lot, Mother,' a voice said, off to one side, and was rewarded by giggles from other unseen people.

90                                    M.J. Trow

The face overhanging Chaucer's withdrew from his limited
field of vision. 'Frivolity is a sin, Sister Lawrence,' she snapped.
There was more giggling and now the voice was positively
acid. 'That goes for all of you. You can all go . . . yes, now,
do not tarry . . . go and say one hundred . . . no, two hundred
Hail Marys. And don't shirk them. I want them said properly,
and with reverence. Send two of the kitchen men out, with a
litter. We must take this poor traveller inside and tend to his
wounds.'

Chaucer tried to get up. He didn't want tending. In fact, he
corrected himself, he did *want* tending. What he didn't want was
to waste time while a lot of nuns flustered around him bathing
bits he would rather a nun didn't see. 'No, Mother, I . . .'

A hand as strong as a wrestler's came down on his shoulder.
'Now, now, traveller. Don't try to get up. My serving men will
be here shortly and we will take you to the hospice. You have
clearly been injured. Tell me, were you set upon by footpads?
We have a lot around here, sadly. Now . . .' she looked up as
the wicket gate sprang open and shut. 'But wait, here they
are. They will take you to bed and Sister Thomas will be with
you shortly. She is very learned in the ways of herbs and
tinctures.'

There was a rustle overhead and Chaucer heard her giving
the men their orders. He briefly toyed with leaping into the
saddle and riding hell for leather back to Clare, but the few
cells in his brain which had not been shaken loose in the fall
told him it was impossible. So he lay there, waiting to be lifted
onto the litter and taken off for the tender ministrations of
Sister Thomas.

# SEVEN

He didn't mean to sleep. But, what with one thing and another, it seemed like the sensible thing to do. He was laid on a bed in a whitewashed room, with a simple wooden crucifix above him. The soft spring sunshine came through the high window and made a square of gold on the rough woollen blanket over his legs. He listened to the birdsong outside and the soughing of the leaves. Somewhere, a long way away, a cuckoo called, hesitant and not yet ready to tell the world that spring had sprung. He closed his eyes again, soaking in the peace.

A door opened gently and he peeped from under his lids. A little nun came in, carrying a bowl and a ewer in her arms. Over her arm hung a bag and she brought with her a fresh smell, as of aired linen and lavender. She put the bowl down on a table by Chaucer's bed and poured some water into it. She sprinkled herbs and powders into the water and mixed them round with her hand. She smelled the water and then added a pinch more of a pale powder that smelled of cut grass. Then she smiled and nodded to herself and, taking a cloth from her bag, wrung it out in the water.

'There's no point in pretending, traveller,' she said. 'You might be able to fool a couple of silly novices you are dead, but you can't fool me.' She flicked a couple of drops of water across his eyes and he flinched. 'Come on. Open your eyes and tell me about yourself.'

Despite the flinch, Chaucer hoped he could carry it off. After all, she wasn't a doctor of physick. How did she know whether a man was dead, unconscious or shamming?

She stood back, looking at him for a moment. Then she rolled up her sleeves and girded up her habit above her knees. She swept the wings of her coif back and pinned them behind her head. 'In that case,' she said to the empty room, 'I suppose

I must just wash the poor man and set him to rights before he meets his Maker.'

Before Chaucer could do anything, she had wrenched back the blanket, which was when he discovered that the nuns had undressed him at some point, hopefully when he was unconscious. He lay as naked as a jay in the bed and she slapped vigorously at his private fundaments with the wet cloth. He sat up with an alacrity he hadn't managed for some time, covering his modesty with his bruised forearms.

The nun stepped back, hands in the air. 'By the Holy Mother Mary,' she carolled. 'If it isn't a miracle!'

She pushed him back on the bed, adjusted the small, straw-filled pillow behind his head and covered him up again.

'Madam!' he said, aghast. 'Where are my clothes?'

'In a box under the bed,' she said. 'And when I have tended your wounds and you have had some nourishment, you can put them on and go. I would confess, though, to the sin of being a nosy old woman with not enough to occupy my mind, and would ask you how on God's beautiful earth you came by such bruises in a simple fall from a stationary horse.'

Chaucer looked at her and couldn't help but smile. The nun was small and soft looking but obviously was as strong as a whip. Her face was creased with smiling and her blue eyes almost crackled with fun. He couldn't imagine what had brought her to the priory unless it really was for the love of God; not necessarily a given, in his experience. 'Sister Thomas?' he checked.

'The very same. Now, are you going to let me look at those bruises? And, perhaps more important, are you going to tell me how you came by them? Because if it was from a little fall from a horse, you need to go and see a physician quickly, traveller.'

Chaucer looked at her. There seemed no way out. She was going to wield her cloth come hell or high water and, if he didn't tell her how he got the bruises, he would be kept in this bed and dosed until his pips squeaked.

'I was beaten by Peter Vickers and his men,' he said.

The nun looked thoughtful. 'The oaf was here yesterday,' she remarked, flicking back the blanket and covering Chaucer's bits and bobs with a cloth in one fluid movement. She caught his eye. 'I have no more desire to look at them than you have for me to see,' she said. 'So let's ignore them, shall we?' She patted her cloth over the worst of Chaucer's bruises, tutting as she went. He was surprised to find that he felt almost instantly better.

'What is that stuff?' he asked.

'Nothing much. Spring water, arnica, valerian root. It will cool and soothe the bruises, make you able to leave before nightfall. Unless you would rather stay. Where are you bound for?'

'Clare.'

'Clare? That's quite a ride. Perhaps you had best stay.'

'No. They'll worry. I've already been too long. Perhaps if one of your servants could come with me?'

'I'll speak to the Mother Superior. I'm sure that can be arranged. But . . . Vickers. Why did he beat you? Apart from the fact that he is a pig and a bully, of course.'

'Do you know him well?' She seemed to have the measure of the man as far as Chaucer could tell.

'No. I saw him yesterday, just briefly. I was on the gate when he came with his daughter. But I have seen her since and from that I conclude that he is a pig and a bully. She is deeply shocked. And also, though I perhaps shouldn't say it, covered in bruises.'

Chaucer held his counsel. With Blanche, there was no certain way of telling how she came by those.

'And I know what you're thinking, traveller . . . what is your name, by the way? We need it for the ledger.'

'The *ledger*?' Chaucer was somewhat taken aback.

'We keep a ledger, of course, of all the poor souls we have helped. We send it to the bishop once a year, to show that we are doing our work for the Lord.'

'Goodness.' Chaucer now felt less like a treasured guest and more like a number in some holy quota.

'Indeed.' The nun decided to take him at face value. 'Goodness is our work. So, your name . . .?'

'Chaucer. Geoffrey Chaucer. Comptroller of the King's Woollens.'

'Of *Woollens*, you say? That sounds important.' She twinkled at him and dabbed away with her cloth. 'That would explain the king's seal, then.'

'You went through my bag?' Chaucer was having his view of nuns somewhat turned upside down by this little woman.

'Of course. In case you died, we needed to know who to tell. But you don't have anything in your bag to help. We would have gone to the king, in the end, I suppose. But now we don't need to, Master Chaucer. But, as I was saying, nun I may be, but I know when a bruise is the result of a strap at the hand of an angry father or some lovemaking that got out of hand. And hers are the former.'

'He *beat* her?' Chaucer was both aghast and unsurprised.

'Indeed he did. And not just now and again. The welts are fresh and also scarred. No wonder she sought comfort with men. She was looking for someone to take her away from her father.'

She put her cloth back in the water and turned the blanket back over him, reaching under it to remove the cloth she had put there for modesty.

'Oh!'

'My apologies, Master Chaucer. I rather overreached myself there.' She smiled at him and he couldn't help but smile back, through the tears. 'What I would suggest is that you rest for half an hour. We will be at None soon and if you want to dress then, you won't be disturbed. I will arrange a man to travel with you. I think that is your best plan. Get away from here, before Master Vickers gets any ideas into his head and wants to beat something weaker than himself again.'

'I can't leave until I have spoken to Blanche . . . er . . . is that still her name?'

Sister Thomas smiled. 'She will remain Blanche until she takes her vows. I say "until" – I imagine, with a young lady like Blanche with her . . . needs . . . I perhaps should say "if". But, why do you need to talk to her? Surely, you are not one . . .'

Chaucer couldn't decide how to take that. He was years younger than Lionel of Antwerp, that he knew, though perhaps the difference of almost twelve inches in height, the lack of an enormous fortune and the fact that he was not related to the king might have been deciding factors in a straight fight. 'I don't know quite what you mean, Sister Thomas,' he said, drawing his dignity around him like a cloak. She had, after all, had a handful of all Chaucer held most dear, so there was no need for levity. 'I need to speak to her because she was . . . or may have been . . . the last to see a very dear friend before he died.'

'Oh, dear!' Sister Thomas quickly crossed herself. 'She didn't . . . kill him, did she?'

Chaucer frowned. For a nun, this woman had quite a mind with but one thought in it. He decided to tell her the facts, unadorned and simple. By the time he had finished, she had tears in her eyes. 'He was a sinner, your friend,' she said, 'but he didn't deserve that. And his poor *dog*.' She leaned nearer. 'We will be at None in a very short while. I just have time to see Blanche and send her to you. She won't be expected at devotions yet. But, Master Chaucer, be quick and be discreet. I will have a man ready with your horse within the half-hour. Get dressed, get ready, speak to Blanche and then go. Will you do that?'

'I will. Thank you, Sister Thomas.'

'*Pax vobiscum*,' she said. 'God will go with you, Master Chaucer, of that I am sure. Whether you will go with him' – she shrugged – 'that is up to you.' And with that, she crossed herself and slipped out of the door, silent as a shadow.

As soon as he was sure she had gone, Chaucer felt under the bed for his clothes and bag and dressed as quickly as he could. He was still doing up his final laces when there was a tap at the door and Blanche Vickers slipped in, closing it behind her with exaggerated care.

'Sister Thomas said you wanted to see me,' she whispered. 'We need to be quick. Those black devils will be out of the chapel soon and I can't be caught in here. They think I want to bed any man I see. They watch me like hawks with a mouse.'

'Well, *don't* you want to bed any man you see?' Chaucer asked, quite reasonably in his view.

'No!' Her voice was a squeak. 'I don't want to bed *you*, tor a start!' She looked him up and down with contempt.

'But young monks, young squires, old men with more money than sense – you will bed them?' Chaucer sat on the bed, his feet decorously crossed at the ankles like a memorial brass, his hands folded in his lap. He looked as innocent as a child.

Blanche's naturally pink cheeks turned scarlet. 'What do you know of young monks?' she asked, truculently.

'I know he likes to be known as Sunex Amures,' he said. 'And you would be Marie Lairre, as I understand it.'

Her mouth was opening and closing like a fish.

'Don't think it's witchcraft,' he said. 'I was put up at your father's house last night, in a small room at the end of . . .'

'Ratcliffe!' the girl spat. 'He *knows* I use that room! Oh, but . . . I won't use it any more.' And she burst into floods of tears, lifting her face and howling to the sky like a soul in torment. 'I live here now.' She dropped her head and then looked at Chaucer through tear-blurred eyes. 'I live here now.' And every word was like a stone dropping into the mouth of Hell.

Chaucer waited until she had collected herself but was aware that time was short. He patted her hand. 'Blanche,' he said, gently, 'I need to know. Were you still with Sir Lionel when he died?'

She opened her eyes wide and more tears spilled. 'No! How can you say such a thing? I would have fetched help.'

'Would you?'

'Of *course*. I know I am not . . . good, Master Chaucer. But I am not an animal.'

'I didn't think you were,' Chaucer said, kindly. 'Can you tell me what happened?'

Blanche looked horrified. 'You mean . . .?'

Chaucer was quick to stop her. 'No, no, not that. Let's take that as read, shall we? No, I mean, well, how can I put it . . . what happened after.' She opened her mouth to tell him, but he stopped her. 'To make myself clear, I mean, some time after. Not the immediate . . . after.' He realized he had used the same word to the point of redundancy, but he wasn't writing poetry now, he was trying to avenge a man he knew and respected.

Blanche sniffed and then rummaged in her sleeve for a cloth

to blow her nose. When she felt more composed, she settled herself in the hard bedside chair and began, like a child reciting a lesson.

'Well, after . . . I must tell you, Master Chaucer, before I begin, that I did *love* Lionel. Li-li I called him, when we were alone. He was like a man of much fewer years. Why, he could—'

Chaucer lowered his brow. 'After,' he reminded her.

'Yes. Sorry. Well, *after*, we talked of this and that. He liked my stories about the town, you know, and what my friends told me. He liked young people, Master Chaucer. He was tired of fighting and worrying about money and what would happen with the king such a boy and all of that. Well, after a bit, I asked him if . . . well, you know, if it was long enough *after* and he said not really, he was a bit tired, so I could stay if I wanted, but there wouldn't be any . . . you know.' She blushed again and Chaucer wondered whether she could do it at will. It was hard to tell through the tears, but she was only an average-looking girl when taken a feature at a time. It was what she did with it all that seemed to drive men to insanity.

'So you left?'

'Yes. I didn't just want Li-Li for . . . you know, Master Chaucer. Please believe that. I loved him for his . . .'

'Castle. Money. Position. Yes, I know. Go on.'

She breathed in hard through her nose and set her mouth. 'If you're going to insult me, Master Chaucer—'

'You know it's true, Blanche. And believe me, I'm not here to judge. But we are running short of time and I need to know. You left, you say . . .'

'Yes. I couldn't get home that night, so I stayed in the castle. There are so many rooms, there is always somewhere to lay your head.'

'I'm sure you have no problem with that,' Chaucer observed, with as straight a face as he could muster.

'I slept with one of Lady Violante's grooms, if you must know,' she said, high on her horse. 'He smells of the stables but . . .'

Chaucer coughed.

'Yes, well, that's where I was. I would tell you his name if I knew it. And I wouldn't recognize him, before you ask. It all happened in the dark.'

'Did you pour Sir Lionel any wine before you left?' Chaucer tried to get back on point.

She closed her eyes and tipped her head back, concentrating. Her breasts strained at her newly modest gown and Chaucer knew she would not be in the priory for long. 'Yes, I did. The bottle was on the side, with a glass.' She looked at Chaucer with a piercing stare. 'Just one glass. I suppose that bitch Violante moved the other one. She was as jealous as a hell-cat.'

'Did she not have every reason?' Chaucer asked.

'No, she did *not*!' Blanche spat. 'She would never visit Li-Li in his chamber. She spent all her time with that priest and that slimy seneschal of hers. Lionel often said how tired he was of it. He was getting rid of the priest anyway, and he would be shot of the seneschal as soon as he could arrange something.'

'Getting rid of the priest?' Chaucer's ears pricked up.

'Going to the bishop, or some such.' She turned her big blue eyes on Chaucer and innocence poured forth. 'I didn't always listen, Master Chaucer, when Li-Li got going. He could be very dull, poor old . . . poor darling.'

'But, the priest . . .?'

'Hmm, yes. Well, Li-Li didn't say, exactly, but I expect it was about what happened with that altar boy. There was quite a stink, but that Violante hushed it up.'

'What happened with . . .?'

'Nothing dramatic. Just the usual. Some pretty boy from the town, I suppose, got himself in difficulties with Father Clement. Some don't mind it, others do, and I suppose this one did. He took a while to complain, though, so perhaps not.'

'Blanche,' Chaucer said with a sigh. 'How old are you?'

'Nineteen.'

'Well, I hope before you are much older, you will discover that not everyone is like you.' Chaucer crossed himself, not something he did often, but it seemed to serve the moment. 'I'll let you go because Sister Thomas will be back shortly and she doesn't want to find us here. Was the wine open or was it still sealed?'

She looked at him as though he were something unpleasant which had dropped from the ceiling. 'Open, of course! Surely, you wouldn't expect Sir Lionel to open his own *wine*!' Clearly, this was the most appalling thing she had heard or seen for many a year.

'Silly of me, of course not.' Chaucer had found out what he needed to know. Possibly more, but a little time might erase those memories. He stood up to go, hefting his bag over his shoulder. 'Thank you, Blanche. May I, before I go, just . . .'

'Oh, yes, I thought I knew your sort,' Blanche said, hauling up her gown. 'Be quick, though. They probably wouldn't like it if they caught us.'

'No, no!' Chaucer was horrified and pushed her hands away so that her gown fell in demure folds. 'I was going to say thank you very much. You have been most helpful and I have just what I need.' He scurried out of the door without looking back.

'Yes,' he heard her voice wafting down the corridor. 'They all say that, more or less.'

Chaucer wasn't often drawn to the clash of steel, but he found himself standing on the edge of Clare's new tilt yard the next morning as the sun began to warm the stones.

'When you like.' John Hawkwood stood in his shirtsleeves, his hands on his hips. A bastard sword stood in front of him, rammed into the Suffolk earth.

Giovanni Visconti was padded in a training doublet, laced at each side and with gauntlets encasing both hands. He lunged forward, thrusting with his own bastard. He sprawled in the dust, having managed to miss both Hawkwood and his sword.

'Again,' the mercenary sighed.

The boy, blushing crimson to his hair roots, scrambled upright and picked up the weapon. He had just begun to attack again, when Hawkwood held up his hand.

'Hoo!' he shouted, and the Italian stopped in his tracks. 'You're starting too far back, lad,' he said. 'You'll be an old man before you reach me. Your balance is all wrong. Look . . .'

He straightened Visconti up and changed the angle of his grip on the sword-hilt. 'Which leg do you lead with?' he asked.

'Er . . . my right,' the Italian told him.

'Do it,' Hawkwood said and stood back.

This time, the attack was better. Chaucer was impressed. From where he stood, Hawkwood had just told the boy how to kill him. Visconti swung the blade at the mercenary's head, annoyed now and blinded with embarrassment. Hawkwood flicked his own sword into his hand and batted the attack aside, sending the lad sprawling to the earth again.

'Better,' he said. He thrust the sword back into the ground. 'Next.'

Next was Hugh Glanville, a year or two older than Visconti, taller and broader. Sir Richard Glanville was proud of his boy; Chaucer was proud of him too. He folded his arms and smiled; this would be interesting. The squire gripped his sword in both hands while Hawkwood, unconcerned, just stood there. Then Hugh screamed out the Glanville battle cry and whirled around like a deranged windmill before slashing through the morning air. Astonishingly, Hawkwood caught the hissing blade with his hand and bowled the boy over.

'What was all that about?' Hawkwood reached out a hand and helped him up. 'All that shouting and jumping?'

'Well, I . . .' Hugh Glanville remembered it as something his father had taught him, but he may not have remembered it accurately enough.

'First,' Hawkwood said, 'if you're going to attack a man, you don't scream at him. You might as well say "Coming, ready or not". And second,' he thumped the boy across the shoulder, 'you never, *ever*, turn your back on an opponent. If you do, he'll kill you. Now, again.'

Hawkwood stood back. Hugh licked his lips and flexed his fingers. There was no shout this time, no fancy leap, just a forward charge, blade gleaming. It was fast – Chaucer didn't see it coming. But John Hawkwood did. He stepped aside, flicking his sword upright and helping Glanville on his way to the ground.

'All right.' Hawkwood rammed his sword home again. 'Both of you.' He beckoned to both squires.

Chaucer's jaw dropped a little. He unfolded his arms. The boys could be Hawkwood's grandsons. They were strong and fast and the Comptroller of Woollens couldn't actually see much wrong with their attacks. This could get ugly. Visconti and Glanville looked at each other. The Englishman nodded and the Italian launched himself. Steel clashed as Hawkwood hacked the sword out of the boy's hand. Then he threw the weapon across to his left hand and disarmed Glanville too. As a final gesture, he threw his sword down and cracked the lads' heads together.

'Not bad,' he said. 'Now get your practice in. No screams, young Glanville – and save your dancing for the ladies, Visconti,' he held the boy at the back of the neck, 'keep that Italian passion of yours in check, eh? All very well to get carried away in the heat of battle – I've known men die that way.'

'You changed hands,' Visconti whined, ever the overgrown schoolboy. 'That's against the rules of chivalry.'

Hawkwood laughed, a sound that Chaucer had certainly never heard before. 'Chivalry, my arse,' he growled. 'How old are you, boy?'

'Sixteen,' Visconti said.

'Well, I'm nearly sixty,' Hawkwood told him, 'and it's because I've ignored the rules of chivalry that I'm still here. Now, away with you.' He glanced across at Chaucer. 'The grown-ups want to talk.' And the boys, bruised but alive, walked away.

'Sir John,' Chaucer bowed his head. 'That was . . . impressive.'

'Chaucer.' Hawkwood bobbed back. 'All in a morning's work.' He pulled his sword out of the ground. 'Er . . . I don't suppose . . .?'

Chaucer held up both hands, laughing. 'Thank you, no,' he said. 'It is a little early for me.'

Hawkwood saw the bruises on the man's hands. 'Quarterstaff?' he asked.

'Tripped,' Chaucer said, crossing himself in his head. 'Forgot that little twist in the stairs by the chapel. Are those boys any good?'

They looked across the tilt yard where blades banged and clashed. 'The Italian, no, hopeless. Young Glanville, he'll make a decent swordsman in ten or twenty years. Did you want a word?'

'Er . . . yes. I couldn't help noticing you chatting to the chaplain at table the other day. Do you know him?'

Hawkwood was cleaning his blade with a cloth. 'Clement? Not really. He attached himself to me for some reason. Rather oily, if you ask me.'

'I do ask you,' Chaucer said. 'In what way, oily?'

Hawkwood thought about it. 'Slimy. Clingy. Kept pawing at me for no reason. He was lucky we were at table – I have hacked hands off for less. If I were to put a name to it, I would say he is not as other priests. Or perhaps he is; I don't know many priests, apart from the ones whose churches I've burned down, of course. But they were French, so there you are.'

'I am indeed,' Chaucer said.

'If that's all, then,' Hawkwood hooked the sword across his shoulders. 'I've got likely lads to recruit.'

'Ah, yes,' Chaucer smiled. 'The White Company. Good luck with that.'

And the man was gone.

Chaucer found himself walking the ramparts later that morning. Richard Glanville, he knew, was checking Lionel of Antwerp's boundaries, trotting along the byways of Suffolk with his own people. The Lady Violante would be with her ladies of the Italian persuasion in her embroidery room, stitching and probably bitching in equal measure. Joyce would be up to her arms in steam, still fresh, still young, as if the years had not passed. He looked down at the paunch that travelled a little before him and sucked it in until he found breathing difficult and had to exhale.

At first, he couldn't make it out. Certainly, there was noise from the forge – the ring of iron on iron and the wheeze of the bellows. He took the steps down to the outer bailey and nodded to the smiths at their work, red-hot metal hissing in brackish water, muscles flexing in the heat. But there was something else; voices, angry, tempers flaring. Either the smiths were ignoring it, or they couldn't catch it above their own cacophony; they carried on as usual.

As he turned the corner, Chaucer was suddenly aware of the source. Seneschal wars were in full flight. Butterfield, standing like an English oak, looked down at Ferrante, the Italian cedar who was poking him in the chest.

'This is *my* castle, you Italian lickspittle!' Butterfield bellowed, pushing the other man away. 'I won't have this muck in my kitchen.'

'It is not muck, Master Butterfield,' the Italian was altogether more reasonable. 'It is called pasta. And it is delicious.'

'Pasta, my arse!' the Englishman growled.

'There are many types . . .'

'I don't give a flying fig how many types there are. It's all stodge – and tasteless, to boot. I've seen the cooks trying to cook it.'

'That, with respect,' Ferrante said, his accent getting heavier as his anger rose, 'is because they are English and have no idea what to do in a respectable kitchen.'

Butterfield's face was white with rage and he grabbed the Italian by the collar of his doublet.

'Hoo!' Chaucer felt he had to intervene. He may not have been impressed by reading Dante, but he had once dined with Petrarch and felt a certain affinity with men who had once been Romans and whose language he nearly spoke. 'Now, now, sirs,' he said. 'What's all this?'

'I'd thank you to stay out of it, sir,' Butterfield snapped.

'I don't think Sir Richard would want me to do that,' Chaucer said. 'Still less the Lady Violante.'

'What are you, Chaucer?' Butterfield snapped. 'A schoolboy threatening to tell the dominus?'

Chaucer pulled himself up to his full height, still at least three inches less than Butterfield. 'Must I remind you, knarre, that I am Comptroller of the King's Woollens. One word from me and you won't have to worry about what is cooked in Clare's kitchens ever again. Now, be about your business, sir. Good morning.'

Butterfield stood, scowling, his knuckles white, his jaw flexing. He spat on the ground near the Italian and turned on his heel.

'Signor Chaucer,' Ferrante said. 'I fear you have made an enemy of that one.'

Chaucer shrugged. 'So, perhaps my bed won't be made as neatly as it should,' he said. 'I can live with that, Master Seneschal. Tell me, this pasta stuff . . .?'

'Ah,' the Italian's eyes lit up. 'It will be my pleasure to cook you some,' he said, 'and with my signature sauce. Oh, but you must have already sampled it. Were you not in Italia recently, according to His Grace Giovanni of Gaunt, on a mission?'

'Oh, ah,' Chaucer flustered. 'In Milan, yes. Yes, indeed. But pasta . . . no, I don't think so.'

'But Milano is the home of pasta,' Ferrante insisted.

'Well, there it is,' Chaucer beamed. 'Missions, eh? You never get to see the people you're supposed to, or eat the delicacies you've always heard about.'

'We'll put that right,' Ferrante said. 'Tonight. And, Master Chaucer,' the man was suddenly serious, 'with Butterfield, you'll watch your back, won't you?'

# EIGHT

Chaucer, as he ambled around Clare, making small talk with people he met, tried not to walk like a man who had been beaten as well as spending the best part of three days on a horse. It was difficult and he carried it off with varying success. He managed to avoid stairs, in the main, and as long as he was on the flat, with something to hold on to now and then, he was sometimes able to forget the pain for seconds at a time. He was ambivalent about going in to the hall for a meal. He could sit down – that was a mark on the side of the angels. But he wouldn't be able to suddenly leap up screaming when the pain in his battered buttocks got too much to bear – and stout English oak was unremittingly hard. He hoped the meal would be short and sweet. With luck, he would be able to have a rest before he tackled Father Clement.

Richard Glanville was already at the board when he arrived, saving him a place as always. He wasn't to know that a wooden chair with no back was not ideal; the man's heart had always been in the right place.

'Geoff!' the knight clapped the comptroller on the back and didn't notice him wince. 'Have you managed to entertain yourself? Sorry I was out. Just checking that the boundaries are intact, you know. Important now Sir Lionel has gone.'

Chaucer thought that seeing John Hawkwood in action and then two seneschals squaring up to each other was about as much excitement as he needed in his condition, and just nodded. He looked up as he lowered himself into his place and Ferrante caught his eye and bowed.

Glanville noticed. 'Not like him,' he remarked. 'He usually doesn't give anyone the time of day, except Lady Violante and her ladies.'

'And her brother, surely?' Chaucer had found that his left buttock was noticeably less painful than the right and was leaning over, to the distress of the woman sitting on that side, who assumed he was making unseemly advances. She flapped at him weakly with her sleeve and had to resort to her kerchief, pressed to her quivering lip.

'Not really,' Glanville said. 'He is a bit of disappointment, I think. Violante loves him, of course. With the age gap, he is more of a son than a brother. But . . . well, he's not like my Hugh, that's for sure.'

Chaucer smiled. He could agree wholeheartedly there. Should there be another war, Lady Violante would be mourning more than just her husband.

'No, I don't know what's going on, Geoff,' Glanville said, nudging him and by some miracle missing all the painful bits. 'Ferrante is really making up to you today. Why is that?' He peered closer. '*What* is that?'

The Italian seneschal was bearing down on them, ushering a small boy carrying a large and laden platter. Steam rose from it and obscured the boy's face from view and he almost walked right past them, as he could hardly see his hand in front of his face.

'Boy!' Ferrante cried. 'Oaf. Stop.' He leaned down to Chaucer and Glanville. 'Gentlemen,' he crooned, 'here is what I promised earlier, some pasta and my signature sauce.'

Chaucer inhaled. It smelled divine. He leaned back without noticing the pain and let the small boy decant some onto his platter. He leaned in and sniffed again. 'Master Ferrante! This smells wonderful. What is in it, may I ask?' He had plans to ask Alice to concoct something as near as she could manage, when he got home to Aldgate.

The boy had dumped some of the food on Glanville's plate and was now off down the table, trying to get rid of the rest on the drunk and the gluttonous. He hated being the pasta boy for Niccolò Ferrante; his friends all served good English fare, pigs' feet, sheep's head, nice nutritious things like that. This slimy stuff wasn't to his liking at all. All the serving lads got to eat the leftovers when they got back to the kitchen, but where was the fun in that? Foreign muck, he called it.

Glanville also leaned forward, then back, then poked it with his spoon. 'Foreign muck,' he announced, looking mutinous.

Chaucer had scooped up a spoonful, using a hunk of bread to balance it, and his mouth was too full to speak. But his eyes said it all. He was in heaven.

When he finally swallowed, he licked his lips and looked at Ferrante as though he were an angel come to earth. '*This* is pasta?' he asked. '*This* is what Butterfield doesn't want in his kitchen?'

Ferrante spread his arms and shrugged. '*Veramente*,' he said. 'Truly, Master Chaucer. You can see now, as I told you, the man is mad.' He turned slightly, as though on wheels, a movement which seemed to be unique to seneschals the world over. 'Sir Richard? What do you think?'

Glanville was not a man to mince words. 'It looks like worms in vomit, Ferrante, if I'm honest,' he said. He took a tiny mouthful and bit it gingerly. 'But it tastes like . . .'

Ferrante watched him, the smile ready to form on his face.

'Yes, it tastes like worms in vomit. Not that I have actually eaten that particular dish, you know; I would just imagine it tastes like this. What in the Virgin's name is in the vile stuff?'

Ferrante lurched back as if he had been bitten. 'Vile?' He stretched out an arm to Chaucer and pointed at him with a dramatic finger. 'Your friend Master Chaucer, Comptroller of Woollens to His Grace the King and a man of discernment, does not find it vile!'

Glanville glanced at Chaucer and, indeed, his friend seemed to be as happy as a pig at slops time. 'Master Chaucer lives in London,' he said, as if excusing a sin. 'He eats slop all the time.'

Chaucer surfaced and wiped his beard clean of the signature sauce with the corner of the table linen, offering a silent apology to Joyce. 'Richard,' he said, 'this is delicious. You should try some more of it, see how you like it. Try . . . this.' He held out a succulent piece of meat with oily fingers. He looked at it. 'What is this, Master Ferrante?'

The Italian leaned forward and turned his head this way and that. '*Cinguettii*,' he announced, with a supercilious smile.

Having failed to interest Glanville, Chaucer popped the gobbet into his mouth and chewed enthusiastically, smiling and nodding. 'Delicious,' he said, with his mouth full.

Glanville was more suspicious. 'And that is?'

Ferrante shrugged. 'It is not always easy . . .'

'Try.' Glanville narrowed his eyes.

'I suppose . . . what is the word? . . . yes, I believe it is . . . chitterlings?'

Glanville's eyes widened again. 'Pigs' guts, you mean?' He looked at Chaucer who seemed unconcerned.

'Thoroughly washed, of course, and seethed in milk. Two changes of milk,' Ferrante said, as if that made it all right.

'Geoff!' Glanville said, nudging him and causing a choice piece to bounce across the table and land in his opposite neighbour's frumenty. 'Stop it! Stop eating! The man's a poisoner! He'll kill us all!'

Chaucer put down his spoon, for the sole reason that he had eaten every morsel and wiped the platter clean with his bread. 'Shut up, Richard, for heaven's sake. You're making a spectacle of yourself.' And it was true; from the top of the table to the bottom, every face was turned towards the pasta pantomime. 'It was delicious. Master Ferrante, could you possibly write down the recipe for me to take home? I can't imagine that Winter – the man who does my food at home, you know – will be able to do it justice, but just a ghost of that delicious dish will be enough.'

Glanville turned his eyes to heaven. It was never pleasant to see a friend go stark staring mad in front of your eyes, but what could he do?

Ferrante lowered himself enough to take the clean platter and wasted no time in brandishing it under Butterfield's nose. Butterfield growled something that was impossible to hear but looked as though it could be some very basic Anglo-Saxon. Ferrante shrugged and took up a proprietorial stance near the wine goblets. Butterfield took up a similar position near the ale.

Glanville, still watching his friend like a hawk, in case of sudden collapse through poisoning, gestured to the two. 'Look at them,' he said. 'Like two rutting stags. And all over a plate of . . . does it have a name?' He raised his voice. 'Master Ferrante?'

The seneschal looked at him and cocked an interrogative ear.

'What was this muck called?'

'*Conchiglie con cinguettii in aglio e latticello,*' he said, with a bow.

'A plate of foreign muck,' Glanville concluded. He took a deep draught of ale. 'So, tell me,' he leaned in closer to Chaucer, 'what did you find out on your travels? I've hardly seen you.'

'I did indulge in a lie-in,' Chaucer admitted. 'Then I went to watch Hugh and young Visconti in the lists.' He paused to think. 'What then? Oh, yes, then I broke up a fight between Butterfield and Ferrante. Then' – he spread his hands – 'here.'

'So?' Glanville folded his hands and looked attentive.

'Well,' Chaucer said, 'I discovered, as if I didn't already know, that Vickers is definitely one bell short of a peal and violent with it.' He looked about him. Ferrante was looking at him but with the blank expression common to seneschals. They seemed able to switch off their brains but leave their faces doing the work of watching.

'Also, that Blanche is . . . well, Blanche, I suppose. That nuns have a sense of humour.'

'Now that I *don't* believe,' Glanville chuckled. 'Wait a bit. Nuns? Don't tell me Vickers has actually put that poor girl in a nunnery?'

'He has,' Chaucer confirmed. 'But she had been practising in advance, by meeting a monk in a disused chamber at Borley Manor.'

'Poor Lionel. Did he know, do you think?'

'I have no idea,' Chaucer said. 'It was difficult to get anything that sounded truthful out of Blanche when it came to her dear Li-Li . . .'

Glanville's eyebrows shot up into his hair.

'Except that I do believe that the wine in his room was already opened and that he was going to get rid of the priest.'

'Clement? Really?' Glanville nodded. 'That doesn't surprise me. Do we know why?'

'Well, she says because he was being a little too up close and personal with boys of the town, but as Blanche has but one thought in her head, that might not actually be the case.

He may have been stealing, or spying, any number of other things. It does give him a motive, though. He is very attached to Lady Violante and won't take kindly to being sent elsewhere.'

'True. I know that Violante has saved him from dismissal at least once before. She is too kind for her own good, I sometimes think. Violante . . .'

Chaucer smiled and moved his attention to other things. Poor Sir Richard – he was like a lovesick boy, needing to hear the name of his beloved, if only from his own lips; Chaucer just hoped it would not end in tears.

Chaucer knew he had to play this one carefully. What passed between a man and his priest in the confessional was known only to God and God – Chaucer crossed himself at the irreverence of his sudden thought – wasn't talking. But the comptroller was less interested in what Father Clement had to say about the late Lionel of Antwerp than what he had to say about himself.

It was late evening before he padded his way up the spiral staircase to the priest's quarters and the brazier on the walls threw wild, twisted patterns of flame onto the stones. Gargoyles leered at him from porticos and he smiled to himself to think of how, as a boy, he had been afraid of them. Belial was there, Lord of the cult of sodomy; Succor-Benoth, chief eunuch of the House of Infernal Princes, jealously guarding his locks and bolts; the three-headed Haborym, commander of the Twenty Legions of Hell. He had scurried beneath them as a child, head down, eyes averted. Now, he looked up and smiled at them, happy that his innate goodness could counter their communal evil. And, anyway, they were just carvings made out of stone, by men with too much imagination.

Damn! Chaucer's way was blocked halfway along the landing by ropes. There must be some work being done at this level in the keep, but no one had mentioned it and he had heard no hammering or sawing in his wanderings. He'd have to go back, cut past the swannery and the Lion Tower. Oh, well, after Ferrante's delicious meal, he needed the exercise.

If the stone devils had scared him witless before his beard

grew, the old lion had been worse. His name, aptly, was Daniel, and you could smell him half a mile away. But as Lionel of Antwerp had told young Chaucer the first time he met the animal, Daniel could smell *you* a whole mile away; *that* was the worry. Daniel was old and his mane was coming out in clumps. He didn't have all his teeth either, and Lionel's party piece had been to stroke his nose and kiss him on top of his head. Both these facts had calmed young Geoffrey, but, even so, those little yellow eyes never left him. Daniel's attributes were superior to Chaucer's in every respect; he was stronger, he was bigger, he ate people given half a chance and, if his teeth were no longer up to it, his claws could rip a man to shreds in two shakes of his great tail.

But that was then, Chaucer remembered. The mangy old boy had dropped dead one day and no one knew why. He was not replaced, but was buried with all solemnity across the moat, at the edge of the orchard in apple blossom time. Chaucer stopped. There was a gurgling sound. He thought he'd heard it the first day he'd arrived at Clare with young Hugh, but he thought his ears were playing tricks. He hadn't had the need to come this way before, but, yes, there was no doubt about it. There was a big cat in Daniel's den, although the comptroller couldn't actually smell anything. Chaucer turned left to the door that led to the stairs. It was locked. Damn all over again! He padded back down. Now, he'd have to take the walkway that ran along the top of the lion enclosure. Well, so be it. How bad could it be? He could hear the king's lions roaring through the night in his bed in the Aldgate, all the way from the Tower. He was far above the thing here; perfectly safe.

The light from the brazier dappled the walls and there was a growl to his right. Chaucer looked down into a black pit. A lioness lay there, ears flat, teeth bared, looking up at him from what had once been a roebuck, its ribs exposed, its intestines stretched along the ground.

There was a slam behind him and Chaucer whirled, his dagger in his hand. The door had closed and there was no wind on earth that could move a slab of oak and iron like that. The cat leapt up, snarling and screaming with the sudden noise. She ran at the wall and threw herself upwards, her claws clashing on the stone, inches from Chaucer's waist. He flung himself backwards, then hurtled along the walkway to the far door. This merited more than a mere damn. It too was locked. No coincidence in the world could explain this – a roped-off stairway; two locked doors. Chaucer's heart was in his mouth; not that that would have bothered the lioness for a moment – especially as her sister undulated out of the shadows and made a lunge at the comptroller too.

Chaucer would never claim to be an expert on wildlife. He lay in bed sometimes and watched the mice chase one another along the rafters of his little room. As long as they weren't eating his food or peeing in his shoes, he found them quite good company. He had played his part in many hunts, of animals from as small as a hare to as large as a boar, and that was all fair in love and war, he felt. But being caught in a lions' den and surviving – he suspected that that might lie above his skill level. He was not a devout man, but at that moment, he began to wish he had been a whole lot more so; he might be having to explain himself to St Peter any moment now.

Chaucer dropped his knife, which bounced off the wall and clattered onto the floor of the pit. The one thing which might keep him alive was now lying uselessly on the ground. One of the cats sniffed it and moved on. The comptroller kept telling himself that he was fifteen feet above the animals roaming the half-light below him. They couldn't possibly jump that high unless . . . Unless there was a tree trunk at a rakish angle against the far wall. Its bark had been stripped long ago by vicious claws in practice for just such a moment as this. Chaucer was suddenly, nauseously, aware of the cat smell. He saw the beady yellow eyes again, as in his boyhood nightmares, and there were four of them this time.

How long he stood there, he never knew. His feet felt like lead and sweat was making his houppelande clammy. One of the lionesses was prowling at the base of the tree. From its top branches, she could reach him in a single bound. It would be a long reach, but then, the lioness was long and she could smell the man's fear.

There was a crash to his left and the door swung wide.

'For God's sake, Geoffrey,' Richard Glanville said. 'What are you doing in here?'

'Shitting myself, Richard,' Chaucer gulped. 'Thanks for asking.'

Glanville remained confused. 'But . . . where were you *going*? This isn't on the way to anywhere.'

'I might ask, then,' Chaucer said, getting on his high horse as he was prone to do when scared out of his wits, 'why you came looking for me here?'

'I can recognize a Chaucerian shriek probably better than the next man,' Glanville said mildly.

'I shrieked?' Chaucer had no memory of that.

'The echoes are still ringing.' The knight hung over the pit and yelled at the cats, who looked calmly up at him with unblinking eyes, opening their mouths in a soundless roar. 'I don't know why we keep these,' he said. 'They take a lot of feeding and it isn't as though you could pet them. But Lionel – well, he didn't like to let the old ways go.'

'He made a lot of changes, though,' Chaucer pointed out. 'I keep getting lost here.'

'Always adding,' Glanville said. 'Never subtracting.' He looked around. 'I'm sorry, Geoff, but even allowing for getting lost, I just don't . . .'

Chaucer was dumbfounded. 'But . . .' he waved his arm. 'There was rope, just here. That door' – he tried it and it opened on silent hinges – 'locked tight. I had no option but to go through the Lion Tower.'

Glanville weighed the options. Either Chaucer was going mad, or someone was trying to kill him. And, what with one thing and another, the latter seemed the obvious choice.

'Did anyone know where you were going?' he asked.

Chaucer thought and shook his head. 'I didn't tell anyone. Only you. And I don't think anyone overheard, do you?'

'I shouldn't think so. It was pretty loud, like it always is when people are eating. Unless Lady Eleanor . . . no, it couldn't have been her. She walks with a stick and is deaf as a badger.'

'Lady who?' Chaucer had enough to contend with without more suspects to litter the path.

'She was the woman sitting next to you. You accidentally

shared your . . . worms in vomit . . . with her. She wasn't happy.'

'I don't think the average person throws you to the lions because of a bit of pasta splashing, though, do they?' Chaucer remembered the woman who was grumpy but seemed to take it as well as could be expected.

'No. I wonder . . . could it be Clement?'

Chaucer raised his eyebrows. 'Let's go and ask him, shall we?' He knew it would be weeks, if ever, before the stink of cat and the gleam of those yellow eyes would leave his nightmares.

The chapel was in darkness, apart from the light burning to guard the Host. The hanging oil lamp was shaded with red glass and gave out a low but steady gleam. Chaucer peered round the door, which had creaked open at his touch, with a sound to waken the dead.

Except that, it didn't waken the dead. Crouched before the altar, folded over like a sleeping baby, was Father Clement, his head almost touching his knees. The sanctuary light threw his face into deep shadow, but there was no doubt in the men's minds, as they padded silently up the nave, that he was dead. There was something about the one extended arm, with its clawed fingers desperately reaching for help that would never come, that spoke of death, and not a peaceful one.

Glanville, as the one with the better-functioning knees, bent to the priest and gently turned him onto his back. The extended arm flung back with the movement and the back of the hand slapped on the stones with a sickening noise that made Chaucer's heart turn over in his chest. The face, exposed to the dim, red light, was that of a soul in torment, the lips drawn back and the eyes staring. Flecks of foam besmottered the clean-shaven cheeks and the smell was appalling. The priest had vomited before he died and it lay, slick and noisome on the flags. Glanville wiped his hand surreptitiously on the priest's cloak, thrown aside onto a chair as he had come in, ready for a man who would not need clothes again, apart from his winding sheet.

Glanville stood up and stepped back, crossing himself. 'What happened here?' he whispered. 'Did he have a seizure of some kind?' He looked around and dropped his voice still more. 'Divine retribution?'

Chaucer sniffed the air. 'Not unless God is a giant mouse,' he said, crossing himself and sending a silent apology aloft. But it wasn't right; he was not an expert in vegetable poisons, he would be the first to admit, but he had never got the impression that poisoning with hemlock caused such contortions and distress. But . . . the smell was unmistakeable. Even if this church was full of the poorest mice in the parish, it couldn't be that strong.

'Mouse? Again? I can't . . .' Glanville sniffed, gingerly. 'Do you mean that acid, musty, metallic, cabbagey, horse-uriney sort of smell?'

Chaucer shrugged. 'I don't know. Personally, I just call it mouse. But you can smell it, can you?'

'I can,' Glanville said. 'Sadly.' He sniffed his fingers. 'It's very clinging, isn't it?'

'I'm afraid so. You might want to wash that hand, though. And' – he turned his foot up and looked at the sole – 'I think we both need to wash our shoes and change the moss. I don't know if anyone ever died from hemlock poisoning through the soles of their feet, but I don't want to discover that by dying.'

Glanville held out his hand to the side, as though by distancing himself from it, he could stop the poison. He looked around him. 'Is there any water here?' He looked at Chaucer. 'Would it be sacrilegious to wash in holy water, do you think?'

'I would say so, yes,' Chaucer said, drily. 'Let's use water from the well just outside, shall we?' He turned to go down the nave.

'What about . . .?' Glanville looked at the body on the floor, the dreadful face turned fruitlessly to the man's God.

'We'll cover him,' Chaucer said. 'Use his cloak.'

They each took a corner and let the woollen fabric encase its late owner gently, as if they were tucking up a sick child.

'We'll send some of the women,' he said, 'to clean him and prepare him. Then a couple of likely lads from the wardrobe, to take him to his cell. Then, we can send him to God, with all the right offices.'

'We must warn the women,' Glanville said. 'Make sure they know about the poison.'

Chaucer looked at his old friend and smiled. It was clear that the knight had never lived with people below his own station, people who used the plants of the ways and highways for good or evil. 'They will know the smell,' Chaucer said. 'They will have been warned as children against hemlock – no real country child will ever touch cow parsley for fear it is hemlock in disguise. They will have warned their children and perhaps even their grandchildren. But yes, I will make sure they know.'

'Will you send Joyce?' Granville was still wondering what, if anything, was left between the two.

'If she is the first I see,' Chaucer said, in dudgeon. 'Otherwise, not.'

'She'd do a good job,' Glanville pointed out.

'Joyce does everything well,' Chaucer rejoined and then wished he hadn't.

'I'm sure she does,' Glanville said, leading the way out of the chapel. 'I'm sure she does.'

It was, of course, imperative that the chapel was tidied and the cleric's body made decent before anyone else stumbled upon it, particularly Violante, who had a habit of visiting the priest between devotional hours. She knew, if he didn't, that tongues wagged, but, as she pointed out to her women when they told her what was being said, it is in the eye of the beholder.

So, Glanville went to head off Lady Violante if need be, while Chaucer went in search of some servants to clean the chapel. After a few false starts, he found the laundry and ran the gauntlet of the washerwomen and headed to the back room, looking for Joyce. As expected, she was there, lovingly smoothing out her lady's linen with her glass slickstone. Her natural smile broadened to a grin when she saw Chaucer.

'Geoff!' she said, not pausing in her work. 'What brings you here? I saw you with that foreign muck at table today. You did a manful job there, pretending you liked it.' She pulled a face, with her tongue out. 'Nasty stuff.'

'I quite liked it,' Chaucer said. 'But . . . can you do me a favour, Joyce?'

'Anything,' she said, resting her slickstone to one side. 'Name it.'

'It's a bit unusual.'

She smiled again. 'I do unusual, Geoff. You know that.'

He coughed and tweaked the shoulders of his houppelande into place. This needed some gravitas and it was hard to have that with Joyce. 'The priest is dead.'

She looked at him, her head on one side, like a bird listening for a worm. 'Is that some kind of code, Geoff?' she asked. 'Some kind of London talk?'

'No,' he said, advancing and putting his hands down on the stretched linen. She batted him away. 'Sorry. No, it means, quite literally, no more, no less, that the priest is dead. Father Clement, in the chapel. Poisoned.'

Joyce's eyes grew wide. 'I only saw him just this afternoon!' she said. 'He does confession, special, for us servants, of a Thursday. I don't go every week. Takes a while and I haven't the time, no more than he has.' She shook her head, looking solemn. 'Dead. Well.' She looked up suddenly, her eyes narrow. 'How do you know he's been poisoned?'

'The smell,' Chaucer said. 'Mice.'

'Ah,' Joyce said. 'Hemlock. Plenty of that round here. Not the season, really, though it will be starting to sprout, where it grows. But I suppose somebody could have saved some . . .'

Chaucer felt a little smug. He wished Glanville were here – all the women would know about hemlock.

Joyce reached behind her and undid her apron, reaching for her rough sacking one which she used in dirtier tasks. 'I suppose, then, that you're here to ask me to clean up?'

'Joyce,' Chaucer said, reaching for her hand. 'You are a gem among women.'

'I know,' she said. 'I'll take . . . how many, do you think? Is it very messy?'

He grimaced. 'Vomit . . . quite a bit of that. And the body is a bit . . .'

'I've never seen a hemlock death,' she said, 'but I know it isn't pretty. Clenched teeth, clawed hands when they try to snatch a last breath, or so I've heard. I'll take three. If you could send some lads along as well, they can carry poor Father Clement to his room.' She shook her head again, tutting. 'What an end for the poor man. Tell me,' she leaned in, 'do you think he . . . did it himself?'

Chaucer had not actually considered that. He hadn't known the priest well, but he hadn't struck him as the kind of man who would take himself out of this vale of tears. 'I don't think so,' he said. 'Let's give him the benefit of the doubt and say no.'

Joyce was as quick as lightning. 'So, the same person killed him as killed His Grace? That's why Ankarette died.' She went over to Chaucer and buried her head in his shoulder. 'When will it end, Geoff?' she murmured.

Chaucer got the definite impression that she was sadder about the dog than the people, but let it go. He patted her back awkwardly and after a moment she let go, wiping her eyes on her apron.

'This won't get the priest laid out, will it?' she sniffed. 'Don't forget to send me those lads. Leave the rest to me,' and she sailed out into the laundry, calling as she went. 'Dorcas! Eleanor! Margaret! Come with me and bring some pails and clothes. We have a job to do!'

A disembodied voice from amid the steam answered. 'Don't tell me that mad old bugger from the stables has done it again! I told you, next time he . . .'

'No, it's not Jack up to his tricks,' Joyce said, then dropped her voice and Chaucer didn't hear the rest.

'Holy Mother of God!' another voice said.

'Something like that,' Joyce said, and led her women off to do what the women of Clare did best; clean up the mess left behind by the men.

# NINE

Chaucer didn't know what to expect when he tapped on the door of the Lady Violante's room. He knew she was attached to her confessor, but didn't know whether she liked him – the two were completely different things. He had heard that she had defended him when Lionel of Antwerp had wanted to get rid of him, but that really told him nothing. The woman was an enigma.

One of her women let him in. She was older than Violante and dressed in a sober gown. Her butterfly wimple was fitted tightly across her forehead and the eyes beneath it were expressionless.

'May I see Lady Violante?' Chaucer asked, waiting to be invited in.

'*Perché no? E' venuto uno venire tutto, se me lo chiedete.*'

As always, Chaucer was frustrated by Italian. It was so like Latin and yet somehow . . . not. He got the definite impression that she wasn't that happy to see him but went inside anyway.

Violante was sitting in the window seat, her back against an embroidered cushion to stave off the cold of the stone. The late afternoon sunshine gilded her hair and outlined the curve of her cheek. She was looking down on Sir Richard Glanville, who knelt at her feet and was holding one hand in a gentle caress. Chaucer was glad to see that her faint smile did seem to have some love in it; though he could never see them as a happy couple wandering off into the sunset, he didn't want his old friend's heart to be broken.

The lady looked up and, seeing Chaucer, disentangled her hand from the knight's grasp and held it out to him. She and Chaucer both tactfully looked away as Glanville regained his feet; it wasn't as quick and lissom a task as it once had been.

'Master Chaucer. Thank you for coming. Sir Richard has just been telling me what . . . what you found. It must have been most unpleasant for you both.'

'But far more unpleasant for Father Clement,' Chaucer pointed out. 'We're sorry to bring such grim news.' He looked at Glanville, who had now taken the other end of the seat and was surreptitiously massaging his knees. 'I must tell you both, I have had it suggested to me that he may have taken his own life.'

Violante was immediate in her protestations. 'Father Clement! He simply wouldn't do anything so wicked. He was the most devout man I have ever known, and, don't forget, I have spent many years in Rome, surrounded every day by the most senior men of the Church.'

Chaucer was not impressed. In his experience, the more senior, the less devout, but he let her make her point.

'He was absolutely,' she stabbed at the cushion with a finger, 'but *absolutely* set against anything which was not in the teaching of the Church. He was . . .' she dropped her eyes for a moment, to collect herself. 'He was so angry with Lionel when he took up with Blanche. He argued with him all the time. Lionel was going to be rid of him, I could tell. I had used all my wiles to protect him, but' – she threw out her arms in a very Italian gesture – 'I don't think, in the end, I could have prevailed.'

Chaucer jumped in quickly, to try and clear up something which had puzzled him all along. 'Did *you* not mind about Blanche?' he asked, keeping his voice flat and inflection-free. He didn't want to seem to be in one camp or another.

She smiled at him and reached out again to briefly hold his hand. 'Master Chaucer, you are kind to be so gentle in your question. Many people have been far more blunt, my brother among them. No, I did not mind. Blanche – whatever she and her vile father thought – was a passing fancy of an old man. Lionel was not what he was, Master Chaucer. His . . . shall we call them glory days . . . were behind him by many a year. But now and again, he wanted to relive them and, to that end, Blanche served her purpose. He didn't want to fail with me. But to fail with some girl he plucked from relative obscurity – that he didn't mind. She should be grateful, he told me, to be chosen at all.'

'So Blanche's stories of—'

Violante laughed aloud. 'Are stories, yes. Perhaps, once in a while, Lionel would have pawed her for a bit before he slept, full of wine. But for the rest, he was just happy to have the stories of beautiful girls creeping into his room go round. If he could still do *that*, then he could still do everything. *Vedete?* Do you see?'

'Did Blanche know that? That she was his . . . I don't know what to call her.' Chaucer, man of many words, was stumped.

'I don't know and, Master Chaucer, I am bound to say I don't care. As Sir Richard will attest, there have been many women in my husband's life. I myself, before we were married, was invited to his bed.' She smiled. 'There is no need to look shy, Master Chaucer. Of course I said yes. My husband was, and remained, a very attractive and persuasive man.' She looked at Glanville particularly. She knew that of all the people on earth, next to her, he knew Lionel of Antwerp best.

'How did we get on to this?' Glanville barked. 'We're here because the priest is dead.'

'True,' Chaucer said. He pulled up a stool and sat down, so he could see the others better. Standing and looking down he had felt like a schoolboy again, called to the dominus's room for a thrashing. 'So, if *felo de se* is not a consideration, we must think of who may have done the deed.'

'Could it have been accidental?' Violante said.

'Hardly,' Chaucer said. 'Unless . . . did Father Clement ever prepare his own food?'

Violante chuckled. 'Dear me, no. Father Clement was many things, but I don't think you could call him humble. He loved to be waited on.'

'So he never ate food made for him alone?'

'No, just what we all ate. Well, not necessarily *me*. I sometimes prefer something other than is eaten at table. He would join me then, sometimes. But if he wasn't sharing with everyone, he was sharing with me.'

'So . . .' Glanville said. 'We can sum it up like this. He didn't do it himself. It wasn't an accident. So . . . it had to be . . .' He looked at Chaucer, not wanting to say the word himself.

Chaucer had no such qualms. 'Murder,' he said.

\*    \*    \*

After that, there seemed little to add. Someone, someone enjoying the comforts of Clare, was killing people and, clearly, that had to stop. As always, when two or three are gathered together, there were five options of how to proceed. Chaucer bowed to local knowledge. There was only one thing for it, Richard Glanville said. The Lady Violante concurred. Hugh was brought in to add the freshness of youth and they all said the same thing. If Chaucer was right about this poison business, it had to be Alban the apothecary. Left off Callis Street, up the hill to where the old gibbet had stood and left again. Alban had an appropriate sign swaying in the least breeze over his shop, a glass phial filled with golden liquid which he refilled from time to time. You couldn't miss it. But better leave it until tomorrow, was everybody's advice. Although Alban was, of course, very respectable, perhaps his shop was not in what might be called the *best* part of the town.

Actually, Chaucer could miss it. And did. Twice. Friday was market day in the town of Clare and half Suffolk seemed to be there. The comptroller turned down the domain bread, tempting though it was, and remained unmoved by the country ale. He did nibble the cheese and patted the head of the little lad hawking fish outside the guildhall. Briefly he caught sight of Nicholas Straits, the dyer, looking terribly important in his civic robes and hobnobbing with the great and good.

Alban's premises were squeezed between a butcher's and a spice shop, so the smells that hit Chaucer's nostrils wrestled with each other before he even opened the door. An unshaven lad was sitting to the comptroller's right, cross-legged on a joint-stool. He was pounding away with a pestle, grinding something unspeakable into the mortar.

'Alban the apothecary?' Chaucer asked breezily. After all, he needed a favour from this man and he knew from experience that apothecaries and favours went together like chalk and cheese.

The lad stopped pestling and scowled up at him. Then he jerked his thumb towards a counter that ran the length of the shop. A head popped up, long-haired and beaver-hatted; business must be looking up.

'Alban the apothecary?' Chaucer tried again.

'The very same, sir,' the man said. 'Roll up your sleeve, would you?'

'What?'

'Your sleeve,' Alban blinked. Surely, this man had to have been to an apothecary before; he had to be the wrong side of sixty. 'You *are* here to be bled?'

Chaucer felt himself turn pale. 'Good God, no,' he said, keeping his sleeve firmly down around his wrists. 'I came for some advice.'

'Ah,' Alban smiled and tapped the side of his nose. 'Cupid's measles, eh?' he winked. 'Quicksilver'll do the trick. Mind you, it's not cheap.' He was scanning the shelves of phials, pots and containers behind him. 'Roger, where's the quicksilver?'

'Out,' the pestler informed him with all the grace and finesse of a sledgehammer.

'Till when?' Alban asked.

'Week next Thursday,' Roger told him. 'It don't grow on trees, you know.'

Chaucer was impressed; clearly, the apprentice was learning fast.

'Sorry, sir.' Alban spread his arms. 'Had a bit of a run on that particular product. Lent, you see.'

Chaucer had always assumed that Lent was a time of forbearance, in all things, so that should make quicksilver *less* in demand, surely, not more.

'However,' Alban was not a man to be deterred, 'if you'd care to leave a deposit, I'll put your name down and if you come back week Thursday . . .'

'No, my good man.' Even a Comptroller of Woollens has an end to his tether. 'I did not come to let blood or to be cured of an ailment I do not have . . .' He was touching the apothecary's wood as he spoke. 'I came for a consultation.'

'Oh, really?' From the look on Alban's face, this was not a frequent request. 'Well, then . . . what seems to be the trouble?'

'In private, if you please,' Chaucer jerked his head in the direction of Roger, whose ears were decidedly pricked.

'Very well.' Alban ushered his client into a back room,

behind a curtain embroidered with signs of the zodiac. The walls here were covered in rows of shelves. There were more phials of garish liquids, with Latin and Greek names painted on them and ancient tomes bound in long-dead calfskin. Alban ushered Chaucer to a seat and took his place behind a low table on which an astrolabe, chased in gilt and silver, had pride of place. It caught Chaucer's eye at once.

'I see you've spotted my little piece of nonsense,' Alban beamed. 'It's a conversation piece, nothing more.'

'An astrolabe,' Chaucer nodded. 'I haven't seen one outside the port of Deptford. No, I tell a lie, I saw one once in Plymouth. Fascinating.'

'How so?' the apothecary asked.

'Well,' Chaucer wondered if this was some sort of test. 'It takes altitudes,' he said, 'marks positions and movements of the sun, moon and stars.'

Alban burst out laughing. 'Oh, come now, sir. You can't *believe* that nonsense.'

Chaucer was flabbergasted. 'Well, the Greeks and Arabs . . .'

'The Greeks,' Alban told him patiently, 'were rather a long time ago, you'll agree.'

'I . . .'

'As for the Arabs, you do *know* about the crusades, do you? You know, holy war for hundreds of years? No, we can't learn anything from them. I keep this here as a reminder of man's folly.'

'Then, I fear we have wasted each other's time,' Chaucer was on his feet. 'Good morning, sir.'

'You were born in the sign of the Ram,' Alban suddenly said, pointing at Chaucer.

'Er . . .'

'The Heavens are better aligned than you know.' The apothecary stood up too. 'Give me your hand,' he said.

Despite himself, the comptroller held it out. Alban took it, noting its firmness and the bruises still on the knuckles. 'Smooth,' he said, 'plain and without hair.' He peered at Chaucer's beard and moustache. 'Short,' he concluded, 'fat . . .'

'I beg your pardon?'

'Large, then,' Alban said quickly. 'Yes, large is a more accurate word. Your dullness of countenance is balanced by phlegm. Take care with that – it can affect the heart. Tell me, do you fall over a lot?'

'Hardly ever,' Chaucer said.

'Good, good.' Alban had relaxed his grip. 'Phlegm and blood. That's probably the best combination. A mix of cold and hot humours, but definitely moist. The moon and Venus contend for your soul, sir.'

'I'll take your word for it,' Chaucer said.

'Oh, not mine,' Alban said and reached a dusty volume down from a shelf. 'Bartolomeus Anglicus.' He slapped the leather cover. 'It's all in here. Hot off the quill.'

'Fascinating.' Chaucer was nearly at the door.

'You came to find out what killed His Grace the Duke of Clarence,' Alban said.

Chaucer spun to face him. 'How did you know that?'

Alban chuckled. 'I'd be a fine apothecary if I didn't, Master Chaucer.'

The comptroller sat down again, his mouth open, his grey eyes fixed on Alban. 'Assume I have,' he said, 'and that I am Chaucer. Can you help?'

Alban looked to right and left. 'I was at the funeral, of course,' he said, 'but more importantly, I came to pay my respects the day after His Grace died.'

Chaucer rattled through the days in his head. Hugh Glanville had been on his way to find him at the Aldgate then; Alban had seen a fresher corpse than the comptroller had.

'He looked peaceful,' the apothecary remembered. 'Of course, I am not a doctor of physick,' he almost apologized.

'I wouldn't be here if you were,' Chaucer said. 'Overrated as a profession, in my opinion.'

'Amen to that, brother,' Alban said. 'In London, of course, I could be earning six pounds a year.' He was glancing in an interested way at Chaucer's purse.

'Make that four pounds,' the comptroller corrected him, 'And Clare isn't London.'

'Even so,' Alban was unfazed, 'a man has to live. Then there's my lad, Roger . . .'

Chaucer fished out a coin that glinted in the light of Alban's candles.

Alban received it gratefully. 'I did smell mice, of course.'

'Mice?' Chaucer could play the ingénu until the cows came home.

'Oh, I know what you're thinking,' the apothecary said, which Chaucer seriously doubted. 'Mice and chapels go hand in glove, don't they? As indeed do mice and most buildings. But this isn't just pure mouse. To trained nostrils such as mine, there's something else.'

'There is?' Chaucer knew exactly where this was going.

'It's hemlock,' the apothecary said. 'Some call it poison parsley. Technically, it's *Conium maculatum*. Pretty plant. You'll find it in Lady Violante's garden up at the castle. Not in bloom as yet, I wouldn't think, though it has been unseasonably warm. You'll also find it in several groves in the countryside about. The roots look like horseradish – that's how I know His Grace was of the choleric humour; leeks, garlic, radishes – anything like that is fatal.'

'But His Grace was a man past middle age.' Chaucer spoke kindly of his old mentor. 'Surely, he would have avoided such things all his life.'

'Assuredly,' Alban nodded. 'Unless, of course, he ingested the stuff without the knowledge that he was so ingesting.'

'Can it be crushed?' Chaucer asked, 'made into a powder, perhaps and added to wine?'

'Certainly,' Alban told him. 'You saw Roger at work with the pestle and mortar. It's the work of moments.'

'And the death is peaceful?' Chaucer was thinking of the nightmare scene in the chapel, something he never wanted to experience again.

'Indeed. If a death by poisoning could be said to be a pleasant one, then I suppose death by *Conium maculatum* could be said to be that. I have never witnessed an actual *death*, you understand, but my small experience of the condition of the deceased seems to bear that out. Quiet. Even with a smile, you might say, though some struggle against it and then you may have a face left with a grimace. But, generally, not a bad way to go.'

Chaucer wasn't helped by that, but even so, smiled as though he were. He nodded. 'Smells of mice,' he said again. He just needed to make doubly sure, to confirm he was at least partly right about the priest.

'Indeed, but do not become fixated on mice, Master Chaucer. Rats, now, that's more worrying.'

'It is? Er . . . I mean, they are?'

'Of course. They carry the Pestilence, you know.'

'Oh, come now, Master Alban,' Chaucer laughed. 'Hemlock is one thing – I'll go along with you on that. But rats and the Pestilence; don't be ridiculous!'

Chaucer had to run the gauntlet again on his way back via Callis Street. He had had his hypothesis confirmed by an expert, albeit one who had a rather pessimistic, not to say nonsensical, view of rats – Lionel of Antwerp had been poisoned by person or persons unknown, using hemlock. Chaucer had deliberately not mentioned Father Clement – that was a killing too far and, anyway, he was still concerned by the violence of his passing. He looked at the ground as he walked, slick with fat and blood near the butcher's, slick with shed fibres and grease near the stalls selling fleeces, slick with crushed cabbage leaves near the farmers' stalls. In short, a trap for the unwary. Chaucer was not built to fall over will-ingly and was hard to raise to his feet again when that happened, so he kept his eyes on his feet. He saw someone in his peripheral vision, standing foursquare in the middle of the pavement, and took last-minute avoiding action.

'Master Ifaywer.' The comptroller had nearly collided with the carpenter, who was pontificating about the rising cost of living and asking, very loudly, what John of Gaunt was going to do about it.

'Oh, Master Chaucer,' the carpenter half bowed. 'Lured out of the castle by the exotic merchandise?' Since both men were looking at rows of pigs' heads and chickens' bums at the time, that didn't seem likely.

'Something like that,' Chaucer said.

'Listen,' the carpenter eased him to one side so that they were half-hidden by a stall, 'about the other night . . .'

'Other night?' Chaucer was making the guildsman squirm. 'Yes, you know, when we were all . . .'

'. . . breaking into the castle,' Chaucer finished the sentence for him, as loudly as he could.

Ifaywer hushed him just as Whitlow the haberdasher came around the corner, three lackeys in tow carrying bales of ribbon. The fancy-goods proprietor nodded in lordly fashion to the carpenter and comptroller and made to walk past.

'I was just about to invite Master Chaucer for a drink,' Ifaywer said; his surreptitious wink to Whitlow could have been seen as far as the old town gate. 'Care to join us?'

'Er . . . delighted,' the haberdasher said. 'You lads,' he spun to face the lackeys, 'lose yourselves for an hour. No drinking. No whoring. Understand?'

All three nodded and one muttered under his breath.

'What was that?' Whitlow leaned forward so that he was nose to nose with the lad.

The boy hefted his burden up a little. 'I said, Master Whitlow,' he spoke in the tones of one who is on the verge of deciding that this apprenticeship is not really for him, 'that it's hard to do either of those things when carrying two stone of mixed ribbon.'

Whitlow stared at him and the lad stared back. Although, as an apprentice he was the lowest form of animal life, he had seen his master's overdue accounts from merchants all over town and knew he would struggle to survive without his fees. After a moment, Whitlow's gaze dropped. 'Speak to me again like that, lad, and you'll feel the strap,' he said. 'Get off with you, all of you.'

Ifaywer watched this with smug glee. He had one apprentice, his nephew, and he knew what side his bread was buttered, so kept a civil tongue in his head. Whitlow turned to the other men and sighed, shaking his head. 'The youth of today,' he said, sadly. 'It wasn't like that in our day, was it?'

Chaucer, whose parents would have seen him dead in a ditch before sending him out as an apprentice, smiled weakly. Ifaywer shook his head in agreement; guildsmen stuck together, through thick and thin. Well, through thick, in any case.

The carpenter suddenly remembered what they were doing.

'Master Chaucer?' he said, holding out an arm in the vague direction of the Cockatrice, the inn sign swaying and creaking in the breeze. 'Shall we?'

'Charmed,' the comptroller said and followed the pair into the inn.

The place was packed, with stallholders in their coloured clothes, shepherds and swineherds up from the country, grubby and smelly in their smocks. Ploughmen had come in from the fields and had brought their families with them. Said families sat on the kerb outside, children running and laughing, women gossiping about the ones who weren't there. Chaucer couldn't see the greasy, flagstoned floor for the wooden clogs and pattens filling the room.

'Not here,' Ifaywer said and ushered Chaucer into a back room. The ceiling was low and the noise reverberated through the oak panelling, but there were chairs here at least and a large, heavy table. Around the walls, the arms of the Clare guilds blazed in painted gold and silver and the illustrious names of guildsmen past stood proudly below them.

While Whitlow ushered Chaucer to a seat, Ifaywer was still on his feet, gesturing to the roll of carpenters. 'My father,' he said, pointing to a name. And then, higher up, 'His father. I can trace my family back as far as Domesday.'

'Fancy,' Chaucer smiled. 'And you're telling me this, why?'

Whitlow was at Chaucer's elbow. 'Whatever you think of us, Master Chaucer, we are not bad men.'

'We just . . .' Ifaywer began.

'. . . want what's ours,' the comptroller finished the sentence for him. 'Yes, I know. You told me.'

A serving wench came in, carrying a tray heavy with tankards and ale. Chaucer noticed that Whitlow watched her closely and patted her hand as she put the drinks down. He also noted that the haberdasher's other hand was stroking the small of the girl's back before sliding a little downwards. She gave a start and snatched up the tray, bobbing before she left the room.

'I'm afraid,' Chaucer said, waiting until the others had sampled the ale, 'that we do not always get our just deserts in this life. Take Lionel of Antwerp, for instance.'

'What of him?' Ifaywer asked.

'Well, he didn't deserve to die, did he?' Chaucer took his time to swig his drink. 'By the hand of another.' He was watching his drinking companions closely.

The guildsmen looked at each other. 'What are you saying?' Ifaywer asked.

Chaucer opened his mouth to say it all again, only louder, when Whitlow interrupted him. 'He's saying, somebody murdered His Grace the Duke of Clarence,' he said in a low voice, looking at the comptroller with hard eyes, 'and he thinks it's one of us.'

Ifaywer's eyes bulged in his head and he swallowed his ale hard, wiping his mouth where half of it had spilled.

'I've met so many people over the last few days,' Chaucer said. 'It's difficult to remember who said what but, am I right that Mistress Blanche is your niece, Master Whitlow?'

'Er . . . that's right,' the haberdasher said. 'Why do you ask?'

'I had a chat with her the other day. She sends you her affections.'

'You did?' Whitlow blinked. 'Where was this?'

'In the convent at Bures. She is a novitiate.'

Ifaywer felt he had to step in, since Whitlow appeared to have been struck dumb. 'Did you know about this?' he asked. 'You didn't say.'

'Of course I didn't know,' the haberdasher said. 'I can't deny that Peter' – he glanced at Chaucer – 'Vickers, my brother-in-law, the girl's father, has threatened – that's too strong – hinted at it once or twice.'

'Not without good cause,' Ifaywer grunted, lifting his tankard again.

'I beg your pardon?' Whitlow frowned.

The carpenter looked askance at him. 'Oh, come off it, Whitlow. We all know about your roving eye. Anything under thirty . . .'

'You'll take that back!' The haberdasher was suddenly on his feet.

'Are you familiar, Master Chaucer,' Ifaywer asked, 'with the story of Susanna and the elders?'

'The book of Daniel,' Chaucer nodded. 'Yes, indeed.'

'The two old men spying on a hapless girl and threatening to tell all unless she lets them have their wicked way with her.'

'Ifaywer!' Whitlow growled, but the carpenter ignored him.

'Well, I'll grant you that Blanche is not exactly hapless; come to think of it, I can't think of anyone with more hap. And in this case, there aren't two lecherous elders, just one middle-aged haberdasher.'

He burst into laughter as Whitlow slammed down his tankard and left the room. Ifaywer laughed until the tears ran down his face. He dried his eyes with his sleeve and caught sight of Chaucer's astonished face. 'I'm sorry, Master Chaucer,' he said. 'It's an unedifying sight, no doubt, when senior guildsmen air their dirty linen in public. But it's a fact, nonetheless. Friend Whitlow harbours less than honourable thoughts about his niece. And I don't know whether you've noticed, but she's not exactly the sort to mind.'

Chaucer felt that, as possibly the only man in the inn ever to have been mistaken in the dark, by a monk, for Blanche Vickers, he was the best to judge and he nodded. 'That's true,' he said, 'but isn't that contrary to God's laws?' Chaucer was a man of the world, but the complex legalities of consanguinity had always rather eluded him.

'Probably,' Ifaywer shrugged and clapped his hands for more ale. 'But there's not much that can't be sorted out via an obliging papal nuncio and a large bung of cash. Whoever the pope is at the moment, he's the best marriage-broker in the business and by far the best paid.'

'Does Peter Vickers know? Come to that, how do *you* know? I wouldn't have thought it was the kind of thing a man would share with even his closest friend.'

Ifaywer spat onto the rushes. 'I know, we all know, because he was planning the Susanna scene as his tableau in the pageant. Blanche would have been perfectly happy to be dragged through the town with nothing but her blushes, always assuming she can still blush. They do something similar in the Coventry Mystery Plays, I believe. But some of our wives found out and that was that. Shame, really, but there you are. As to Peter Vickers, who knows? I wouldn't be surprised, myself.' He tried to take a swig from his empty tankard and looked around vaguely for the girl. 'Blows hot and cold, that one. Happy enough to let his little girl be squired by the squire, young Hugh Glanville, but as soon as His Grace gets involved, he comes over all holier-than-thou about it. Doesn't make any sense at all.'

The girl came back with another tray and was relieved to find that Whitlow of the wandering hands was not there. Ifaywer fell on his drink as if he were dying of thirst.

'Anyway,' the carpenter went on, after she had gone, 'all this is just country matters. So you think Lionel of Antwerp was murdered?'

Chaucer nodded, sipping his new ale. 'It had crossed my mind,' he said.

'You . . . er . . .' Ifaywer became confidential, peering into the froth of his ale. '. . . you haven't any idea by who, I suppose?'

'Job for the sheriff,' Chaucer shrugged.

'Old Gower?' the carpenter snorted. 'Fat chance of that. Man couldn't find his arse with both hands.'

'You were at the castle quite a bit,' Chaucer ventured.

Ifaywer frowned at him. 'You're not telling me Whitlow's right?' he said. 'About you thinking one of us did it?'

'No, no,' Chaucer reassured him, 'but I am a stranger here, Master Ifaywer, like a ship on an uncharted sea. Tell me, how well did you know His Grace's chaplain?'

'Father Clement?' the carpenter sipped his ale, then looked askance at Chaucer. 'How do you mean, *did* I know him?'

'He's dead,' Chaucer said.

The carpenter crossed himself. 'All my eye of a yarn and Betty Martin,' he muttered.

Chaucer knew the Latin original of that, but it wasn't the time to pull rank.

'Murdered?' Ifaywer was barely audible.

'I'd say so,' Chaucer told him.

The carpenter took a huge swig of ale and clapped his hands again, downing the last drop. 'If I tell you what I know about them up at the castle, Master Chaucer,' he said, 'it *will* stay between us, won't it?'

'In this very space,' the comptroller waved his hand between them. Then the girl was back and the room was strangely suddenly silent. Even the noise from the barroom seemed to have ceased. Ifaywer watched her go and grabbed his flagon again, taking a huge gulp before he went on.

'Full of smilers, is Castle Clare,' he said. 'On the surface of it, everybody friendly, open, above board. Talking of which, I even played queck with them. Not the priest, of course – Clement told me it was the Devil's game and asked me if I'd join him in the confessional. His Grace was no slouch – showed a rare skill on the Rhythm Turn. Young Hugh was a dab hand – neat as you please on the Counting Frame. Sir Richard had played before, so he knew his Deal Brush from a handsaw. Young Giovanni, the Italian boy, Her Ladyship's brother . . . he'd played something similar he told me, in Milan, and he was coming on well, when . . .'

'When?' Chaucer had glazed over with the finer tuning of this nonsensical game, but Ifaywer had pulled up short.

'Well, he changed. Oh, he's only a lad, I know, still shitting yellow pretty much, but . . . he told me one night I was up at the castle he couldn't play any more. Wasn't interested, didn't have the time. He just stopped playing.'

'When was this?'

'Ooh, let me see. It'd be soon after Sir John Hawkwood came to stay.'

'Hawkwood?' Chaucer frowned. 'That was only a few days ago.'

'What?' If was Ifaywer's turn to look confused. 'No, no, that was the second time. He'd been before. Around Christmas. I remember because there was a Yule pageant and I was the Lord of Misrule – oh, I know you wouldn't think to look at me now, but my Misrulery is legendary in these parts, Master Chaucer. And I was coming out of the embroidery chamber, having just goosed the ladies, who all pretended to be disgusted, and I bumped into him.'

'Hawkwood?'

'Yes. Well, I don't know it you know, but he's a

short-tempered bastard. Never met a joke he liked. Threatened to slit my throat if I got in his way again. Needless to say, I didn't.'

'So . . .' Chaucer was trying to disentangle the guildsman's gabble and the ale wasn't helping. 'It was after this that Giovanni seemed to change?'

'That's right. As I said, he didn't get on with His Grace.'

'Who?' Chaucer was confused again.

'Giovanni,' Ifaywer said, as though to an idiot.

'You hadn't said,' Chaucer told him.

'Hadn't said what?' the carpenter asked.

'That Giovanni and His Grace didn't get on.'

'Well,' Ifaywer leaned back, wiping his ever-grubbier houppelande sleeve across his mouth. 'You know these Italians. To be honest, after Christmas, everybody seemed to be off hooks with everybody else. His Grace was growling like a bear with a sore head. Then there was Blanche and the Lady Violante. Not to mention Butterfield and his Italian opposite number.'

'Ferrante.'

'That's the feller. I'm not exactly looking forward to the pageants, to be honest.'

'You mentioned the pageants earlier,' Chaucer remembered. 'When do they occur?'

Ifaywer looked aghast. He could hardly bring himself to believe that there was anybody in the world who had not heard of the famous Clare pageants. 'High spot of the year, Master Chaucer,' he said. 'From May Day to Midsummer. Not all the time, of course, just on the saints' days that fall within that time. Over the years, we've dropped some of the saints or we'd never get a day's work done. We just do the main ones now – you know, Philip, James, Bede, Dympna – then do the big finish with John the Baptist. Strictly speaking, that's past Midsummer's Day, but it seems disrespectful to leave him out.'

Chaucer didn't think of himself as an irreligious man, but he was struggling to see how anyone could spend the best part of two months dragging carts with tableaux on them round the town. With the best will in the world, it would get a little dull.

The carpenter was in full flow. Chaucer could see why; presumably, he and his guild members had rather a major role in making the stages and scenery. 'My old pa must be turning in his grave,' he said, solemnly. 'Much bigger in his day, the pageants were. And as for *his* old pa! Well! Every quarter day. Easter. Advent. Christmas. Epiphany. Some of the guilds even had people just for the pageants. Didn't know a thing about their trades, just chosen for how like Moses they looked, or the Virgin, as it might be.' He sighed and swigged his ale. 'I thought in view of His Grace, Her Ladyship might call them off, but no, she wants it all to go ahead in his memory, apparently. So there it is.' He drew himself up to sit at his full height. 'I shall be Noah again, building my Ark.'

'Do all the guilds take part?'

'They do,' the carpenter said, 'each according to their calling. The castle comes alive then, with torches and flames, drums and tabours. Clare sees nothing like it from one year to the next.'

'And Master Whitlow?' Chaucer leaned back, smiling. 'What part of the Bible story does a haberdasher play?'

Ifaywer sniggered. 'With all that swish and tit up at the castle on Pageant Nights, rest assured that Bob Whitlow'll have his hands full, all right, even if Susanna doesn't come across.'

And that went almost without saying.

# TEN

C haucer had never been comfortable even staying with friends. He always felt that it wasn't polite to open a drawer or a press, in case he found something untoward which would make things awkward the next time he saw his host. He had actually once found something in a guest room in Bodiam which could make him blush to this very day. But someone had to look through the room of the late chantry priest, and when he had raised this with Glanville, Violante and Hugh, somehow, they all had more important things to do. The women of the laundry had wrapped the body in the cleanest linen they could produce, with rosemary between each layer, and it had been sent off, tied to a board, in the family's coach, drawn by a matched pair of black horses, back to the house he had been born in, to parents who never thought they would have to bury their son.

So, here Chaucer was. As he had expected, the priest's room was simplicity itself. There were none of the rich hangings with which the rest of the castle was furnished, and the floor was swept clean, with no rushes or even straw. There was a stool by the bed, which held a candle stub, stuck to it by the ghostly wax of its predecessors. One spare habit hung on a hook behind the door, complete with hair shirt lining, a pair of sandals beneath it as though waiting for an owner they would never see again. The walls were plain whitewash, a wooden crucifix above the bed. Even this was as plain as it could be, with no ivory Christ adorning its stark lines.

It was hard to see in this spartan place where anything could be hidden. Chaucer stood in the middle of the floor and turned by degrees so he had scanned everything from as big a distance as was possible in that tiny space. He was never more than six feet away from anything and even his shortening sight was comfortable with that. He tentatively felt all down the robe and there was nothing, not even a thickened seam or hem that could hide a note or coins. The sandals were worn almost through, so there was no room in the thickness of the sole for anything untoward. The underside of the stool was innocent of any paper stuck there and, when Chaucer bent down with some effort to look under the bed, there was nothing between the mattress and the stringing.

The comptroller sighed. He and Glanville had hoped that he would find something that might give a clue, however slight, to whoever had killed him and thus, hopefully, to whoever had killed Lionel of Antwerp. Chaucer was worried about the violence of Clement's death. Why, when hemlock was not usually known to cause anything other than a peaceful but permanent sleep, could that have happened? But until they found the murderer, unless he – or, at a pinch, she – talked, that would remain a mystery for ever.

With a sigh, Chaucer plumped himself down on the bed. The first thing that surprised him was that it wasn't a straw pallet as expected, but soft goose down. So the Father was not quite the ascetic he tried to appear. The second thing was that it crackled. Goose down, apart from its heavenly softness, was known to give a silent night's rest. Straw rustled and crackled all night long; Chaucer was not a rich man by Lionel's standards, but it was goose down for him or nothing. And he had never heard it sound like this before.

He got up and felt carefully along the length of the mattress. About a third of the way up from the foot, the crackle was most pronounced, and he stripped off the simple coverlet. Nothing there. He probed more carefully and found a cleverly concealed pocket and, in it, a sheaf of papers, wrapped around a simple vest. Taking the papers over to the window he began to read. Clement's writing was clear; too clear, in Chaucer's opinion, after he had read the first few lines. Blanche's guess that he had . . . Chaucer decided to call it 'feelings' . . . for one of the serving boys was spelled out in intimate detail; all in Church Latin, of course. Chaucer was a married man, indeed, a married man of the world, but even so, he blushed to read what Clement had written. Apparently, the folded vest belonged to the lad and Clement kept it by him for . . .

Chaucer folded the papers up and thrust them into his

purse. He would have to share this with Richard Glanville, though he didn't want to. His old friend had a heart as big as the great outdoors, he would defend the weak and defenceless till he had no strength left in his body, but he had little knowledge of the sins to which a man could sink. It seemed odd to call a man who had lopped off heads without a qualm innocent, but it was the only word for Richard Glanville. Chaucer sighed. Sometimes, even he, a Londoner, who saw things out of his very window which would make a strong man blanch, was overwhelmed by what his kind could do. The only slight ray of light in the whole dark business was a small, scrawled note from the lad, who seemed to return Clement's love. But that was still no excuse and it was clear that, even as he stood in the bare little cell, Clement was burning many miles below his feet in the hottest fire Hell had to offer.

Chaucer remade the bed and opened the door carefully, looking right and left before he slipped out, closing it silently behind him. He leaned against the wall for a moment, regaining such composure as he could. He tried to hear the jingling bridles, the birdsong and the merry chatter of pilgrims on the road to Canterbury; his happy place. But it was drowned out by the sound of the blood pounding in his ears, the sound of dark deeds done in broad daylight.

And it was still broad daylight when Richard Glanville flagged the comptroller down. He beckoned Chaucer into the stables. No one tended to his horses but Glanville himself and here he was, in leather apron and shirt sleeves, sponging the nostrils of his chargers.

'Well?' the knight asked, kneeling now to trim the hair around the bay's feet. 'Anything?'

'Sorry?' Chaucer was scanning the stable for any sign of lads. Grooms were believed by many of the nobility and gentry to be deaf and dumb, but Chaucer knew differently.

Glanville stood up, closing to his friend, bringing wafts of horse liniment with him. 'The priest, man,' he hissed out of the corner of his mouth. 'Father Clement's chamber.'

'I don't know.' For a man of words, Chaucer was infuriatingly reticent.

Glanville's face said it all. 'You don't know, Geoff?' He blinked. 'What's that supposed to mean?'

'I mean, I do know, but I need time to weigh it all up. By the way, did you know that John Hawkwood was here last Christmas?'

'Hawkwood?' Glanville was looking for his curry comb. 'Christmas?'

Chaucer nodded.

'No.' Glanville was certain. 'I'd have seen him.'

'Not if he didn't want to be seen.'

'Let's ask him.' The knight was already undoing his apron strings.

'No,' Chaucer said. 'No offence, Richard, but this is one I think I'll do alone.'

Of all the nights for John Hawkwood not to be at dinner, this was the most annoying. The man had been out and about in darkest Suffolk looking for his likely lads, but his horse was back in the stables by that Friday, so he couldn't be far away.

So the Oxenford Tower it had to be. All the way up the stairs, Chaucer kept telling himself that this was pointless. So what if John Hawkwood had stayed at Clare at Christmas; what had that to do with the deaths of Lionel of Antwerp and his confessor? The mercenary was hardly the garrulous type; he wasn't likely to have said, 'Didn't I mention, Chaucer, that I was here at Yuletide?' Chaucer was mimicking the man in his head, but even in that enclosed space, it wasn't very convincing.

There was a pearly glaze in the night sky as the days had lengthened and a pale glow filtered through the arrow slits onto the spiralled stones. Hawkwood's door was at the far end of a long passageway and Chaucer half-expected him to have a couple of guards flanking the oak. Instead, the door was open just a crack, and candlelight shone through onto the flagstones. The sound of a lute came through and Chaucer found himself smiling. Who knew that a man so handy with a knife, a man who butchered people for a living, was also a soft tunesmith? It was a melody Chaucer knew, too, a love song which had been one of his Pippa's favourites, back in the day.

He knocked on the door. There was no response. The lute played on regardless. Perhaps Hawkwood had not heard, lost in some reverie to the music. Chaucer tried again, louder this time. Nothing. So the comptroller pushed the door open. The lute stopped, suddenly and with a jarring screech, and there was a hiss and a thud. A crossbow bolt had pinned Chaucer's houppelande sleeve to the open door and had taken the comptroller with it. However hard he tried, Chaucer couldn't pull it out.

'Mother of God!' he screamed at Hawkwood. 'You nearly killed me!'

The mercenary crossed the room in what seemed like a single stride and looked at the bolt embedded in the oak. 'It missed your arm by three . . . no, four inches, Chaucer. Even had it been closer, the most you'd have got would be a scratch. You'd have been *very* unlucky to have died from that.' He yanked the bolt free with one hand and pushed Chaucer into the middle of the room. 'What can I do for you?' he asked.

The comptroller stood quaking, not sure whether he could control his voice. Managing his bowels had just about exhausted him for now. 'I heard a lute,' he croaked.

Hawkwood chuckled. It sounded like pebbles thrown onto a coffin. 'Not exactly,' he said and pointed to a frame in the corner of the room. It looked like an upright loom, but its warp threads were at once the strings of a lute and the cord of a bow, its crosspiece still quivering slightly with the slam of the shot. 'I can't play a note myself,' Hawkwood went on, replacing the bolt in its groove, 'but the man who made this for me can. Or could,' he looked levelly at Chaucer. 'He's dead now.'

'What is it?' Chaucer approached as close as he dared, keeping out of the arrow's line.

'A companion of a mile,' Hawkwood told him. 'I picked it up in Italy. Clever fellows, the Italians, eh, Chaucer? You'll have noticed that on your mission to Milan.'

Chaucer stared blankly back. Playing the idiot was probably the best defence with this man. Then, he cracked. 'About that,' he said.

'You didn't go, did you?' Hawkwood looked at him through

knowing eyes. 'I'm guessing you didn't get much further east than Deptford.'

'I'll have you know I got to Thanet,' Chaucer countered. A Comptroller of Woollens has his pride, after all. 'There were tidal issues and the inn they put us up in was *very* comfortable. So . . .'

'So you lied to John of Gaunt,' Hawkwood finished the sentence for him.

'Well, I . . .'

Hawkwood shook his head, a glimmer of a smile on his lips. 'That's all right,' he said. 'I didn't go either. Now, about my gadget – you wind this turnkey,' Hawkwood suited his actions to his words, 'and lo . . .' little wooden fingers clicked into place, flicking the warp of the frame. 'It only plays one tune,' he said, 'but it works. It lulled you, didn't it? You thought I was sitting, engrossed in my music, perhaps even with my back to the door. Instead of which,' Hawkwood moved Chaucer aside and flicked a switch. There was the screech again and the bowstring jerked back to send the bolt hissing across the room to bite into the door again. Chaucer jumped.

'See,' Hawkwood retrieved the arrow once more. 'I'd adjusted it that time.' He tapped the hole the iron bolt had made. '*That* would have been your head. Now,' he put the bolt back again, 'enough of this tomfoolery. I can't go on making holes in Lionel of Antwerp's woodwork. What do you want?'

'To know how His Grace died,' Chaucer said.

Hawkwood poured some wine into two goblets and ushered his nervous guest to a chair. When he hesitated, Hawkwood put the goblets down. 'I have no more murderous devices, Master Chaucer,' he said. 'There is no sudden poignard that will split your arse when you sit down.' He took a sip from both goblets. 'And there is no poison in the wine.'

Chaucer was grateful to hear all that, but even so, he sat down gingerly. 'You were here at Christmas,' he said, accepting Hawkwood's cup.

'Was I?' the mercenary asked. 'Who told you that?'

'Butterfield.' Chaucer saw no need to implicate the guildsman at this stage.

'Really?'

'Yes. When you arrived for His Grace's funeral, it was clear that you and he knew each other. Although no one else seemed to have seen you here before.'

Hawkwood was secretly impressed. 'Very perspicacious, Master Chaucer,' he said, sitting opposite his man. 'But one other saw me. He was in disguise as the Lord of Misrule at the time, but I believe he is a carpenter called Ifaywer. That's the only way you would know it was specifically Yuletide.' He sipped his drink and looked at Chaucer over the rim of his cup. 'You don't have to worry,' he said. 'I won't hurt him.' He smiled his usual basilisk smile and Chaucer was none the wiser whether he meant that or not.

Chaucer's mouth hung open. In his heart of hearts, he had always considered himself the cleverest man he knew, but John Hawkwood could leave him standing. *And* he knew how to kill people. 'Do you deny you were here?' the comptroller asked.

'Of course not,' Hawkwood shrugged. 'Why would I?'

'Why were you here?' Chaucer asked him. 'And why keep your visit so secret?'

'That's my business,' Hawkwood snapped.

'Not if it involves the murder of Lionel of Antwerp,' the comptroller snapped back.

'You think it's murder?' The mercenary put down his goblet.

'Don't you?'

Hawkwood shrugged. 'I'm not so sure,' he said. 'The priest, now . . . yes, that was murder all right. But then, the priest had a murkiness about him – nothing would surprise me there.'

'Why did you come to Clare at Christmas?' Chaucer persisted. He had lost count of the ways that Hawkwood could kill him if he chose, but, be that as it may, he had to know the truth.

Hawkwood sighed. This plump little quill-pusher was like a leech, refusing to be shaken off. 'Christmas had nothing to do with it. In fact, ever since the Pope excommunicated me and my entire company, I don't even pay lip service to holy days any more.'

Chaucer toyed with crossing himself but thought better of

it; the mercenary had nearly killed him moments ago – what would he do if his blood was up?

'All right,' Hawkwood said, taking up his goblet again, 'I'll tell you. It hardly matters now anyway. You fought alongside Lionel, didn't you? Back in the day?'

'Under, rather than alongside,' Chaucer chuckled. 'And that was twenty years ago. I was a child.'

'Well, I fought *alongside* him last year. And I was a man. I won't bore you with my war stories, Chaucer, but let's say I had a bit of bad luck. You've only had your sleeve torn by one of those.' He pointed to the crossbow bolt. 'I had my shoulder drilled.'

Chaucer winced at the prospect.

'Usual thing,' Hawkwood went on. 'Dirty bandages, gangrene. I went down with the mother of all infections and I had to leave my company under Lionel's command. This was in Tuscany, arse end of 1378. The stupid bastard got himself cut off, somewhere near San Gimignano. Half the Company were wiped out. I blamed Lionel.'

'So you came to have it out with him?'

'I did,' Hawkwood said. 'I tried to find him in Italy, but by the time I was well enough to travel, he'd already gone home. So by the time I got here, I was spitting feathers, I can tell you.' Hawkwood looked at Chaucer. 'And you wouldn't like me when I'm angry,' he said. 'That arsehole Butterfield told me His Grace was indisposed. Actually, of course, he was making the beast with two backs with that little trollop Blanche. It wasn't my finest hour, Chaucer, but I went to Violante – well, she is my sister-in-law, albeit on the wrong side of the blanket. I told her just what I thought of her bloody husband – and I threw in the fact that he'd killed her father, just for good measure.'

Chaucer was pulled up sharp. 'He had?'

'No, as it happened. A misunderstanding, but at the time I didn't know that.'

'How did she take it?' Chaucer asked.

'Like an Italian woman – and I should know, I married one. She threw furniture around and smashed windows. All very predictable, really. The brother just stood there, like a rabbit with a stoat; he had never seen her so angry before. She spoils him – he'll never amount to anything. Too much like his father. It didn't take a man like Lionel of Antwerp to put the old bastard away – and he was so dishonest, it could have been any man in the town. I was wrong to tell her something I wasn't sure about, but I was angry.' He spread his hands as if that explained it all.

'And did you find Lionel?'

'The next day, yes. That idiot carpenter bumped into me on my way to his quarters and, by this time, I'd cooled down. Revenge, they say, is a dish best served cold. I barged into the old man's room and kicked him out of bed. Then I put my poignard to his throat and we had a frank exchange of views.'

'And Blanche?'

'Gone by that time,' Hawkwood said. 'I understand she was rather good at creeping around the castle in the wee small hours; goes with the territory, I suppose, of being a mistress, I mean. I wouldn't know. Never been one. Never had one, though don't tell anyone; I have my reputation to consider.'

'What did Lionel say?' Chaucer was all ears.

Hawkwood sighed. 'He told me what I believe was the truth. It was all down to an ally of ours – Marco Blanco, Count of Perugia. He sold us out to the enemy and Lionel was lucky to escape with his life.'

'And you believed that?' Chaucer checked.

'I did. I've locked horns with the toughest and best, Chaucer. I believe I am a good judge of character. Lionel of Antwerp told me the truth that morning, even after I'd put my dagger away. All a bit of an anticlimax in a way. But it had to be done.'

'And Marco Blanco?'

'Died,' Hawkwood told him. 'Some two weeks after Christmas.'

'Pestilence?' Chaucer hardly dared ask.

'War hammer,' the mercenary said. 'through the right . . . no, I lie . . . left eye.'

'Which Pope did you say excommunicated you?' Chaucer asked.

Hawkwood broke the habit of a lifetime and laughed out loud. 'Both of them,' he said. 'Oh, I know, when my time comes, I'll be facing the Lord of Wrong and his legions, but I think I'll give the old bastard a run for his money.'

'I'm sure you will,' Chaucer said.

'Was there anything else, Chaucer?' Hawkwood asked.

There was a lot, but Chaucer didn't want to push his luck. However, there was one thing. 'How did you know it was Ifaywer the carpenter dressed up as Lord of Misrule who told me?' he asked. 'Was it the smell of pine? Did he have sawdust adhering to a sleeve? Was it the shape of his mouth, from holding nails in it all day long?'

Hawkwood looked at the man and shook his head. 'You people with brains,' he said, 'make everything so difficult for yourselves. Afterwards, when I went to tell the Lady Violante that Lionel had not after all killed her father, I asked her. I had sworn all the others to secrecy.'

Chaucer was crestfallen. What a tediously humdrum answer. 'Well,' he said, getting up, 'you've been most helpful, Sir John.'

Hawkwood grinned. 'That's a myth, Chaucer,' he said. 'A bit like the travels of John Mandeville. I'm not a knight and never will be. Popes and kings and nobles have need of men like me, but they don't make us knights. It's plain John Hawkwood.'

'I find that hard to believe,' Chaucer said. 'You are, at the very least, Giovanni Acuto.'

'Ha!' Hawkwood scoffed. 'They don't come any sharper, it's true. By the way, how are the quarterstaff bruises?'

Chaucer looked down at his hand and at the marks, now fading to yellow. 'It was the doorframe,' he insisted.

'Yes,' Hawkwood smiled. 'And I am John of Gaunt's left bollock. See yourself out.'

As Chaucer turned the second twist in the stair, plangent lute music filled the air behind him, followed by a screech, a plunk and a low chuckle.

Pippa Chaucer had often told her husband about the days of the week and the planets which ruled them. She believed in it implicitly and, on one memorable occasion, had refused to give birth to the baby who turned out to be her son Thomas until midnight struck, because she didn't want him born on a Wednesday. Chaucer had often applauded her strength of will, but as the last minutes of the day ticked away and the midwives had stopped shouting and begun crying, he had wished she were otherwise. Although he scarcely listened, some of it had sunk in. So he knew that Friday was ruled by Venus and, on that day, all things to do with love, money and possessions would take centre stage. He wasn't sure whether any of that had been true but, one way and another, it had been one hell of a day. As had Thursday, come to think of it, but Chaucer was trying his best to live in the present. And he had designated Saturday, the day ruled by Saturn, a day of rest, against all astrological teaching. He didn't intend to rush about or indeed do anything beyond, possibly, a gentle amble around the orchards of Clare.

Setting out for just such, he kept his eyes peeled and his wits about him. By this method, he managed to avoid Hugh Glanville, striding ahead with his hand – ready for anything – on the hilt of his sword. He sidestepped Richard Glanville and Lady Violante walking through the physick garden, bending occasionally to examine a plant here and there. John Hawkwood didn't need avoiding; unless he wanted to see you, he would walk straight over you and not even break his stride. Even so, Chaucer slipped inside a dark doorway as the man swept past, cloak cracking in the breeze of his passing.

A hand coming down on his shoulder almost made him swallow his tongue.

'Master Chaucer,' a voice hissed him his ear. 'I have been looking for you.'

Chaucer twisted his head and saw the Italian seneschal, Niccolò Ferrante, standing there, bent over, as always, in his slightly deferential pose. The smell of garlic was enough to make Chaucer's beard curl. 'Master Ferrante,' Chaucer said, trying not to breathe in. 'I was . . . I was, umm . . .'

'Do not worry yourself, Master Chaucer,' Ferrante said, in a conspiratorial hush. 'You want a quiet day, a day of rest after a busy and distressing time.' His voice dropped lower. 'You find the priest, I hear.'

Chaucer nodded.

'Not a nice thing to find,' Ferrante remarked. 'No, not at all.' He waved an eloquent, continental hand which Chaucer took to be a gesture of sympathy. 'I have spoken with my kitchen and they have come up with a suggestion to make you happy, Master Chaucer. They say, why do I not cook you a special meal, one which would make the angels cry?' He leaned back, beaming. 'Would that please you, Master Chaucer? Hmm?'

Chaucer was about to refuse when he realized that actually, yes, yes it *would* please him. He nodded, with a smile.

'Then, it is settled. If you would like to bring Sir Richard . . .' Ferrante held up his hand. 'I know, I know, I will not forget the worms in vomit for a while. In fact, for a joke, I have named a dish such, but in Italian, no one will know. *Vermin el vomito.*' He clapped his hands and laughed.

Chaucer was about to say that, in fact, it didn't take a linguist to guess the joke, but Ferrante had moved on. 'Come to my chambers at midday and I will cook you a feast such as you have never had before. And Sir Richard will never scoff at my pasta again!'

Chaucer smiled. 'We'll be there,' he said. 'But I can't guarantee Sir Richard's response, I'm afraid.'

Ferrante laughed. 'I can. Wait and see.'


Chaucer had not reckoned with Glanville being quite so averse to giving Italian food another try.

'Whenever I have lunch with Vio . . . with the Lady Violante,' he protested, 'we have normal food. Being Italian doesn't mean eating that muck.'

'Has it occurred to you,' Chaucer wheedled, 'that the Lady Violante might be longing for a nice plate of pasta, for a taste of home, but she eats food she considers to be foreign muck but which she knows you like, just to be polite?'

Glanville looked staggered. It had never occurred to him that boiled hare could be considered foreign muck. 'Do you think so?' He wasn't convinced.

'How lovely would it be,' Chaucer continued, in his guise as devil's advocate, 'If one day you asked her to share a meal with you and it was something that reminded her of home? I'm sure there is something in Ferrante's repertoire which would be suitable for both your tastes.'

Glanville never liked to give in. His friends said he had a will of his own. Those on the other side of the divide said he was a cussed old bugger. His son often said both. 'We'll see,' he said, eventually. 'But if I don't like it, I won't eat it.'

'Agreed,' Chaucer said. 'Now, which way to Ferrante's chambers? He is entertaining us there.' He lifted his nose and sniffed. 'Are they nearby? I believe I can smell sautéeing garlic.'

Glanville sighed. 'Just up this stair,' he said, leading the way. 'Good God, Geoff, it's only just along the passageway from you. Oh, and down a bit. And, remember . . .'

'You don't have to eat it, Rich, if you don't want to.' Chaucer had a momentary pang of loneliness. It seemed many years since he had said that to one of his children and he missed those days. Especially little Elizabeth, though he knew he shouldn't have favourites. But before he could sink too far into familial misery, they were at Ferrante's open door, with delicious smells emanating from within.

Ferrante stood at the fireplace, which had been fitted, by a very bemused blacksmith, with a cooking device of Ferrante's own design. A flat area, not unlike Joyce's smoothing table, stuck out into the room, with various perforated areas spread across it. Below it, pans and skillets rested on bars made to measure. All of it was radiating an intense heat which made the air above it wobble.

'Come in, come in!' Ferrante was in expansive mood. He loved to cook and did all too little of it these days. He wore a smith's leather apron to shield him from the heat and his hair was tied back in a cloth. 'Excuse my attire, gentlemen,' he said, 'but the heat of my . . .' he struggled for the word – '*fornello*, my cooking device, is quite uncomfortable in my usual garb. This is also why the door is open – I hope you don't mind.'

Chaucer and Glanville were grateful for the slight breeze coming up the stone stair. Without it, the room would have been stifling.

'As you see, our table has been set for us already and is under the window. After this week, I doubt I will be able to cook again until the winter – this room is really too small, but I do love to cook so much and the castle kitchen is no place for an artist.' He tried to look suitably humble but failed. '*Ecco* . . . here we are!' He extended a hand to his guests. 'Take your seats and help yourself to wine. This dish is one I cannot make until my guests are arrived.'

Chaucer approached the fire and was driven back by the heat.

'Charcoal,' Ferrante explained. 'The only way to cook, in my opinion.'

Chaucer nodded. He had seen street vendors use it at home in the Aldgate.

Glanville didn't go near the business end of the room. He was already apprehensive about what might turn up on his plate and had his nose in a goblet of wine before Chaucer could even sit down. Poison could always be on the menu in Sir Richard Glanville's view, and everything was all the better for having had a good sniff first. No smell of mice, so it should serve.

Ferrante had a small, flat pan in his hand, held with a folded cloth by the handle. 'You will see that I am using a part of my cooking place away from the flame. This is because I will be slowly adding fresh eggs to new cream and I must be gentle,' he explained. 'Then, I will lightly coat my *strozzapreti* and then – we dine.'

Chaucer was struck again by how similar and yet how different Latin and Italian were from each other. He did a rough translation in his head, as far as he could. His eyes popped. 'Priest strangler?' he asked.

Ferrante laughed and held out a handful of pasta to him. 'They look like collars such as country priests wear in Italy,' he said and stopped, suddenly. 'I am so sorry. What a very thoughtless choice! Poor Father Clement!' He looked around wildly. 'I have no other pasta prepared!'

'Don't worry,' Chaucer said. 'It was a surprise, but . . . it all tastes the same, so it makes no difference.'

Ferrante glowered. Why did all these English clods say that?

But he had made an error in judgement, charmingly deflected, so he let it go. He broke six eggs into a bowl and beat them furiously with a bunch of twigs. Then, he added cream, pouring it from a great height. 'It incorporates air,' he said to Glanville, who was looking somewhat askance. 'It makes the sauce as light as a lady's kiss.'

Glanville looked even more uncomfortable. Ladies and their kisses were not subjects for general conversation, in his view.

'I have already made lardons of fat bacon,' Ferrante said. 'They will be added at the last moment. Along with my signature addition, which I will reveal as we eat. Now, you must excuse me – I must concentrate on the food.'

It was certainly something to watch. Ferrante's brows wrinkled and he bent to his task, beating the eggs and cream for all they were worth over the hotplate and adding small pinches of this and that, tasting as he went. Finally, he was satisfied and leaned perilously close to the fire to reach for the pan of bacon. He took a bowl of pasta from beneath the plate, keeping warm furthest from the fire, and mixed it into his pan. Finally, he added the bacon, tossed the whole thing in the air, catching it effortlessly on another dish he had snatched from a handy shelf and he brought it to the table with a flourish.

He took off his apron and discarded the cloth around his head and sat at the third place. 'Shall I serve, gentlemen, or will you take your food yourself, as is the Italian custom. Not in great houses, you understand, but when we invite friends to dine, as I hope I have done today.' He smiled at the two men and seemed a different person to the self-possessed and somewhat oily seneschal to the Lady Violante.

Chaucer's mouth was watering too much to wait and he dug into the creamy, velvety mass with his spoon. The smell was wonderful, savoury and with an underlying sweetness. He gestured at Glanville.

'Take some, Rich. You saw it cooked. Cream and eggs and bacon – you eat all those daily.' He took a mouthful and rolled his eyes heavenwards. 'This tastes like . . .'

'Nothing else on earth, probably,' Glanville muttered, but took some anyway. He had been brought up at Clare to be honourable and a gentleman and he could eat a plate of foreign

slop if he had to. He licked his spoon tentatively and Chaucer
and Ferrante waited, breaths bated, for his decision. 'Mmm,'
he said, and mumbled on a morsel of bacon. 'It will serve, I
suppose. If a man is hungry enough, he could eat it.' He took
a mouthful. 'Cream and eggs, you say.' He washed it down
with a mouthful of wine. 'And bacon.'

Ferrante nodded.

'And what else?' Glanville was always suspicious when it
came to food but especially so now.

Ferrante laughed. 'Oh, no, Sir Richard,' he said, taking a
mouthful himself. 'When we have finished eating, then and
only then will I disclose my secret ingredient. Unless you
guess it, of course.'

Chaucer looked at his friend and had to stifle a smile.
Glanville was shovelling the food in as if his life depended
on it, the silky sauce running down his chin. The wine was
also of the very best, brought from Lady Violante's private
cellar and, before that, from the hills of Tuscany. It slipped
down like honey, and soon all three men were on the very
merry side of merry. After the pasta came a plate of fresh
cheese and fruit, figs from Lady Violante's fields in Italy,
seethed in honey and bottled in the sun. Several empty wine
flagons were under the table and the three men leaned back
in their chairs and surreptitiously loosened their belts.

'Well, Sir Richard,' Ferrante said, after a suitable pause for
recuperation. 'What was my secret ingredient, do you think?'

Glanville closed his eyes and, after a few minutes, Chaucer
began to wonder whether his friend had fallen asleep. But no.

'There was a warmth, there,' he said, 'which eggs and cream
could not give. Was it . . .' he licked his lips reminiscently,
'unless I miss my guess . . .'

Chaucer and Ferrante leaned forward, intrigued to hear his
answer.

Glanville held up a finger. 'It was . . . horseradish!'

Ferrante leaned back and applauded. '*Meraviglioso*, Sir
Richard! Wonderful. What a palate you have.'

Glanville bowed as well as his full stomach and position
would allow, belched and fell fast asleep.

# ELEVEN

'Time, as the guildsmen would say, to put our quecks on the table.' Richard Glanville leaned back in the chair in his solar and closed his eyes. He hoped that his companions would assume he was thinking, but in fact all he wanted was for the flashing lights to stop. 'I must confess, Geoff, I am none the wiser now than when you came to Clare.'

Chaucer looked at the Glanvilles, father and son. He knew them both, trusted them both, loved them both, but although they were beacons in a world of chaos and storms, both of them, in their different ways, were out of their depth. The solar was still swimming a little in Chaucer's vision and he realized that he should not be drinking the senior Glanville's Gascony wine after the amount of Tuscan wine he had drunk at his midday meal. His history was not at its best at the moment, but he did wonder whether the two regions had ever fought each other – their wines certainly did. Still, drinking yourself under the table was sometimes the only way to face the demons of the night. And facing them, they were.

'Lionel of Antwerp,' the comptroller said. 'Young Hugh, you first brought me the news of His Grace's death. Your views?'

A squire's role was to be polite, obedient, loyal and, above all, silent. But Hugh Glanville had not been brought up that way. If he lacked the wise counsel of his father, he more than made up for it with the exuberance of youth. 'He was poisoned,' he said, 'by persons unknown, with a concoction, perhaps in his wine, composed of hemlock.'

'Who served the wine?' Chaucer asked.

'The serving woman, Joyce,' Hugh told him, blissfully unaware of Chaucer's history with the lady in question. 'She seems to be everywhere you look, at table, in the laundry – suspicious, if you ask me.'

'And she did subsequently kill Ankarette the hound,'

Glanville chimed in. His moment with his eyes closed had refreshed him and the next stage would be loquacious.

'Not intentionally.' Chaucer hurried to Joyce's defence. 'She was very upset.'

'No, no, not intentionally, of course not.' Richard Glanville shook his head and instantly regretted it. 'No one is suggesting . . .' He caught Hugh's eye. 'I think, saving Geoffrey's blushes, Hugh, that you ought to know that Joyce and Geoffrey were very much an item back in the day. He'd have been younger than you are now and she—'

'I don't think we have to wander down young love's lane, Richard,' Chaucer interrupted.

'No, no, quite.' Glanville looked suitably chastened.

'All the same, Geoffrey,' Hugh slapped the comptroller's shoulder. 'Good man!' And he winked.

Time to turn the tables, Chaucer thought. 'Who was the last person to see Lionel alive?' he asked.

'Blanche Vickers,' Richard said and, in the interests of fairness, added, 'She and Hugh were very much an item not so long ago.'

'Thanks, Pa,' Hugh winced. 'For the record,' he pulled himself up in the chair as straight as the wine would allow. 'I have come to realize the error of my ways. I was young and shallow . . .'

The elder Glanville stifled a snort.

'. . . And I see now that I clearly dodged an arrow with that one.'

'But His Grace didn't.' Chaucer got them all back to the night in question. 'Blanche was in his bed, but had apparently gone before he became ill. In that she appears to have suffered no ill-effects, we can assume that she wasn't poisoned too.'

'So, we come to motive.' The elder Glanville topped up everybody's drink. 'That list I gave you, Geoff,' he said. 'Any good?'

'Yes and no,' Chaucer said enigmatically. 'To be sure that Lionel alone swallowed the draught, surely it had to be administered by somebody inside the castle. Merely having it delivered, say in a bottle of Gascony, would target everyone and might not even reach Lionel at all. In fact, depending on the trustworthiness of the chosen carrier, it might not reach the *castle* at all.'

'Off the list, then.' Glanville knew when he was beaten. 'Who would want to see Lionel dead?'

Chaucer hated himself for saying it, knowing his old friend's feelings, but he really had no choice. 'Violante,' he said.

'Now, just a minute . . .' Glanville held up his hand.

'You can call "Hoo" as often as you like, Richard,' Chaucer said, 'but we've got to face it. Lionel was trying to regain his lost youth with Blanche, and, as I understand it, there had been plenty of others.'

'Granted,' the knight said.

'How must that have made Violante feel? A scorned woman, Richard, with the volatility of an Italian thrown in.'

Chaucer and the squire looked at Glanville.

'And poison *is* a woman's weapon,' Hugh said, and the other two now looked at him.

'No,' Glanville said, after a moment's hesitation. 'She'd have used a stiletto or whatever they call poignards in Italy. I will concede that I harbour feelings for Violante – what full-blooded man would not?' He glanced at Hugh, who was trying not to smirk at his old pa's admission. 'But I agree with you, Geoff. Wouldn't a woman scorned, wronged beyond endurance, want to watch the old bastard's face as she plunged her knife into him?'

Chaucer's face said it all. There was clearly a side to the Lady Violante that the comptroller had never seen. Speaking for himself, he had always sought out placid women, when he sought one out at all. His Pippa could be annoying from time to time, but if she had a temper, he had never seen it. He bowed to Glanville's superior knowledge.

'All right,' he said. 'We'll set Violante aside for the moment. Who else might want Lionel of Antwerp dead?'

There was a pause.

'Richard Glanville,' said Richard Glanville.

The others exploded in a flurry of denials, but the knight held up his hand. 'I know you dismissed it when you first arrived,' he said, 'but you've got to be dispassionate, Geoffrey. With Lionel out of the way, I can continue in Violante's service, living here rent free with my horses and my hawks. *And*' – he watched his companions' faces for a moment – 'I *may* have a chance with the lady herself.'

'Well, if it's suspects you want,' Hugh said, not wishing to be outdone, 'what about me?'

More explosive denials.

Hugh's hand was in the air too. 'My knighthood has been delayed for too long. Loyal to His Grace as I was, his involvement with Blanche – *my* Blanche as she once was – meant that I have still not yet won my spurs. With him gone, the honour passes to you, Pa, and I've achieved my goal – a knighthood *and* revenge for losing Blanche. It works perfectly.'

There was a silence. It was the Comptroller of Woollens who broke it. He held out both his hands and took the right hands of both Glanvilles. 'My dear friends,' he said. 'I have known you, Rich, since I was a boy and you, Hugh, all your life. A kinder, straighter, more noble pair of comrades in arms I could never wish to meet this side of Paradise. If either of you wanted to kill Lionel of Antwerp, you would have done it face to face, with a sword in your hand. Then you would have taken your own lives and gone to Hell for doing both murders. He leaned forward and winked. 'You'll have to do better than that, you know.'

All three chuckled.

'Father Clement,' Glanville said, leaning back and cradling his cup.

'Did not die by hemlock alone,' Chaucer told him. 'Perhaps it wasn't working for some reason; perhaps it was too slow; perhaps whoever our killer is, came to check on him, found him still alive and strangled him.'

'His face,' Glanville remembered, with a suppressed shudder.

'Contorted,' Chaucer said. 'Terrified.'

'Who knows about poisons?' Hugh asked. 'What hemlock can do?'

'I'm glad you asked that,' Chaucer said. 'An apothecary would know and you kindly put me in the direction of one.'

'Alban,' Glanville clicked his fingers. 'Did you find him all right?'

'Eventually,' Chaucer conceded. 'And his amanuensis, Roger.'

'Who?' the Glanvilles chorused.

'Something I need to pursue,' the comptroller said. 'But first, we're overlooking somebody, right here in the castle.'

'Who?' Glanville asked.

Chaucer's eyes swivelled to Hugh. 'How's Giovanni's swordplay coming along?' he asked.

'Giovanni?' Hugh was confused. 'Well, he's not bad, but too hot-headed . . . Wait; how do you mean?'

'John Hawkwood told Violante that Lionel had been responsible for her father's death; Giovanni's father too, right?'

'Right!' The knight's eyes lit up. Suddenly, it was all falling into place.

'Violante, for all her flashes of fury, is a nuanced practitioner of politics,' Chaucer reasoned. 'You don't survive long in the Visconti family without that. *She* understands how the world works. All right, so Lionel killed her old man. That's what Italian, not to mention English, politics is all about. But Giovanni now, sixteen, naïve, hot-headed . . . You see the way my mind's working?'

'And *he* wouldn't use a sword,' Hugh said. 'Hence the poison.'

'The whole thing hinges,' Chaucer said, 'on whether Giovanni was privy to the *second* conversation that Hawkwood had with Violante. In the first one, he was furious, accusing Lionel of all kinds of things. Then, having had a chance to talk to him, man to man, he realized that he'd been wrong. It wasn't Lionel who killed Violante's father, it was Marco Blanco, the Count of Perugia. In the *second* conversation with Violante, Hawkwood put that right.'

'But . . .' Hugh was confused.

'But was Giovanni there then?' Chaucer threw back at him. 'We know he was there for the first; but what of the second? What if he *was* there, but didn't believe him? Either way, he would have a clear motive for wanting Lionel dead.'

There was a silence while the Glanvilles wrestled with the information.

'So, how do we—' Hugh began.

'*We* don't,' Chaucer stopped him. '*You* do, Hughie, my boy. Tomorrow, first thing, take him out to the lists. Oh, damn, it's Sunday. After Mass, take him out to the lists. Let him win a few passes, bolster his ego, praise his swordplay. Then get him talking about Hawkwood.'

'He does that anyway,' the younger Glanville muttered. 'Sun shines from the man's arse.'

'Good, good,' Chaucer said. 'And let me know what he says about Lionel and his father. And put that bloody bottle away, Richard; I'm never going to find my room again as it is!'

It was pleasantly warm in the private chapel to the right of the nave in the church of St Peter and St Paul in the town. Chaucer had told the local priest that he was in need of solitude while attending the service and the chapel, with its slanted prayer-slit that faced the altar, would be perfect. The local priest fully understood that and he also fully understood the fistful of coins that Chaucer passed his way.

Instinctively, because he'd done it all his life, Chaucer went through the motions of the Mass, although he was grateful that there was insufficient room in the little chapel for him to lie flat on the ground for the prayers. The priest's Latin was audible and surprisingly accurate for a provincial cleric and not too many of the congregation left part of the way through. They had been seen by their peers and that was the important thing.

But Chaucer was not there to prostrate himself before his God. He was there to watch the censer-swinger, the former altar-boy turned apothecary's assistant, called Roger. The lad looked much more angelic that Sunday, soon after dawn though it was. His hair was combed and the stubble on his chin was shaved. Above all, he had adopted this holier-than-thou appearance as he swung the brass censer, the cloying smoke drifting across the church to the annoyance and dismay of the consumptives. Roger knew his business at St Peter and St Paul as well as he did in the apothecary's shop and Chaucer waited until the service was over.

He emerged from his hiding place once the priest and his people had gone to the robing room, bobbed on one knee before the altar, crossed himself and loitered outside, making small talk with the great and good of Clare. Yes, the young king was shaping up nicely; time he got himself a wife, however. That Anne of Bohemia seemed a nice girl, so the merchants said. But what about that John of Gaunt, eh? About to make himself king of Castile, or so some merchants had testified. Then there was du Guesclin. Hanging, Chaucer was told, was far too good for the French bastard. He was supposed to be a knight but had no chivalrous ideals at all. Anyway, he'd had his bollocks cut off in a clash with the Burgundians, so that would cramp his style a bit. That would explain, one of Chaucer's chatterers contended, why du Guesclin had been caught wearing women's clothing – at least sixteen local merchants had seen that with their own eyes.

By now thoroughly exhausted with current affairs, Chaucer was glad to catch sight of Roger sauntering down the church path and gratefully took his leave.

'Good morning,' the comptroller hailed the censer-swinger.

Roger took a moment to realize who Chaucer was and that he was talking to him. 'We ain't open today,' he said. 'Master Alban is a God-fearing Christian, despite what you might have heard. It's the Sabbath.'

'It is indeed,' Chaucer smiled. 'But I have no business with the apothecary, not today. It's you I wanted to talk to.'

Roger was already striding towards the town and Chaucer had to increase his pace too. 'Why?' the apothecary's assistant asked.

'Father Clement,' Chaucer said.

Roger's step faltered and his eyelids fluttered. Then, he gathered his composure and decided to brazen this one out. 'What of him?'

Chaucer took the boy's arm and stopped him in his tracks. 'Do you want me to tell you that here?' he asked. 'In the public highway, on the Sabbath?'

Roger's eyes swivelled from left to right and back again. 'In here,' he muttered and led Chaucer beyond the pig pens and the tanneries to a door in a high wall. He fumbled with the lock and pushed it open. The pair stood in a yard, open to the sky, and reeking of pigswill. 'It's the outbuildings of the priory,' Roger said, in response to Chaucer's expression. 'We won't be disturbed.'

A little shiver ran up Chaucer's neck and threatened to dislodge his liripipe. What had Roger in mind? And could the lad have so misread an upstanding pillar of society, father of three – or was it four? – and Comptroller of the King's Woollens? In all his forty-odd years, he had never been placed in such a tricky position – and so near a nunnery, too. However, the comptroller needed answers and he might not get a second chance.

'I found writings,' Chaucer said, 'in Father Clement's room at the castle. I'd have to call them love letters.' He was whispering now, imagining the ears of thirty or more sisters pressed to the stone on the other side of the wall. 'Letters addressed to you, Roger.'

'I never got any letters,' the boy said.

'Did you write any?' Chaucer asked.

'No.'

'Can you write?'

'Of course. I'd be a fine apothecary's assistant if I couldn't. Tinctures don't mix themselves, you know; you've got to know what you're doing.'

This was going better than Chaucer had expected. 'There you have it,' he said. 'Tell me about tinctures.'

'What do you want to know?' Roger asked.

Chaucer narrowed his eyes. 'How old are you, boy?' he asked.

'I shall be nineteen next Michaelmas,' the lad told him.

'Right. Now, I don't care what you and the priest got up to. That's between the two of you and your Maker. If you want to risk Hellfire . . .'

'We loved each other!' Roger suddenly blurted out so that the words rang around the walls. The sisters must have recoiled at that, their ears throbbing with the noise.

Chaucer saw silver tears drop from the lad's eyelashes. What a tortured soul. A less kind man would have dragged the boy to the bishop's consistory court where his abominable crimes would be exposed to the world. Roger's back would be raw with whipping and he would stand outside the church of St Peter and St Paul in a white sheet on three successive Sundays. Undoubtedly, Alban the apothecary would have to let him go. And how would he pay the crippling fine then? But Geoffrey Chaucer, whatever else he was, was a kind man and he let it go.

'Good for you,' he said quietly, crossing himself in his head. 'But the sad fact is, Roger, that the man you loved is dead. And he was poisoned.'

Roger blinked back the tears. 'Poisoned?'

'Hemlock,' Chaucer said. 'Poison parsley. Do you know it?'

'*Conium maculatum*; yes, I do.' Roger was still trying to take in what Chaucer had told him, crossing himself and sobbing. 'Who would want to kill Father Clement?' he wailed.

'My question precisely.' Chaucer consoled the boy with a pat as manly as he could make it. 'Tell me,' he said, 'did the Father mention anyone who had taken a dislike to him?'

'He was the loveliest of men,' Roger sobbed. 'Kind and loving.'

'Yes, yes, of course, but priests hear things – you know, in the confessional. They acquire secrets, secrets which are sometimes dangerous. Was there someone who the Father was wary of? Suspicious, even?'

'The secrets of the confessional remain so,' Roger said. 'Clemmie wasn't a gossip. He took that kind of thing very seriously.'

'I understand,' Chaucer said. 'Of course he did.'

'Master Chaucer,' Roger looked at the comptroller with fear in his eyes.

'Yes, dear boy?'

'I know that His Grace Lionel of Antwerp was murdered. But . . . two men in the castle of Clare in as many weeks. Is it all by the same hand?'

'That would be my guess,' Chaucer said. Roger said nothing.

'So you can't help me further?' the comptroller checked.

The boy shook his head, his shoulders hunched, his eyes red. The loss of the love of his life was bad enough, but to lose him in so vicious a way to a killer was too much. Chaucer was just glad that the lad hadn't found him – that would have murdered his sleep for the rest of his life.

Chaucer turned to go, believing that the listening sisters had heard more than enough for one day. 'Have you come across Signor Giovanni Visconti?' he asked. 'The Lady Violante's brother?'

Roger was wiping his eyes on his sleeve. 'Sixteen or so?' he sniffed. 'Blue eyes, fine hair, neat feet? No, not really. Why do you ask?'

'Er . . . no reason,' Chaucer said. 'No reason at all.'

The three of them stood on the battlements of Clare as the sun dipped below the great elms beyond the river: Richard Glanville, knight of great renown; Hugh Glanville, the squire of endless promise; and Geoffrey Chaucer, poet and, always, Comptroller of the King's Woollens.

'It's not Roger.' Chaucer was sure. 'I thought perhaps he had the knowhow – a man of tinctures, after all. And I thought perhaps a lover's tiff . . .' The elder Glanville cleared his throat uncomfortably – he was the wrong generation for all this. 'But I don't think so, unless the lad is a better actor than anyone I've seen.'

'Let's see how he performs in the pageant,' Hugh smiled. 'I understand the apothecary's people are joining forces with the goldsmiths – frankincense and myrrh; magi in the morning.'

They looked out over Clare as the torches were lit and the bell tolled in the priory for Vespers. The church of St Pater and St Paul looked as if it were made of beaten bronze in the dying sun. Filling every open space, it seemed to Chaucer, the great wagons of the pageant stood ready to be yoked to the oxen, one tier above the other where Adam's tree stood dripping with Satan's evil and Hellmouth yawned for the unwary. From somewhere in the shadows, they heard the solemn thud of a drum and the rattle of a tambour.

'Shawms,' the elder Glanville muttered suddenly. 'God, I hate shawms.'

The others ignored him. 'What happened with Giovanni this morning, Hugh?' Chaucer asked.

'He wasn't exactly talkative,' the squire said. 'As you

suggested, I let him win the odd bout.' He rubbed his right shoulder and flexed it gingerly. 'Damn near broke my arm into the bargain. Even so, I got the impression he was rehearsing for a mummer's role in the pageant.' He used both hands to mime the Italian's mouth being sewn shut. 'Then I remembered, and that's thanks to you, Pa – Romonye; it never fails.'

'Don't blame me,' Glanville chuckled. 'I didn't shell out a small fortune to turn you into a tippler.'

'Ah, the sweet wine of the Hellespont,' Chaucer smiled. 'We owe the Greeks a lot.'

'Romonye'll get a man under the table faster than anything else I know,' Hugh said. 'Sure enough, a quaff or two and Giovanni was singing his head off.' He clicked his tongue. 'So young,' he smiled. 'So young.'

Chaucer and Richard Glanville were smiling too, but for an altogether different reason. They were remembering warm nights of their youth, the empty bottle lying on the grass between them as they watched the sun set through the boughs of the orchard at Clare. The drowsy feeling when they felt that they could move mountains, while at the same time being unable to stand up unaided. Good times.

'And,' the knight placed a gentle fist on his son's smooth chin, 'old greybeard, what did you learn?'

'Nothing,' the squire had to confess.

'Ah!'

'I eased the conversation round to His Grace and to John Hawkwood and he didn't bite. I tried the Lady Violante, you know, wishing I'd had a big sister like her, that sort of thing. I even said how sorry I felt for him that he had lost his father and asked him outright who he thought might be responsible for that.'

'And?' Chaucer said.

'Nothing, again. By this time, of course, he was crying like a baby.'

'Romonye will do that,' Glanville nodded, looking at Chaucer with a reminiscent smile which the comptroller chose to ignore.

'So will guilt,' Chaucer commented. 'So, the upshot is, we don't know what Giovanni's attitude to Lionel was.'

The squire shrugged.

'Don't blame yourself, Hugh,' the comptroller said. 'In my experience, a murderer only confesses to two people – his priest and his torturer. And I don't suppose we're any of us in a position to use the red-hot pincers?'

The others shook their heads.

'As for the priest,' Chaucer sighed, 'is that why Clement had to die? For what he knew? For what Giovanni, in a moment of guilt, had told him?'

'Does he have any knowledge of poisons, though?' Glanville asked. He and Chaucer looked at Hugh.

'We didn't get on to that,' the squire said. 'Drunk or not, it's not an easy subject to bring up.' He looked thoughtful. 'Particularly when you're drinking, come to think of it.'

'It's not usual,' the comptroller was thinking aloud. 'Members of the nobility aren't often, in my experience, of the Scientia persuasion. And with the best will in the world, you can't accuse the lad of having any brain.'

'But he *is* Italian,' Hugh ventured.

'True.' Chaucer nodded.

'Stilettos,' the knight muttered. 'Your Italian uses stilettos, poignards sharper than ours. Remember, Geoffrey, the smiler with the knife.'

'How could I forget?' the comptroller said. In his heart of hearts, the poet in him was pleased that his phrases were known and remembered the length and breadth of Suffolk, but this phrase was different. It implied that he, Geoffrey Chaucer, could get results. And so far, he had precisely nothing. 'We'll have to watch him,' he said at last. 'I can't get this Hawkwood story out of my head. The boy heard him tell Violante that Lionel had killed his father. There's a code, isn't there? In Italy, I mean? Some family thing.'

'Blood's thicker than water,' Glanville shrugged.

'Yes, but there's more to it than that. It's a blood-feud thing. We used to have it in this country before the Conquest. Ethelnoth kills Eadwald. Egbert kills Ethelnoth. Eosterwine kills—'

'You're making this up,' the knight grumbled.

'I most certainly am not,' Chaucer told him. 'My grasp of

Old English is second only to my grasp of Middle English. I have *written* poetry, you know!'

There was a silence. It wasn't often the comptroller got on his high horse about literature, but woe betide his audience when he did. 'Sorry,' he said. 'Just making a point.'

There was another silence.

'So, what do we do?' Glanville asked. 'Follow Giovanni?'

'For a while, yes,' Chaucer said. 'Unless and until anything else breaks. We've had two deaths as it is – three, if you include the oaf John Hawkwood dispatched. Can we risk another?'

'I think you can best answer that, Geoff,' Glanville said.

'Me? Why?'

'It must be common knowledge by now why you're here,' the knight said quietly, checking the crenellations for eavesdroppers. 'And can I remind you about the Lion Tower incident?'

'I'd very much rather you didn't, Richard,' Chaucer said, but he took the knight's point absolutely. All those locked doors and roped-off stairways. Was that someone's way of telling Geoffrey Chaucer to keep his nose out of somebody else's business? Or was it someone's attempt to kill him?

# TWELVE

The priest of St Peter and St Paul was of the old school. A man of certain years, he had watched, as his tonsure greyed and his rheumatism get worse, the world around him fall apart. In his youth, as he took his vows, the Lord had sent the Pestilence, to vent His wrath and purge the world of its undesirables. Miserable, wild and violent, the worst people alone had survived to bear witness. Had something gone wrong with the Lord's plan? It was not the priest's place even to raise the question. He would leave that sort of thing to the heretic Wycliffe and his Lollards. And they, assuredly, were not the work of the Lord. Lollardy was the creation of Satan and he walked the earth. The priest had seen him once, all fire and cloven hoofs, striding through the churchyard in search of souls to torment. The man of God had confronted him, holding the crucifix to his face, but the Devil had laughed at him and had run away, unafraid, unashamed. What was the world coming to?

So, yet again, as he did every year, the priest of St Peter and St Paul dipped his quill into his ink and wrote his annual letter. This time, it could not be to His Grace Lionel of Antwerp, the Duke of Clarence, because the Lord had taken him to His bosom. So he wrote to the Lady Violante instead.

The Lady Violante broke the priest's seal and unrolled the parchment. She clicked her tongue and shook her head. 'You'd really think,' she said, 'that this year, of all years, the man would give his rants a rest.'

She passed the letter to Richard Glanville, standing next to her in the great hall at Clare. Now that Lionel of Antwerp was no more, his widow, still in her black weeds, was carrying out as much business of the estate as she could. Dealing with turbulent priests was just a small part of it. Glanville was about to tear it up, but Violante stopped him.

'No,' she said. 'Show it to Master Chaucer; he might find it amusing.'

Glanville did as he was told and the comptroller ran his eyes down the page.

'Read it out, Master Chaucer,' Violante said. 'I'd welcome your views.'

'"April Fool's Day is bad enough",' Chaucer read, '"with the world turned upside down. Did you know, my lady, that in French universities, the scholars teach the Fellows on that day? The young rule the old. The lowest riff-raff is served at table before his betters. Those who can write, do so backwards, to be read in mirrors. Even, and I blush to think of it, some priests say the Holy Mass backwards."' He paused.

'Well, Master Chaucer?' There was a smile on Violante's lovely face.

'I know priests who cannot say it forwards, my lady,' he said, 'and as for writing backwards, I really must try that.'

'Read on,' Violante said.

Chaucer cleared his throat. '"May I remind you, my lady, that the first pageant this year is to celebrate the feasts of St Philip and St James. It happens to fall on May Day, as always, but I hope we will not see, as we did last year, a maypole erected on Clare Green" . . .'

'Butterfield?' Violante turned to her English seneschal.

'Already erected, my lady,' he said. 'In the coloured ribbons of His Grace, as per usual.'

Violante nodded and Chaucer went on. '"As the maypole is" . . .' his voice tailed away.

Violante burst out laughing despite her black robes. 'Say on, Master Chaucer. I *have* heard all this before.'

Chaucer cleared his throat again. '"As the maypole is the member of the Devil and those who dance around it are forni-cators and adulterers."'

'Quite,' Violante chuckled. 'Butterfield, are the nuns of the priory to dance this year?'

'They are, my lady,' Butterfield beamed. The seneschal was not a man of many amusements, but seeing the priest's face as the sisters pulled on their ribbons was one that he particu-larly looked forward to.

'Master Chaucer,' Violante nodded and the comptroller read on.

'"There must be no green boughs on doors, for green is the colour of evil."'

Violante turned to Ferrante, her Italian seneschal. 'Is that true?' she asked him.

'Black in Italia, *donna bella*,' he told her.

'I thought so.' She waved Chaucer to continue.

'"No one should be eating those disgusting biscuits called Jack-in-the-Greens."'

Violante turned to Ferrante again.

'Not in *my* kitchen, *donna bella*,' he assured her.

'They shall be in *mine!*' Butterfield bellowed, and the two men glared at each other over Violante's head.

'"Running races,"' the priest, via Chaucer, ranted on, '"hurtling to Hell with bare feet. Rolling hoops, the circles of Hell" . . .'

Violante held up her hand. 'Thank you, Master Chaucer. We've heard enough.' She stood up and moved to the supplicants in the hall, who rose with her. 'We'll hear the rest after dinner,' she said. Then, in a loud voice, 'The feasts of St Philip and St James,' she announced proudly, 'will merge with the Clare pageant. There will be the mystery plays and the mummings, the guisings, music and dancing.' Her voice dropped a little. 'We have need of that.' She half-turned in the doorway below the dais. 'And of course,' she said, 'we'll have the maypole. And I'll race everybody to it.'

Cheers and laughter filled the hall.

The bells. Why did everything have to begin with bells? Having lived over the Aldgate for ever, Chaucer should have been used to them, but it hadn't happened yet. Some men, men like Chaucer, of the poetic persuasion, rejoiced in the sound of birdsong in the morning, as the sun warmed the earth and the search for worms and grubs began. But Chaucer himself was oblivious to that; the London cocksparrows were made mute by the cacophony of brass. On such a morning, the whole air seemed alive with joy and it seemed wrong that two men lay dead by the hand of another. Perhaps, before May Day became merely another spring day, they would have laid that other by the heels.

The priory of Clare clanged first, then the peal of St Peter and St Paul, followed by the other half-dozen churches in the town. It was, after all, the Feast of St Philip and St James and the Church held priority over all that. But the cities of God were not going to have it all their own way. As Chaucer took up his position on the crenellations of the Auditor's Tower, he could hear the boatmen on the Stour calling to each other and he could see the bunting and the banners being stretched from prow to prow. He heard the thump of the dancing drums and the whinny of horses, mingling now with the deep lowing of the oxen; heavy, melancholy beasts whose shaggy heads were plaited this morning with flowers and garlands.

From somewhere in the tiny tangle of streets, a solitary rattle hissed about the thatch of the roofs and a single voice sang out: 'Oh, it is the First of May, oh, it is the First of May. Remember, Lords and Ladies, it is the First of May.'

The lords and ladies were not abroad as early as this. The mist had not yet left the river and the sun had yet to clear the great elms that stood sentinel along the Stour.

Chaucer turned at the arrival of Richard Glanville. 'Any sign?' he asked.

The knight was dressed for a feast day, without his telltale heraldry, so that he could blend with the crowd. His liripipe was scarlet and his tired old houppelande had been replaced by a dashing doublet of silk and taffeta which had clearly been made for a much younger man. Chaucer was impressed.

'Giovanni's still breaking his fast,' Glanville said, and caught the look on his old friend's face. 'Don't say it, Geoffrey; I am not in the mood.'

'I was going to say how very fetching you look, Rich. Been taking a few tips from the boy, eh?'

Glanville pulled himself up, looking slightly down to the poet's hairline. 'The day Hugh Glanville can show me how to dress is the day I'll hang up my sword . . . Talking of which . . .' He adjusted his fluttering sleeve so that his poignard hilt remained within easy reach. Whatever happened today, it *was* the start of the Clare pageant. There'd be laughter and merry-making, for sure, but there'd be drinking too and one man's light-hearted quip was another's deathly insult.

'Hello,' Chaucer was looking down to the Nethergate where the castle's guard was surrounded by a knot of ladies from the town, more than one of them wearing the yellow hoods of their calling; well, it saved the embarrassment of accosting the wrong girl and meant that deals could be struck straight away. 'Looks as though breakfast's over.'

Sauntering out of the gate, and being pestered immediately by the yellow ladies, Giovanni Visconti was making his way down the hill towards the action in the marketplace and along Callis Street. By the time he had jostled past them, he had flowers sticking out of his hair and his tunic and codpiece were both unlaced.

Chaucer shook his head. 'You know, Rich, the more I look at him, the less sure I am that he's our man.'

'I'll let you know,' the knight said, slapping his friend's arm. 'See you at the Cockatrice at midday – and don't be late. I'll have had shawms ringing in my ears for five bloody hours by then and I'll be ready to kill somebody myself.'

The problem for the relay of men following Giovanni Visconti was that it was important they should not be seen. That was why Glanville had helped himself to his son's less-than-cutting-edge finery and why he hung back by the Nethergate until the boy had all but disappeared into the crowd.

'Hello, dearie,' a gap-toothed hag pawed Hugh's satin as Glanville brushed past her. 'Got a kiss for a lady on this bright May Day morning?'

'Unhand me, madam.' Glanville brushed her off.

The old girl pulled up with a jolt. 'Oh, it's you,' she said. 'How can I have been so rude, forgetting myself like that? Let me try that again.' She cleared her throat. 'Hello, Sir Richard; got a kiss for a lady on this bright May Day morning?'

She puckered up and closed her eyes, but the knight who had fought in France and Italy and Latvia and Prussia, was already retreating down the hill.

Once Glanville had gone, Chaucer went to his room to put on his costume. He had not brought anything with him, but he had taken part in pageants before and he always wore the same thing – as behove his role as Comptroller of the King's

Woollens – a shepherd's simple garb, with a lamb in his arms. He had sought out one of Lady Violante's seamstresses and with much giggling on her part and misunderstanding on his – *why*, he had wondered often in the conversation, was Italian not more like Latin? – they had come up with something of which they could both be proud. It took some donning, but the seamstress had clever fingers and it was both comfortable to wear and eye-catching, to Chaucer's mind the most important elements of any costume a man must wear all day. He tested his laces and found they were easily accessible, for a man must still piss, no matter how important the day. He hitched up his lamb and set out for a wander around the castle, until such time as Richard Glanville returned or sent word that it was Chaucer's turn to keep watch on Giovanni Visconti.

He found a quiet spot in the inner bailey and sat down, his lamb in his lap. Although he knew it was made of lambskin with a sewn-on leather nose and glass beads for eyes, he was becoming quite fond of it. His stay at Clare had not been the most restful he had ever spent and he sat back, letting the spring sun warm his face and fancying he could feel his lamb breathing gently on his lap.

'Geoff?'

His eyes flew open and he looked around, trying to get his bearings from his light doze. A figure was between him and the sun and he squinted up to see who it was.

The figure stepped aside and plumped down beside him, stroking his lamb. 'I love May Day,' she said. 'I can talk to you without fear. What a wonderful day. And, if I may make so bold, that is a wonderful lamb. It looks real from a little way away.'

Chaucer focused. 'Joyce,' he said with a smile. 'You like him, do you? I had him made yesterday. I like to join in.'

'Clare's Pageant is for everyone,' Joyce said. 'It's quite famous hereabouts. We have a float, you know, we ladies of the laundry and table. I'm not dressed for it yet, but you'll like it, I feel sure. But' – she patted Chaucer's lamb again, snuggling up to his chest, encircled by his arms – 'aren't you going to get a bit tired, carrying that around all day? What's it stuffed with?'

'Straw,' Chaucer said. 'It does look lifelike, doesn't it? I am the shepherd who went after the one sheep that strayed.' He smiled. 'I've done it for years. Pippa has always said it suits me.'

Joyce patted his arm. 'And she's right,' she said. She stopped, looking puzzled. 'Is that . . .? What *is* that? Oh!' She gave a sudden shriek. 'And what was *that*?'

'To take your questions in turn,' Chaucer said, 'the first, that is stuffing in my sleeve, sewn around the lamb with stuffed gloves attached at the ends. The second, that was me, giving you a pinch.'

She looked down to see his hand, waggling its fingers out of the side of his smock, through an undone seam. 'That's so clever,' she said, pulling at the sewing to see how it was done. 'No wonder the lamb isn't heavy.'

'Not at all,' Chaucer said. 'It's hung round my body on a harness. It doesn't really weigh me down at all. It's a bit of a swine to put on and I may need to be cut out of it at the end of the day, but it has to be securely stitched and I think that Moderata has done me proud.'

Joyce's nose went up in the air. 'Moderata? Oh, *her*! What a name for a woman who doesn't know the meaning of the word moderation.' She leaned forward to check under the lamb. 'I suppose she insisted on arranging your lacings, too.'

'To be honest, Joyce,' Chaucer said, 'I have little idea what she was insisting on. Her Italian was far too fleet for my Latin to recognize more than the odd word. So, who knows what she had in mind? But she was sorely disappointed, I can tell you that. She made the lamb and stuffed the arms to my drawings, made from the memories of many a pageant in London. My lamb never fails to amuse. Little Richard loves it and always asks for it.'

'Little . . .?' Joyce was confused. She knew that Chaucer and Glanville were friends of longstanding, but even so . . .

'The king,' Chaucer said. A silence fell between them as they considered what he had said. Simple enough in itself, it had reminded them both of the gulf between them. Chaucer broke the awkward spell.

'So, what is your costume, Joyce?' He gave her another pinch for good measure.

'Geoff,' she said fondly. 'You will always be a boy to me, you know. But I would much appreciate it if you stopped doing that.'

'Sorry.' Chaucer dipped his head and looked up at her through his lashes. He had almost forgotten how to flirt, what with his work, his paunch and his Pippa.

She nudged him and his lamb wobbled, making it look more lifelike. 'Does he have a name?' she asked, apropos of nothing. 'Your lamb?'

'No,' Chaucer said. 'I've never thought of naming him. Why don't you?'

'All right,' she said, and bit her lip. 'Why not call him . . . Arthur? I've always wanted to call one of my boys Arthur, but their fathers never seem to like the name.'

She was so matter-of-fact about it that Chaucer wanted to weep. The women of London would never sit beside him like this, letting him pinch them through a hole in his clothing. Pippa would slap his hand away and go off on some house-hold task. But Joyce . . . once *his* Joyce . . . was a jewel among women. He cleared his throat. This business of chasing down a boy who would have to die at their hand . . . it was making him melancholy. 'You didn't tell me, what is your costume?'

'You'll find out soon enough, Master Geoffrey Chaucer. My old pa, he says I should be ashamed at my age – there, that's all you'll be told, until you see us tonight! We'll be down in the town later, putting the finishing touches. But I think I can safely say, it will be our best float yet!' She patted Arthur the lamb and jumped up. 'I still have work to do, but I'll see you later – and you will definitely see me.'

And with that, she was gone. Chaucer stuck one arm out of the side of his smock and aimlessly scratched Arthur the lamb behind the ear. It was strangely soothing and he leaned back in the warmth again, thinking over what was to come.

They did things differently in Milano; so this was, essentially, Giovanni Visconti's first pageant. In the square, surrounded as he was by townsfolk and people who had crossed the fields from the countryside around, the great wagons which were the moving stages of the mystery plays were limbering up. Guildsmen and their companies were hopping on and off the lurching floats, their wheels creaking and groaning under the weight. The oxen's muscles bunched and their eyes rolled and the drovers cursed and cracked their whips.

The Italian had come upon the first play by accident, to be performed outside the mayor's house. His Excellency and his very large retinue of family and servants had all crowded into the upper balcony of his townhouse as the great tree of the Garden of Eden ground to a halt under the eaves. Visconti was hemmed in on all sides by the throng, determined as they were not to miss the first pageant of the day. Halfway up the tree with its twisted, bark-covered trunk, the lad playing Satan peered evilly out of his scaly suit, with every scale lovingly sewn on by his mother. He was eternally grateful to whoever wrote the book of Genesis for making it clear that serpents had arms and legs in the good old days so that at least he could cling on for dear life and fend off some of the offal that he knew was bound to come his way. The Corpus Christi Guild was paying him over the odds for this, and everyone knew it was danger money.

A great roar went up as Eve came demurely onto the wagon's upper platform. She looked suspiciously like Agnes Toogood from Clare's largest bakery, but she looked the part in her huge fig leaves. Most of the roarers, it is true, were the menfolk, shepherds from the fields and ploughboys from the furrows, who might volunteer to fetch the bread themselves a little more often in the future.

Satan curled seductively as best he could, encased in his embroidered oilskin, and he held out an elderly apple to Eve. May was not a good time to find apples which looked anything other than wizened from overwintering, but the pair did their best.

'No! No!' the crowd shouted.

'Don't take it!'

'He's the Devil, he is. Just walk away!'

But Eve knew the story and her role that day. She hesitated coyly, holding her finger up to her dimpled chin. Then she took the fruit and bit into it.

'Abomination!' one of the churchmen shouted. Everybody looked at him; surely, he knew how this one went?

Adam stumbled on to wolf whistles, mostly from the women in the crowd. 'He can give me an apple any day,' somebody shouted and there were hoots of laughter. Eve passed him the fruit.

'No,' the churchman bellowed. 'That's forbidden!'

But it was all too late. Predictably, Adam bit the apple. Satan gurgled triumphantly and raised both hands in sheer happiness, gripping the tree with his thighs and trusting to the God whose arch-enemy he was. Sure enough, missiles began to hiss through the air, thumping onto the Eden set and bouncing off Adam and Eve as well as the object of the crowd's hatred.

Even before the angel Jophiel appeared to rebuke the first humans to walk the earth, Adam and Eve engaged in a sensual embrace which threatened to unglue Adam's fig leaf.

'Abomination!' the churchman bellowed again. 'That's not in the Corpus Christi script!'

But he was drowned out by the mob who were loving this impromptu moment. Even the mighty Jophiel just had to stand there until the passion had cooled. Up on the balcony, the mayoress was doing her best to cover the children's eyes and explain to her elder offspring that the evil of Satan could even be found here in their own dear Clare.

Richard Glanville had seen it all before – in fact, he mused to himself, the Eve wasn't half as luscious this year as the year before, though even so, he could understand Adam's enthusiasm – and he eased his son's doublet which tended to cut in under the arms, before sidling off behind Visconti towards the fish market by the river. The Flood was a series of blue-painted boards rolling over a cylinder at the front of the wagon, and David Ifaywer of the Carpenters' Guild of St Anne stood like an ox in the furrow at the prow of the Ark. Gone was the finery of the Guild and in its place was a rough carpenter's smock and apron, dangling with nails, awls and chisels. His own beard was covered in a false one, great strands hanging down to his waist. Shem, Ham and Mrs Noah all stood behind him, praying to the Lord for an end to the driving rain. Japhet, who had been a weak link through all the rehearsals, had failed to turn up and he would be sorry when he did; Ifaywer took his play-acting seriously and being left a son short was nothing short of a sacking offence in his eyes. Because the sun was shining, the lads of the guild threw buckets of water over the front row of the crowd, who shrieked with delight or outrage, depending on their mood. Visconti found himself with a face-full and wasn't sure how to react; as the young master from up at the castle, he had something of a reputation to keep up, he knew. In the end, a pretty girl at his elbow took his hand and that made up his mind for him, and he followed her in and out of the crowd, twisting and turning like the fish beneath Noah's bow.

'Jack-in-the-Green, master?' A cake seller stopped Richard Glanville, who refused with a grunt. The knight did, however, fall to the temptation of a pint of cuckoo-foot ale, his eyes crossing slightly as the combination of basil and ginger hit his tonsils. He fell for it every year, a perfect example of the triumph of hope over experience, and he always regretted it in the end.

The girl who had attached herself to Visconti showed no sign of losing interest in her new beau and that, Glanville knew, would cramp the lad's style if, as he and Chaucer suspected, he would use this day of days to work his evil once more.

There was a shriek near the knight's left ear. Instinctively, his hand dropped to his dagger-hilt, but it was nothing. 'Leave off!' a woman shrieked. She was a buxom lass and she was talking to Bob Whitlow, ironically of the Guild of St Mary the Virgin. As they swept past, Glanville heard her whisper, 'Oh, all right, but up at the castle, later. My mama will have gone to bed by then.'

Cain and Abel were a different matter. At the northern end of Callis Street, outside the house of the sheriff, the crowd was silent and gripped by the horror on the stage. Even the oxen stood rooted to the spot as the first murderer in the world went through his paces.

'Arrest him, my lord!' one of the crowd shouted to old Gower, sitting on his balcony like a gargoyle.

There was a roar of terror as Cain struck home, a butcher's cleaver flashing in the morning sun and genuine pig's blood spraying the audience. Children were crying and Cain was lucky to get off the stage alive, even when the slaughtered Abel got up and bowed to the audience in an attempt to diffuse the situation.

Glanville was near enough now to Visconti to hear what he was saying to the girl. In his borrowed finery, in the pressing crowd and with the lad clearly smitten with his unexpected companion, the knight thought it was probably safe to get closer. Visconti was leaning close to her and explaining, in his less-than-perfect English, that this was an allegory. The girl had no idea what that was in her own tongue, let alone Italian. She was altogether happier, however, as the Saviour came into the world in the churchyard of St Peter and St Paul, the crowd pleased to leave the dismal scene of fraternal carnage. No one was happier on that occasion than Cain, who peered out from the curtains of his wagon's lower tier, glad to be alive.

The drums and tabours and shawms that had thudded and rattled and jarred in Glanville's ears all morning were suddenly distant and peace came to Clare. The lads of the choir, hair brushed and cassocks gleaming, gave forth over the rooftops, their treble voices bringing fresh purity to the glory of the psalms. The devils in the crowd, all black leather with horns and forked tails, slunk away from the glow from the church porch. Shepherds trooped up the slope as the crowd sat irreverently on the tombstones and three kings came from the east of the town, dripping with jewels made of finest paste.

The girl with Visconti stood wide-eyed and open-mouthed as the magi knelt before the boy-king in his manger. The child was a stuffed doll, because even the best-behaved infant could not be trusted to play the part *that* well. Mary and Joseph were a real-life couple from the south of the country and the mothers in the crowd oohed and aahed as the little hunted family sat divinely among the donkey shit.

William Aske of the Goldsmiths' Guild placed his gift before the little Jesus and bowed to kiss the straw. His was a present

befitting a king of all the world. Then came Alban the apothecary, with his phial of frankincense, the essence of divinity.
Finally, as if his camel had been playing up outside, Roger
his assistant bowed before his young Lord. 'Mine is myrrh,'
the crowd heard him say. 'Gathering gloom is bound up in its
bitter perfume.' And Hector Bazalgette, who owned the town's
spice shop, beamed with pride, telling everybody that both
these exquisite perfumes were available at surprisingly reasonable prices in his emporium.

With a final 'aah', Visconti and his girl jostled through the
crowd to the increasingly frenzied rhythm of viols and shawms.
Alban the apothecary watched them go, a gleam in his eye.
There was always a bit of a spike in sales of sundry mercury
and other goods after the pageants; he almost rubbed his hands
together, then thought twice – he took his role as Second
Magus very seriously.

Word was spreading that the Guild of Plumbers was putting
on The Woman Taken in Adultery and that, mysteriously, Bob
Whitlow of the Haberdashers' Guild was starring in that one.
Every year, the plumbers thought long and hard about changing
their Bible story but every year, the woman and her adultery
won the day. Once upon a time, there had been a good reason
given for it having anything to do with plumbing, but it had
been forgotten long ago. And now Bob Whitlow was of
the company, the costumes, where worn, were the best in the
entire pageant.

As the festivities and the drinking went on, it became
increasingly difficult for Glanville to keep his quarry in sight.
The boy was cuddling the girl now and kissing her, oblivious
to Judas hanging himself from a tree and the dragons
and gryphons belching fire dangerously near to the straw and
timber, dry in the long spring days. The nuns of the priory
were tripping daintily around the maypole, blissfully ignorant
of the fact that it was the Devil's pizzle.

Then, it was midday by the tolling of the priory bells and
never was a knight more grateful to see the sign of the cockatrice swinging over the swaying crowd. Chaucer was there
already, less red in the face than Richard Glanville.

'Well?' he asked the knight.

'As well as can be expected,' Glanville told him. 'A few clouts to the shin, elbows in the ribs, the usual pageant crush.'

'No, I mean, what news of Visconti? What's he been up to?'

'I don't know her name,' the knight said, nodding in their direction. 'But he's certainly giving her his full attention.'

'Is that it?' Chaucer frowned. 'All morning?'

'Love's young dream, I suppose,' Glanville said. 'And I think you were right; the Italian boy isn't our man. Or else today he is not in the killing vein. Didn't seem remotely interested when Cain slew Abel. Incidentally, Geoffrey, you seem to be clutching a lamb to your chest.'

Chaucer looked down as though previously unaware of the fact. Beyond the shepherd's smock with its Suffolk weave, the lamb, with its glass eyes and its leather nose looked meekly up at Richard Glanville, who looked solemnly back. 'It's all about disguising and mumming, Richard,' he said, reaching out through his side placket to reach his ale and take a sip. 'If I'm wrong about Visconti, then God help all of us. Our killer could be any one of these people,' he pointed to the tumblers in their reds and whites and greens, the wild men in their leaves, the music-makers in their caps and bells, the devils winding through it all. 'And we chose this day, of all days, to catch him.'

Glanville, tired to his bones with the sound of shawms and voices, drained his ale, patted the lamb and left, heading for the peace of the castle and an afternoon's lie-down.

# THIRTEEN

Chaucer had noticed before that a man with a lamb clutched to his chest becomes more or less invisible, especially in a crowd of other people dressed in unexpected costumes. A few of the shepherds from the Nativity scene were wandering around and almost unconsciously welcomed him as a brother. It was easy to sit almost next to Giovanni Visconti and his new light o' love, without drawing undue attention, and he listened in, to see if he could hear anything to his advantage.

In the excitement of having a pretty girl on his arm and being away from the strict gaze of his sister, her seneschal and various masters at arms, and also being under the influence of a large volume of sundry alcoholic drinks, Visconti was becoming both voluble and more Italian by the minute. Chaucer watched him carefully but knew that the difference between a man on the verge of an alcoholic stupor and a man who is pretending to be on the verge of an alcoholic stupor is but a hair's-breadth. Chaucer had no idea whether Giovanni Visconti harboured any histrionic talents, so for the moment his judgement was reserved. But he could see, because the girl was not drinking at all, the predatory gleam in her eye. If they could find any privacy, this could be the day when a boy, murderer or not, became a man.

He had not been eavesdropping for long, when the cry rose up for 'Queck!' and anyone in the inn who still retained the power of movement rushed outside in a body, Visconti and his paramour well to the front. Chaucer shook his head. This ridiculous game had hovered in the air like a ghost ever since his arrival at Clare. The guildsmen had threatened him with it from the beginning and, to his horror, he saw young Visconti being drawn into the nonsense in the square. The great wagons had moved on now, ready to lumber up the hill to the castle for the evening's festivities, and the square was full of tables laid end to end with square, chequered boards on them. The crowd was thickest at the far end, where the self-appointed Queck Master, David Ifaywer, sat nodding his approval at the mob's adulation and flexing his fingers as he prepared to play. He still wore his Noah robes, but had taken off his beard and tucked it into his belt to don again later – nothing must be allowed to interfere with his game. He wore the air of the Man To Beat.

The girl with Visconti pushed him into a seat and stood at his shoulder, playing with his curls and whispering encouragement and other things which made him blush.

'Let the tournament commence!' Ifaywer roared and the trumpeter's fanfare was all but drowned by the crowd, jostling and pushing as the contestants faced each other in the knock-out trials. One by one, underscored by the sound of clicking quecks, the weaker players fell by the wayside, until only the Italian and the carpenter were left. The boy had already found to his delight when playing the game with Lionel of Antwerp that queck was almost exactly the same, except in a few minor plays unknown to these yokels, as *Gomitate*, which had been all the rage in Milano the year before he had joined Violante at her new home in Clare. Soon he had become more than a little flushed with the English ale and success, the girl enjoying every minute as her new beau was lauded by all and sundry. Then, Visconti faced Ifaywer and it was suddenly all over. The lad took it in good part and shook the carpenter's hand. Even defeat had its compensation; the girl was all over him.

'Master Chaucer!' Ifaywer recognized the shepherd and his lamb in the crowd. 'I promised you a match.'

'No, I . . .' Chaucer shook his head. He couldn't lose Visconti now; there was no telling which way he would go as the afternoon wore on. The crowd all but lifted Chaucer off his feet and plonked him down opposite the Queck Master. He could see that Visconti was still there, watching the outcome, his arm around the girl. All was well . . . so far.

'Best of three, Master Chaucer?' Ifaywer suggested.

'I really don't know how to . . .' the comptroller began.

'Come, come, sir,' the Queck Master thumped him on the

lamb. 'You've been watching play for a while now. It's *so* simple, that little sheep of yours could do it. Apt costume, by the way, for a Comptroller of Woollens.'

'Thank you,' Chaucer smiled, not taking one eye off Visconti for a moment. 'I think it works.'

The carpenter produced a coin from his purse. 'Father?' he called to a Dominican standing nearby. 'Would you do the honours?'

The monk checked the coin and bit it, showing it to Chaucer to prove that it was not loaded. 'A fair likeness of His Late Grace King Edward III, sir?' he asked.

'Undoubtedly,' Chaucer agreed and the priest spun it in the air.

'Call,' he said.

Ifaywer gestured to Chaucer.

'Heads,' the comptroller said.

The coin clattered onto the queck board.

'Bad luck,' Ifaywer crowed. 'It's tails.'

There was a groan of disappointment from the crowd. David Ifaywer was nobody's favourite. He had virtually invented this game and was obsessed with it. To see him toppled by a novice now, that would be marvellous. It would also be a miracle. The carpenter raised his queck piece and slid it sideways, knocking the other pieces to one side.

The monk bent over the board. 'That's nearly a queck in one,' he announced.

The crowd cheered and bellowed in equal proportion. Now, it was Chaucer's turn. He flicked his piece, feeling it warm and clammy in his hand, and realized how difficult this game was with your arms pinioned in a lamb-carrying disguise. The crowd roared with delight and Chaucer had no idea why.

'Queck mate,' said the monk and the comptroller wondered what sort of priory was being run just up the road.

There were claps and whistles; Chaucer was pleased to see the Italian boy joining in the fun. All was still well. Ifaywer was smiling. 'As I thought, Master Chaucer,' he said. 'You're a natural. Queck ho!' he shouted and flicked his piece again. This time, it spun in the air for what seemed an eternity before landing on the edge of the board. Howls and applause again.

'Leaning queck,' the monk said, apparently impressed. 'You'll have to go some to beat that, sir.'

Chaucer was sure of that, but exactly how he had no clue. He flipped the piece and the crowd went wild. Ifaywer was still smiling and he extended his hand. 'Well quecked, Master Chaucer,' he said. 'You've played this before.'

'No, I . . .'

'Well, there it is,' the carpenter said, resetting the board. 'Second round.'

'One up to the fat shepherd!' somebody shouted, and Chaucer couldn't help noticing that money was changing hands in the crowd. And the whole farce began again. This time, although Chaucer couldn't see anything different, the mob became quieter, if a little more mutinous.

'Queck in four,' the monk observed.

'Never!' somebody shouted and a little Suffolk jostling broke out.

'Replay!' somebody else demanded.

'No, no,' the monk said, holding up his hand to calm the situation. 'Arbiter's decision.'

There were still murmurs of discontent, but only the most inebriated would go up against a man of the cloth at the Clare pageant; it just wasn't done.

'He's lost it,' someone commented, 'the shepherd. Concentrate, man!'

Chaucer was trying to do just that and flicked his piece. It rattled down the board's edge, jumping onto the table and back again. Howls of derision and groans of disappointment. Ifaywer's hand was out again. 'Bad luck, Master Chaucer. That's queck evens. Third round, now. The big one.' He closed to his opponent. 'Er . . . you wouldn't care to put some money on this, I suppose?'

'Um . . . well, I . . .'

But the crowd was more than insistent, patting Chaucer on the back and thumping him on the lamb. Ifaywer's bulging bag of coin was already on the table.

'I'm not sure I can match that,' Chaucer said.

'Whatever you have,' the carpenter beamed, magnanimous when it came to somebody else's money.

The comptroller retrieved his purse from under the lamb and put it alongside Ifaywer's, with a feeling akin to saying goodbye to someone very dear.

'Quecker's friend!' a female voice rang through the mutterings and everybody looked up. Joyce stood there, scowling at Ifaywer.

'Out of the question,' the carpenter said. 'Round three. Play on.'

'Father?' Joyce stood her ground.

The Dominican blinked. He wasn't often called upon to play Solomon, except every year in the Clare queck championships. Even so, he had never encountered *quite* this situation before. He turned his back while he fished under his robes and produced a little, leather-bound book. He flicked through the pages. 'She's right, Queck Master,' he said. 'It says here, on page sixteen "In the event of a stranger taking part in the championship, he shall be allowed a quecker's friend to advise".'

'Don't quote that to me, you idiot,' Ifaywer snapped. 'I wrote the damned thing.'

'Well, then . . .' Joyce stood like an ox in the furrow, hands on hips. Chaucer was suddenly very glad she was there.

'Doesn't apply to women,' the carpenter snapped.

'Father?' Joyce wanted confirmation.

The monk flicked the pages backwards and forwards. 'There's nothing here about the . . . gender . . . of the friend,' he said.

'Even so . . .' Ifaywer said, getting flustered, 'when I wrote that, I . . .'

Joyce fixed him with her special glare. 'When you wrote that you . . . what, Master Ifaywer?' she asked. The carpenter tried to stare her down, but failed. Only she knew what he was about to say and perhaps it wasn't for mixed company, some of them her children. 'Father?' Joyce now swivelled her special glare to the monk. Chaucer had never seen this side of her; he was impressed. Solomon quaked a little, then he remembered that he was one of the greatest kings of the Old Testament as well as a Dominican and pulled himself up to his full height.

'There is nothing to preclude the lady,' he said. 'Round three. Play on.'

Ifaywer was furious, but he saw a metaphorical noose swinging in front of his eyes if he crossed a man of God *and* the baying mob in one petty move. He sat back in his chair.

Joyce pushed her way through to Chaucer and placed a gentle hand on his shoulder. 'The Ipswich Deferential,' she whispered, miming with her fingers what Chaucer's attack should be. He flicked the piece as she indicated and it clattered in the centre of the board. The crowd became hysterical but settled down for Ifaywer to make his play. He did, with consummate skill, and the mob roared.

'Hm, he's tried the Colchester Malfeasance,' Joyce whispered in Chaucer's ear. 'Clever. Very clever. Happily for you, he has missed a perfect CM by a whisker. That means . . . now, careful here, Geoff; he's not called the Queck Master for nothing. Try . . .' she was wrestling with the tactics in her head, gnawing her lip, 'try the Bungay Straight,' and she mimed the action, 'but be *very* steady with your aim or you'll have somebody's eye out.'

The sweat was forming on Chaucer's moustache. What possessed him to play this stupid game with a lamb clamped to his chest? And why were half his life's savings sitting in an inviting heap on the table to one side of him?

'Go for it, Signor Chaucer,' Visconti shouted and his girl reached up on tiptoe to kiss his cheek, flinging her arms around his neck. Chaucer glanced up; at least that was one worry off his mind, the Italian was still visible and going nowhere fast, to judge by the crowd at his back.

Chaucer quecked, straight and true, and Ifaywer thumped the table in annoyance.

'Rule Thirty-Eight,' the monk said, the book still in his hand. '"Any examples of bad temper that affect the balance of the board, or—"'

'Yes! Yes!' The carpenter cut him off. 'Play, Chaucer, if you can, after this.'

Ifaywer's piece spun in the air, clattering along the board and sliding into the corner. There was a silence, followed by a deafening shout. Chaucer heard Joyce breathe in. 'The

Saxmundham Speculation.' Her voice was almost inaudible. 'I've only ever seen that done once. It didn't end well.'

The carpenter was beaming like Nicholas Brembre's cat with the cream. 'Nobody comes back from the Saxmundham Speculation,' he said, smugly.

Chaucer believed that. He had had no idea what he was doing for the past half-hour. He had no idea what he was doing now, but a look at Joyce's stricken face warned him he would be saying goodbye to his money any second. For all her skill, Joyce had no answer this time. He squared his shoulders, making sure that his right arm was as free as the lamb would allow and quecked for all he was worth. The piece soared through the air, slicing everything in its path, bouncing on the board rim and ricocheting past Ifaywer's piece. The little town of Clare had never heard a noise like it. Chaucer's shoulders and back were pounded with congratulatory slaps until he was black and blue. The girl and Visconti embraced. The Dominican put away his little book. 'I believe we have a new Queck Master,' he said, and shook Chaucer's hand.

Ifaywer slumped back in his seat, a beaten man, and said nothing as the monk slid his ample purse across to his conqueror. Eventually, he recovered something of his composure. 'I've never seen a move like that,' he murmured, 'and I invented the game. What do you call that, Master Chaucer?'

Chaucer would have called it a miracle if it wouldn't offend the monk, but the poet in him took over. 'That?' he said, getting to his feet with difficulty as Arthur the lamb had got caught in the trestle leg. 'That old thing? Surely, you know the Clare Clarification?' He turned to Joyce. 'Madam,' he said loudly, 'I don't know who you are, but may I thank you for your help today?' and he placed Ifaywer's purse in her hands. Her eyes widened at its weight. She looked at him.

'I don't know who you are either, Geoffrey Chaucer,' she smiled and loosened the purse's strings. With a glance at Ifaywer, she threw the purse into the air, the coins cascading down on the hysterical crowd, struggling with each other to catch the tinkling silver as it fell on them like manna from heaven.

But Giovanni Visconti, who from his cradle had never had

to worry about money, was leading his new conquest by the hand, striding up towards the castle. And, at a suitable distance, the fat shepherd turned Queck Master, walked that way too.

The slope from the town up to the castle was not very steep, but it was long and before very many minutes had elapsed, Chaucer was lagging. The day was drawing to a close and the sun was low behind the castle and the air was cooling. Even so, Chaucer could feel the sweat beading under his moustache and he would have given his hard-won purse to be rid of the lamb riding on his chest. He could see Giovanni Visconti and the girl ahead of him, the white flash of her kerchief sometimes disappearing as the lad wrapped her in his arms. From time to time, they leaned on a tree by the side of the road and Chaucer could stop to catch his breath.

Standing with his hands on his hips and flexing his aching back, Chaucer looked up to the high crenellations of Clare and saw the unmistakeable outline of Hugh Glanville silhouetted against the sky. His costume for the day was an even more outrageous version of what he wore usually, so he was an arresting sight, with frills, furbelows and floating plumes to further order. He waved and saw the boy's head turn towards him. Hugh put his hands on the stone, still warm from the sun of the day, and leaned forward, to be sure. He was confused at first; the comptroller seemed to have put on a great deal of weight during the afternoon, but when the man on the road waved to him, pointing in front of him in dumb show, he was sure he wasn't mistaken. Closer to the castle, stepping out of a patch of deep shade into the twilight, was Giovanni Visconti, entwined, it would seem, with a girl from the town. Hugh was as red-blooded as the next squire but had been nicely brought up and thought that this behaviour was perhaps a little coarse. But he had not had the advantage of being the brother-in-law of the uncle of the king, so perhaps things were different for such as Visconti. He waved back to Chaucer, to tell him he had seen and understood and, within a minute, Visconti and his conquest had disappeared under the black shade of the castle gate.

Chaucer, his charge handed safely over, sat on a log at the

side of the path and lifted the weight of his lamb away from his stomach and chest, letting his sweat cool and dry. He made himself a promise that the next time such an occasion arose, he would choose a lighter costume. Perhaps he could go as a poet, a simple couplet on the lip, a quill behind his ear. Perhaps a line or two of doggerel pinned to his chest; *I wol nat letten eek noon of this route; Lat every felawe telle his tale aboute; And lat se now who shal the soper wynne; And ther I lefte, I wol ayeyn bigynne* – it needed work, but it was a start. Smiling at his own thoughts, he looked up at the castle again, hoping that Hugh had understood and was watching Visconti. For a moment, his heart leapt – a figure still stood there, looking down. Chaucer squinted into the dying day; it wasn't Hugh. It was taller, for a start, broader in the shoulder. His father, perhaps, waiting to let Chaucer know that Hugh was on watch. He squinted again. No, not that; this was a bigger, stronger man altogether and he was wearing a loose garment, not Glanville senior's tight-fitting borrowed garb. As he watched, the man – it couldn't possibly be a woman, it was far too tall – seemed to look straight into his eyes. The right arm extended in greeting and, above the noises of the town, of oxen bellowing and wagons beginning to rumble forwards, crushing the cobbles under their iron-shod wheels, he heard the Marshal at Arms' 'Hoo!' ring out. He raised an arm as best he could and returned the call. The figure gave a bow and, as quick as a blink, was gone.

In the inner bailey, all was bustle. At the far end, opposite the big double door, a dais had been set, with a short row of chairs for Violante and some honoured guests. They could watch the wagons arrive and see a brief recreation of each show, best bits only. Flanking the dais were two long trestles, with chafing dishes along their lengths and sweating kitchen boys behind each one. A lad had been given the job of delivering glowing coals to each as they needed it and he was trundling a heavy cart to and fro, in answer to the calls from the cooks. Behind one trestle stood Butterfield, arms folded and eyes everywhere. Cooking was demeaning; he did not intend to get himself covered in flour and grease, but if his boys didn't beat that

Italian in the battle for hearts and stomachs, heads would roll. He had been tasting and sipping all afternoon, making sure that every posset, fritter and dumpling was the peak of perfection. Because of this, he was now feeling very much less than his best. His head ached and his stomach was very rebellious, growling and gurgling and doing its best to let him know that the odds against the evening ending well were small.

Niccolò Ferrante also stood to the rear of his people, arms folded and eyes everywhere. But not for him the flurried tasting and worry that was ruling Butterfield; he knew that his food was the best and had, for that reason, little boys waiting on the customer side of the table to load up plates and – for the great unwashed – explain what the dishes were. He had already reduced six of them to tears over their pronunciation of *cozze impanate* and was prepared to go to any lengths to make his buffet table something to delight and amaze the clods of Clare in a way that mutton dumplings and lampreys could never manage. He had positioned himself in such a way as to be able to watch the dais to make sure Lady Violante had everything she needed before she knew she needed it and also watch Butterfield as he careened off into the depths of despair. Ferrante was not by nature much of a smiler, but he smiled that night in the inner bailey of Clare, surrounded by the smells of home and bathed in the warmth from the old stone and the newly lit braziers, still a little smoky but festive and bright. This evening would go well, of that much he was certain.

The noise of the wagons drew nearer and the Lady Violante and her women stepped onto the dais and curtseyed politely to the townsfolk as they poured in through the gates. The smell of food was almost deafening, but they waited, as they had for years without number, to see the Guilds all strut their three minutes upon a stage. To those on the dais, it all seemed to be going like clockwork, but they didn't know how much wrangling, shouting and – on at least one occasion – physical injury had gone into working out the pecking order of the wagons' arrival. The saner counsel was that they should arrive in chronological order, starting with Adam and Eve and ending with stories from the Gospels. The Corpus Christi Guild, very naturally, agreed with this and cast their votes accordingly.

All the other Guilds complained that in the natural order of things, tapicers were the lowest of all of them, making things which any competent housewife could achieve with both eyes shut and one hand behind her back, so they should not enter first. The Goldsmiths, who always considered themselves the major Guild, stepped forward and offered their Magi as the leading wagon, Alban the apothecary standing in their lee and ready, as clearly the most intelligent man in Clare, to speak up as required. All the other Guilds had shouted the Goldsmiths down – what was the point of having the leading wagon telling the story of an event almost at the end of their story? Whitlow the haberdasher had slithered to the front and the thought rose in more than one breast that he would make a better Serpent than that daft lad whom the Tapicers had chosen.

'I think,' Whitlow said, portentously, 'that the woman taken in adultery should come first. It's got a lot to say to any crowd, especially on May Night when,' he chuckled and many husbands' blood ran cold, 'let's be honest, gentles, men and women have been known to . . .' and another chuckle said it all.

A member of the Guild of St Brigit, a midwife of the town, took umbrage and lashed out at Whitlow with a birthing stool. 'You vile knarre!' she shrieked. 'Demeaning and debauching, that's all you do. I've lost count of the babies I've delivered with your vile nose and single eyebrow. The Nativity should come first, with its message of hope for the world.'

After that, the meeting had broken up in disarray and the more sensible Guilds had gathered outside the inn where they had all met and had drawn lots. Thus it was that anyone wanting to learn something of Bible lore from watching the Clare pageant that year would have been hard pressed to know what exactly was happening to whom, and when. But then, the Old Testament was so full of begetting that perhaps Bob Whitlow had been right. By chance, though, the first wagon through the gates would be difficult to beat. It was not the biggest, by any means, but all jaws dropped as it rumbled under the archway and turned to present its best side to the dais. Chaucer, with his lamb still in place, had climbed onto the dais, helped by Moderata, who was worried about her stitching. She smiled to see everything still in place and patted the seat next to her. So Chaucer had a bird's eye view.

The women of the laundry, with little time and no money, had come up with a simple but ultimately spectacular float. Across the top, picked out in bunches of dried herbs, was a stanza from Psalm 51 – 'wash me, and I shall be whiter than the snow'. Under it, a row of half-barrels had been bolted down to the bed of the wagon and filled with water and much soap of the kind that gave the most bubbles. A small boy was standing on a platform behind the yoked oxen and, in the voice of an angel, he was intoning the psalm, every note as clear as crystal. The women each wore a simple shift, the badge of their craft, and were furiously slapping a cloth in their barrel so that the suds flew and the water splashed them and any watcher unwise enough to step near. It was a simple and beautiful sight, certainly not marred – as far as the men in the crowd were concerned – by the fact that the water and soap moulded the shifts to the women's torsos, outlining every contour and detail. Mothers covered their sons' eyes – and their husbands', if they had a spare hand – and the spontaneous applause made the women grin and wave to the crowd. This made things even more spectacular and when the wagon trundled on to make room for the next, there were sighs of regret from everywhere in the bailey, not least from Chaucer, who had had eyes only for Joyce, looking to him as she had in the hayloft so many years ago, fresh, beautiful and innocent. Violante reached down and tapped Chaucer's shoulder, smiling and nodding towards the float. Chaucer smiled back, though he had hoped that the old gossip had not reached quite everywhere.

As the last strains of the psalm died away, the next wagon was pulling into position. The Serpent clung to his tree as Eve stood nearby, fig leaves at the ready. The Serpent's mother nudged those next to her and pointed out how every scale had been individually attached by her own hand. Moderata and the other embroidering women nodded approvingly to each other. Excellent sewing skills were all too rare at the Clare pageant. Chaucer sat cradling his lamb, watching the stories unfold. In and around the floats, devils danced and pranced.

Some held small torches and the more daring occasionally threw them in the air, catching them with deft hands. Their leather costumes gleamed and shimmered and Andrew Trumpington of the Guild of St Agnes stood to one side, beaming with pride.

The bailey was like a melting pot of every Bible story Chaucer had ever heard of and it was hard to know where to look next. He was trying to keep his eyes away from the laundresses; he was not as young as he was and the lamb was an encumbrance. Besides, he had a murderer to catch and, as he scanned the crowd, he constantly watched for Giovanni Visconti, his paramour and – hopefully – not far behind them, Hugh Glanville. He couldn't spot them, but wasn't worried; in such a press, it would be almost impossible to slip anyone poison.

At the edge of the light, at the edge of his vision, he kept seeing a figure he thought he knew. It was indistinct, dressed in black from head to toe, the robes not unlike those of the Saracens of the desert, enveloping and yet easy and flowing. Sometimes, light from a dancing torch would pick out a glint of silver, as of a blade held above the figure's head. It seemed to Chaucer that the harder he stared, the less he could see. He rubbed his eyes and closed them for a moment against the glare and, when he looked again, the figure had gone.

Finally, the last float was inside the bailey and the Guild of St Augustine, featuring the whole family of a very proud Nicholas Straits the dyer, delivered themselves of the Feeding of the Five Thousand. As crowd scenes went, it was perhaps a little short on numbers, but they made up for it in verve and got a huge round of applause. It was also a very serendipitous final offering as, just as the oxen took the strain and moved the float over to the side of the bailey to join the others, the Lady Violante stood, clapping her hands and asking for silence for a moment.

When all eyes were turned on her, she spread her arms and smiled with the smile that had captured hearts the length and breadth of Italy before she had followed her husband to this tiny corner of Suffolk. And now, she captured their hearts too. 'I have lost a lot this year,' she said, in her warm voice which seemed to be underscored by the bees in the lemon blossom of her native Pavia. 'But' – and she leaned forward as if she would scoop them all to her bosom – 'I have gained much, too. New friends' – she indicated Chaucer who blushed and bowed as far as Arthur the lamb would allow – 'and old' – she extended a hand to Richard Glanville, standing to her left – 'have helped me through this very difficult time. And now you, the townsfolk of Clare, have brought the joy of your Pageant to soothe me. As you know, my husband always gave a token of his esteem to the best float in the Pageant, in the shape of a gold coin for every participant, and this year the prize goes to . . .' a serving woman handed her a fat purse and the crowd held its breath. Violante took a step forward and lowered her voice so that the crowd had to strain forward, 'Just to tell you, this float was chosen by the gentlemen of my company, but I agree with them, if only for the beauty of the charming child's singing – the prize goes to . . . the women of the laundry of Clare, with their Fifty-first Psalm. Simple and beautiful and very well done.' Again, she extended her arm, to where the laundresses dimpled and waved, their shifts still damp enough to warm the coldest heart.

Violante stepped back as the applause swelled, then stepped forward once more. 'I forgot to say,' she said, 'that the food is now also ready for you all. *Buon appetito* – a good appetite to you all; eat, drink and be merry. And,' she blew the crowd a kiss and everyone went wild, 'goodnight.'

There was a surge towards the trestles and Ferrante and Butterfield urged on their people from their vantage points. The seneschals had different ways to please when it came to serving food. Butterfield stood back, staring balefully at anyone who looked askance at his fritters. Ferrante darted here and there, tempting anyone who wasn't sure, bolstering up the shaky pronunciation of his lads, wrapping a tempting bit of this in a delicious piece of that and popping it into mouths as eager as a baby cuckoo's. Butterfield's staff were like him. In their view there were always two options; take it, or leave it. To Ferrante it was take it or try it another way, dipped in something delicious. The crowd in front of his trestle grew at an extraordinary rate and Butterfield's depression deepened by the mouthful.

Lady Violante turned to Chaucer and handed him the purse. 'Please give this to Joyce and her women, Geoffrey, if you would. I . . . I am tired. I need to rest.' She smiled at him and stroked his lamb. 'Richard told me that you were a friend in a thousand and so you have been. Even if you never find' – she choked on tears and looked down, fingering the lambswool – 'the person, it has been good to have you here. I shall be sorry to see you go. I don't suppose . . .'

Chaucer held her hand gently. 'Madam,' he said, 'I am Comptroller of the King's Woollens. I have already been away too long.'

'I understand.' She turned away. 'Richard?'

Glanville had been looking at the food laid out before him and was realizing how hungry he was. 'Yes, my lady?'

'Could you escort me to my rooms? I need to . . . I need to be alone for a while.'

Ferrante, who thought of everything, had made sure that the dais was constructed in such a way that the door into the Great Hall was immediately behind it and the two slipped away and no one was any the wiser.

# FOURTEEN

Chaucer looked over the edge of the dais and knew that he would never make it through the throng, so he cut round through the hall. He found Joyce and her women drying off as best they could behind their wagon and handed her the purse.

'That's the second one to come your way today,' he said. 'Please keep this one.'

She weighed it in her hand and smiled. 'I earned this one, Master Chaucer,' she said, keeping it formal. 'We will all be grateful for this.' She reached behind her and pulled the small singer forward. 'I don't believe you have met my Wilfrid, have you? Come on, Wilfrid, don't be shy. Say hello to the gentleman. This is Master Chaucer.' She gave him a gentle shove. 'Say good evening, Master Chaucer.'

The boy looked at Chaucer with eyes like organ stops. 'G'd evenin', Master Chaucer,' he muttered, and bolted towards the food. Joyce watched him go, fondly.

'He's a good lad,' she said. 'A lot like his father, as I recall.'

Chaucer nodded. There didn't seem much else he could do. He looked around him, his hands tucked away inside his smock; he had been forgetting to do that lately and had frightened quite a few small children into fits by apparently having four arms. Out of the corner of his eye, he saw a black figure slip away behind the nearest float. 'Did you see that?' he asked Joyce.

Joyce looked about her, spread her arms and laughed. 'See what, Geoff? All the town is here, most of them dressed as something they are not. Be a little more specific, please.'

Chaucer sighed. How to describe a shadow? 'It's a man . . . I think. Tall, but broad in the shoulder. Dressed in black. Seems to have something silver over his head.'

'It's not daft old Hubert, is it?'

'I don't know,' Chaucer said. 'What does daft old Hubert look like?'

'Bit taller than you. Bit hunched.' Joyce leaned forward and her shift bagged at the front, making Chaucer suddenly a little short of breath. 'No, perhaps not. He's not really tall or broad. Ummm . . . it's not Death, is it?'

'Death?' Chaucer's eyes popped.

'Yes. There's usually one or two Deaths in the Pageant. I think . . . yes, I think I see one over there. It's the one off of the Lazarus float, I reckon. His scythe's only made of wire and paper and it's a thought bent now. Look – over there. Is that him?'

Chaucer peered into the crowd. 'It's similar, but . . .'

Joyce's Wilfrid was back at her side, carrying handfuls of food; dumplings and fritters jostled fried rice balls and hunks of bread dotted with rosemary and olives.

'Wilfrid!' She looked at his savoury haul. 'You're not eating all that! You'll make yourself sick! Now, give it to me. Come on!' She held out the front of her shift to make a pouch. 'In it goes. All of it, now.' She looked sideways at Chaucer. 'Sorry,' she said. 'He'll have me up all night if he eats all this.' She took the sting out of his dismissal with one of her most special smiles. 'I'll see you later, I'm sure.'

'I'm sure you will,' he said, realizing not for the first time how much he would like to stay, to bathe in the warmth of Clare and Joyce's smile. He reminded himself of his Pippa and tried to be strong. 'One thing, though,' he said. 'I was wondering about those herbs on your float. What are they?'

Joyce looked up. 'Blessed if I know,' she said. 'Just this and that from the hedgerows. Meant to be hyssop, of course, but we couldn't get hold of that. Old stalks of keck, I suppose, bits and pieces we could find.' She smiled proudly. 'They look quite good, if I say so myself.'

'Indeed they do,' Chaucer said and ruffled Wilfrid's hair. 'That food smells good. I think I'll go and see if there's any left.'

'There's a lot left on Master Butterfield's stall,' Wilfrid piped up. 'That Master . . .' he looked up at his mother, who mouthed the word he needed, 'That Master Ferret, his food has almost all gone.' And he dived into the mixture in his mother's skirts with the aplomb of a born gourmand.

\*    \*    \*

Chaucer made his way to Butterfield's trestle with reluctant steps. Wilfrid was right; Ferrante's people were beginning to bring on sweetmeats and wine to replace their chafing dishes. The crowd still seethed around the table, their mouths full and fingers slick from the delicious dishes. Butterfield's trestles were far from full – a crowd the size of the entire town of Clare takes some feeding – but his food had been picked at rather than demolished at a stroke and his dumplings and hunks of grey mutton were not that enticing. Even so, Chaucer had a kind heart and a stomach empty enough to eat anything.

As he walked towards the table, he noticed that Butterfield was sitting on a barrel, his head sunk into his hands. He looked the picture of dejection and Chaucer felt another pang of compassion. He approached the table and stood looking for a moment, then spoke the man's name, in as gentle a tone as he could. Butterfield looked up and saw a miraculous sight. A shepherd, cradling the Lost Sheep, was looking at him with gentle eyes. He was outlined by a light from behind him that seemed to dazzle.

Butterfield had not had the best day. He felt nauseous and bilious and just generally sick to his stomach, not to mention more than a little drunk. His good English food had taken a poor second place to that foreign muck on the other trestle. His people had largely deserted him in favour of mingling with the crowd, including the nice little serving wench he had had his eye on for months, waiting for May Night when all prayers were answered, if only once. He had things on his conscience no man should have to bear. The groats added here and there in the right column of his accounts books which found their way into his pocket; the wine which never reached the lips of Lady Violante and her household; the little bribes, nothing big, but a nice little extra, which he took from the merchants of the town. And, of course, the worst thing he had ever done, which was his last thought on sleeping and his first on waking. And now, look, the shepherd had come to find him, the most lost sheep in the whole of Clare. He looked up and the words tumbled out of his mouth.

'I didn't mean it, Lord. I didn't mean to send Master Chaucer to the lions, just because he prefers foreign muck to the Lord's

Own good English fare. I am an evil, evil man and deserve to be punished.' He bowed his head and waited for the lightning to strike him dead.

Chaucer, rather startled, took a dumpling and a gobbet of the less gristly looking mutton with his spare hands and wandered softly away. Before he had gone far, a soft thump and a grunt made him turn. Butterfield had slumped bonelessly off his barrel and was lying prone behind his trestle. Matter-of-fact hands moved him out of harm's way and the sweetmeats were brought out, hunks of jam tart and pease pudding drizzled with good English honey. Chaucer caught the eye of one of the scullions.

'Don't you worry, master,' the lad said. 'He'll come to no harm down there. He's a devil for the sack, is Master Butterfield.' He clicked his tongue and deftly lifted a pile of plates, still laden with half-eaten food. He glanced at his burden. 'If it wasn't for Master's own-recipe dumplings, there'd be some skinny pigs in Clare, without a doubt.' And with a laugh, he ducked behind the dais and was gone.

Chaucer, feeling faintly traitorous, went round to the other trestle and chose a fragment of pastry topped with marzipan and a glaze made of preserved lemon rind and something so delicious he could hardly believe it came from earth. He popped it into his mouth in one and let it explode there. He closed his eyes with the sheer pleasure of it and so missed the dark figure which slipped unseen and unheard round behind the dais and disappeared into the hall, the torches glinting off the scythe carried proudly above its head. Recovered from his trance, Chaucer turned back to the crowd, wandering this way and that, watching, watching, always watching for Giovanni Visconti and his follower, but it was hard to do, with so much colour, clash and clangour. Better to just let his eyes wander and see what they would see.

The fireworks soared into the night, stars bursting over the battlements of Clare, taking Chaucer's eyes skywards. The castle was alive tonight, for sure. It had not been this full since John Hawkwood's White Company had camped in the baileys, inner and outer. Some of the crowd had dispersed, but many stayed, not wanting the night to end. Lovers frolicked in the orchards, children gambolled dangerously near the moat. Tumblers and acrobats cavorted among the crowds, pushing past the wagons and their tethered oxen, throwing their ribbon sticks in the air. Flutes and tambours and rattles filled the night with sound. It had been a perfect day – a day to be with friends and family, a day to laugh at adversity and to welcome May with all its hope and promise.

But there was one celebrant of the day who walked alone. Chaucer stopped dead in his tracks. Wandering past the chapel, trailing a garland of wilted flowers, was the girl who had been with Giovanni Visconti all day. And if she was here, where was he? The comptroller scuttled over to her and bowed, as best he could.

'Oh,' she started, 'it's you.' She had been dimly aware of the fat shepherd who had been in her peripheral vision for the best part of the afternoon.

'None other,' he smiled. 'On your own?'

She looked at him quizzically, the smock, the greying hair, the lamb stitched to his clothes, now wilting a little and shedding straw. One glove was gone and the subterfuge was less convincing; she wondered fleetingly where his hands were, because she might need to know that in the next few minutes. 'Look,' she said, 'if it's all the same to you . . .'

A glance at her face told Chaucer all he needed to know about the sudden misunderstanding between them. 'No, no,' he reached out and patted her hand, answering her question without realizing it. 'I was looking for Giovanni.'

The girl suddenly burst into tears and Chaucer didn't know where to put his hands, always assuming he could free them from his smock in time. 'There, there,' he said. 'Where is he?'

'I don't know!' she wailed. 'And I don't care. He had his wicked way with me in his room . . . those Italians are only after one thing, aren't they? He done that and then he kicked me out. Probably chasing a trollop somewhere. Well, he's dead to me now.'

Chaucer's ingratiating smile vanished. He dashed away, making for the Confessor Tower where he knew the boy's chambers were. On his way, he half-turned, staggering a little as his lamb spoiled his balance. 'If it's any consolation,' he called to the girl, 'May is an unlucky month for marriages.' And the girl burst into tears again.

The comptroller found himself running, not his usual habit. A cold sense of dread had gripped him and he had to find Visconti quickly. He skirted the Lion Tower with its ghastly memories and dodged past three devils, roaring drunk and trying to catch their own tails. A little girl, who had been a shepherdess in Bethlehem earlier in the day, ran past him in the opposite direction, dragging the stuffed rag that was the baby Jesus behind her.

'Seen him?' Richard Glanville nearly collided with the comptroller at the foot of the stairs.

'No,' Chaucer said, 'but he's ditched the girl he was with. I'm trying his rooms.'

'I'll come with you.'

'Pa?' Hugh hurtled round the corner, out of breath and sweating. 'Any sign? I lost him at the—'

'We're trying his rooms,' the knight shouted.

'Hugh,' Chaucer shouted as he ran, 'try the Great Hall. If we're wrong, he might be there.'

The squire ducked back the way he had come as the others struggled up the spiral twist. Visconti's door was shut and all seemed quiet. Chaucer put his ear to the oak and didn't like the sound he heard. He knew he'd regret it but he put his shoulder to the door anyway and all but fell into the room.

Giovanni Visconti lay writhing on the bed, gasping for breath. There was a garland of flowers still at a rakish angle on his head and his doublet was undone, as were the points of his hose. His face was a ghastly white and milky saliva dribbled down his chin.

'Hemlock,' Chaucer shouted and rammed two fingers into the boy's mouth. He vomited immediately, but his eyes still rolled in his head and he wasn't responding. 'Giovanni.' Chaucer held the boy's face between his hands. 'Listen to me. Focus. Here.' He shook the boy's head, but the eyes were glazed. '*Giovanni!* What have you eaten?' Chaucer tried to keep his voice calm, hard though it was. 'Who gave you food? Wine? Have you drunk anything recently?'

The comptroller knew what futile questions they were. The Italian had probably been eating and drinking all day and Chaucer had no idea how long hemlock took to work.

'Rich,' he looked up at the knight. 'Fetch Violante.' He looked back at the lad, who was snatching at breaths far too far apart for his liking. 'He hasn't got long.'

The knight dashed away along the passageway. The Lady Violante was probably still in her chamber, resting. Chaucer tried the two-finger technique again, but this time, the boy didn't react at all. The comptroller fumbled with the lad's wrist. He couldn't feel a pulse. He pressed his ear to his chest. Nothing. Finally, he put his cheek against the boy's nose and mouth. There was no breath. He had gone.

A scream shattered the moment. Violante looked as if Hellmouth had yawned before her. Her dark eyes were wide and staring, her mouth working in silent shock. Behind her, Ferrante stood stony-faced, the perfect servant, reduced to silence like his mistress. She stumbled forward and Chaucer moved aside. The Duchess of Clarence, widowed, bereft of her husband, had now lost her little brother too. As realization dawned, she suddenly felt very afraid and very alone.

'*Stanno cercando di ucciderci tutti?*' She looked up at Ferrante, with tears trickling down her cheeks and her voice trembling.

'What?' Glanville said to Ferrante. 'What did she say?'

'She wonders, Sir Richard,' the seneschal said, 'whether you intend to kill us all. All us Italians.'

'What?' Glanville was speechless. If a man had said that, whatever the circumstances, he would have felled him where he stood.

'It's the grief talking,' Chaucer said. 'Ferrante, find a priest, will you? The last rites?'

The seneschal nodded and turned to go.

'Richard,' Violante held out her hand and the knight helped her up, away from the young body that suddenly looked so small and helpless. Glanville held her close, her hand to his chest, and she raised her face to his. Neither of them was quite themselves at that moment and they kissed, their lips touching softly in the midst of grief and shock.

Chaucer didn't know exactly what to make of it, but there were things to be done. 'Ferrante!' he snapped. 'The priest, man. Get on with it.'

'Signore,' and the seneschal was gone.

Chaucer couldn't see Violante's face. It was pressed against the strongest, safest chest that the comptroller had known. Whatever was happening here at Clare, it was easily the best place for her to be. Glanville, with the strength of ten and the touch of swansdown, led the lady away, leaving Chaucer alone with death.

Chaucer was no stranger to death; the battlefield ones were hard – the beardless boys the French called the Goddamns – but he had been with both his parents when they shuffled off the mortal coil and he had found it strangely comforting, to see the years fall away, the worries, the stresses and strains. They had led exciting lives, one way and another and Chaucer smiled at the memory of it. How many men alive today, for example, could say that his father had been kidnapped to secure the family inheritance? He had escaped that fate worse than death and had married his Agnes, an heiress far richer than he was; Chaucer had wanted for little in his childhood except for the loving touch of his mother's hand. He had gone to Clare when a boy and had never lived at his parents' home again. He looked down at the face of Giovanni Visconti, smoothing out now in death, another beardless boy far from home. Chaucer had closed his eyes and straightened his limbs just as his sister had entered the room, a loving touch that no one had noticed, but had he done this kind thing for a murderer? They might never find out. Hearing a noise behind him, he turned, breaking away from his thoughts.

'Queck Master?' It was the arbiter Dominican from the afternoon's game who stood at the door.

'You get around, Father,' Chaucer commented; perhaps it was not the most charitable comment.

'Just enjoying a little cuckoo-ale when the Italian seneschal stopped me. Apparently, there's been a . . . Oh, Holy Mother of God!' He saw Visconti's body, and crossed himself. Despite Chaucer's limited ministrations, it was still clearly not the corpse of a man who had died quietly in his sleep. 'What happened here?'

'I could speculate until Domesday, Father,' Chaucer said, 'but let's keep it simple and say a man is dead. I can leave his soul with you, I trust?'

'You can,' the monk said, and went about his ministrations. He shook the holy water over the dead boy's head, holding his rosary beads in his other hand. He turned to Chaucer as the comptroller stood to leave. 'Did he die in sin?' he asked.

Chaucer shrugged. 'Don't we all?' he asked.

'When was his last confession?' the monk enquired. 'It would help if I knew.'

'Well, I'm afraid I don't,' Chaucer said. 'His confessor died only this last week.'

The monk frowned. He had heard things, of course, but still. 'I will assume the worst, then,' he said, with the same dispassionate delivery he had brought to the game of queck. He turned again to the bed and lowered his head. '*In nomine patri . . .*'

But Chaucer had gone, hurtling along the passageway, pushing the lamb as far to one side as it would go, hearing some of Moderata's careful stitching finally giving up the ghost. From a silent room of death and torment, the comptroller emerged into a wild party. The fireworks were still exploding overhead and the castle guard were handling their fire sticks and mortars with consummate skill or sheer luck or both. No one had burned to death in the Clare Pageant for the best part of seventy years. A group whom Chaucer recognized vaguely as Noah's family from earlier in the day, now augmented by the absent Japhet, stumbled past him, laughing and hooting.

'Yeah,' one of them called out to somebody else. 'We was in a float, yeah? Get it? Noah? Flood? Float?' He caught Chaucer's eye and shrugged. 'God, I'm wasted here.'

In more ways than one, Chaucer thought. In this sea of faces, with masks of every colour, feathers and furs, sackcloth and ashes, stalked a murderer. And he was fresh from a kill. The comptroller collided with someone he thought he knew.

'Master Chaucer!' It was Andrew Trumpington, the cordwainer of the Guild of St Peter. 'I hear you trounced old

Ifaywer today.' He shook Chaucer's hand. 'Good for you.'
He looked closer. 'Are you well, Master Chaucer? Your
hand feels . . .'

Chaucer released his left hand from his smock and waved
it at the cordwainer. He was beginning to wish he had asked
Moderata to make the lamb easier to remove. But then, he
hadn't expected today to work out quite the way it had.

'Did you see my devils, Master Chaucer?' Trumpington
asked, reassured that Chaucer wasn't dying of some strange
stiffening disease. 'Their costumes are all my own work.'

'Excellent,' Chaucer said, one eye still on the crowd. 'Tell
me, did you also do the costume for Death?'

Trumpington laughed. 'Which one? Death's a popular character at the Clare Pageant. I know I've seen at least three
tonight, not counting the one with Lazarus. His scythe fell to
bits before the judging and he's lost the stomach for it.'
Trumpington looked around, trying to be helpful, waving to
people he knew in the crowd. 'Look!' He grabbed Chaucer's
real arm. 'There's one . . . oh, no, my mistake. It's just daft
old Hubert.'

'Anyway,' Chaucer said, as if he had stopped Trumpington,
rather than the other way around. 'Don't let me keep you.'
And he walked off, still looking right and left. There were
faces everywhere, some familiar, most not. All of Suffolk
seemed to have crowded into the castle of Clare, letting down
their collective hair now that summer was almost here and the
world had turned. But there was one face which stayed oddly
in Chaucer's mind. He had seen it often in the past weeks,
but tonight he had seen it in a different light. There had been
something about the eyes that had rattled him, a cold stare of
contempt that had made the hairs on his neck prickle and
meant that, for just a moment, he'd forgotten to breathe.

Chaucer glanced up to the high window in the Confessor's
Tower and saw a solitary candle flickering there – the
Dominican was lighting young Visconti's way to God. A breath
of wind hissed past him, a dark shadow in funereal black, and
it vanished behind the inner wall of the barbican. The comptroller was caught in a dilemma now. He needed all the help
he could get, but Hugh had disappeared like a will o' the wisp.

Richard Glanville would still be comforting Violante. And when it came to it, those were the only two whom Chaucer could truly trust. Or could he?

He ducked under an archway along from the Nethergate and all but fell over a couple writhing together against the stonework. The man half-turned with a snarl. 'Do you mind?'

'Sorry, Master Whitlow,' and Chaucer retreated, leaving the haberdasher alone with the woman taken in adultery, typecast as ever.

'Ooh, this stone's cold,' he heard her squeal as he ran for the steps to the keep. It was no good; he had to find a Glanville of one generation or another. And quickly.

'Where's Hugh?' As if by magic, the knight was forcing his way through the throng of laundresses, emboldened by their new-found popularity and their windfalls. Some of them went so far as to clutch at Glanville's silken sleeves, but he didn't even seem to notice them.

'I hoped you'd tell me,' Chaucer said. 'How's Violante?'

'Lying down,' Glanville told him. 'I left her with her ladies. She'll be all right soon. The Italian in her will kick in and it'll be time for the flying furniture. Um . . . look, Geoff . . . what you may have witnessed . . .' The knight was shifting his weight from foot to foot and looked down, embarrassed as a lad of fifteen. 'I mean, you mustn't read into it . . .'

Chaucer smiled. In some ways, there was nothing more gratifying than watching an old friend squirm. He patted Glanville's arm. 'If you're apologizing for loving a lovely woman,' he said, 'don't. We've all had our moments.' And as if on cue, Joyce swung past and winked at him.

'What do we do now?' Glanville asked out of the corner of his mouth.

The comptroller would have liked to have lain down on a feather bed and covered his head with a pillow until all this madness had gone away, but that didn't seem a likely option. Again, the black shape he had felt at his elbow all night flitted into his gaze. It was a cloak, not even that, the whisper of a cloak, vanishing up spiral stairs like smoke up a chimney. Daft old Hubert it most certainly was not.

'Who had access to Visconti's rooms?' Glanville was still trying to apply what logic he could muster.

'Not relevant.' Chaucer shook his head. 'Whatever the boy swallowed, he got it outside – in the town, in the castle – I don't know. The last time I saw the girl he was with, she seemed all right. A bit disconsolate, perhaps, but not gagging on poison. So we have to assume that only Giovanni partook of something nasty.'

'You're the mouse-smeller,' Glanville said. 'Try the kitchens. Stick your nose into a few pots.'

Chaucer blew an outward breath. Even if that worked, it was pointless. In theory, *anyone* had access to the kitchens, especially when Butterfield and Ferrante had turned their backs. Even so, it *might* yield results and was better than rushing around Clare in circles, fighting his way through an army of drunks.

'Where will you be?' he asked the knight. He didn't want to have to try to find him in this melee again.

'Looking for Hugh,' Glanville said. 'For a start, I want to give him this wretched outfit back.' Chaucer couldn't help but notice that the knight had unlaced his doublet completely and it hung indecorously from both arms. 'Give me a few minutes. Meet me at the chapel entrance and we'll put some sort of plan together. One thing, Geoffrey . . .'

Chaucer waited for it.

'No one else dies tonight. Is that understood?'

It was understood by Geoffrey Chaucer, Comptroller of the King's Woollens. But would that be good enough?

He was making his way to the kitchens where the scullions, all sweaty and crimson in the heat of the fires, were at that horrible stage of any busy night, when the dishes still going out and the dirty dishes coming in collide. He was almost there when a surly looking carpenter accosted him. 'I want a rematch, Master Chaucer,' Ifaywer said.

'Not now, Master Carpenter,' Chaucer moved the man to one side. He had no intention of playing queck ever again; life was just too short. Around the corner, he collided with Simon Fawcett of the Corpus Christi Guild, who grabbed Chaucer's smock collar and bumped his own paunch against the lamb.

'Stocks,' the tapicer slurred. 'You were going to put us all in the stocks.'

'Was I?' Chaucer frowned. Suddenly, that all seemed to be a long time ago.

'Well, I don't see any sign of it.' Fawcett breathed ale all over him. 'I was having a laugh with old Sheriff Gower earlier and he didn't mention it. He didn't mention it at all.'

'Lovely,' Chaucer smiled. 'Now, another time, Master Fawcett. I'm a little busy just now.'

'It's all your fault, you know . . .' Fawcett was in full flow, bemoaning his lot in life. He'd fallen off his wagon earlier in the day and – from the look on his face – he was doing it again.

Chaucer knew that, but he hadn't time to argue the toss. Behind the tapicer, he saw the shadow swirl through an archway, making for the chapel. The fireworks burst suddenly in a riot of lights overhead and the crowd oohed as they'd been doing now ever since darkness fell. With no moon, their light was all the brighter and the sparks seemed to hang in the warm spring air like stars. Chaucer looked at Fawcett, who was desperately trying to make his eyes move in the same direction as each other. He brought his knee up under the lamb and felt it thud into the tapicer's crotch. The man groaned and went down. Chaucer beamed briefly; he had wanted to do that to somebody all day – and if it was a guildsman who got in the way, so much the better.

The dark shape was ahead of him now. He had seen it on the battlements as he came back from the town, vague, ill-formed, unreal. He had seen it on and off all night, flitting around corners like a spectral crow, black, sharp and frightening. And it was making for the chapel where Chaucer had promised to meet Richard Glanville. His hopeless quest for answers in the kitchens forgotten, he turned the corner, just remembering to duck in time as the steps went down to the chapel door.

There was a groan from the floor and a candle lay on its side on the flags, still alight and throwing jangling shadows onto the wall, making it hard at first for the comptroller to work out what it was he saw. Richard Glanville lay there, blood oozing from his son's doublet, dark crimson besmottering the satin.

'Rich!' Chaucer knelt, despite his knees and the ever-present lamb, and cradled the man's head.

'It's all right,' the knight croaked. 'I've had worse cutting myself shaving.' He tried to laugh but it didn't work too well, making him cough and double up in pain. His eyes rolled up into his head and he took one enormous breath and then – for what seemed to Chaucer an age – finally he exhaled again and his eyes flickered back to look into the distance. He raised his arm as best he could and pointed to the stairs. 'There!' he wheezed. 'There! After him! Go on!'

There was no dilemma now. Richard Glanville was a survivor. He had come through more wars than Geoffrey Chaucer had had hot dinners and, if he said it would be all right, it would be all right. And Chaucer sensed that this was the last chance he'd have to bring a murderer to book.

As Chaucer bolted for the stairs, Richard Glanville let his head drop back. If this was to be the end, it was a good day to die. He knew that Violante loved him and he knew men who had died for less; he was content. But a spark at the back of his head told him that it would be better to live loved by Violante than to die; he hugged that thought to him and hung on to life by a thread.

Chaucer had no light with him and no poignard at his hip. He knew who was at the top of the stairs and he knew he was armed. What happened now was in the lap of God.

A dark figure stood in the shadows.

'Master Seneschal.' Chaucer didn't risk a bow. He couldn't afford to be caught off balance.

'How did you know?' Niccolò Ferrante emerged into the half-light from the brazier at the turn of the stair. 'How did you know it was me?'

'I didn't,' the comptroller admitted. 'Not at first. It had to be someone familiar with the castle, able to come and go unnoticed. That ruled out the guildsmen and Peter Vickers. It had to be someone who knew his herbs – not the apothecary or his lovesick assistant but a man quietly obsessed with the haute cuisine of his own country. If I'm not mixing my languages there. And of course,' he edged forward, 'that wasn't your only obsession, was it? I saw it on your face tonight.'

'What?' Ferrante sneered. 'What did you see, Fat Comptroller?'

'The look of hatred when Richard Glanville and the Lady Violante shared a kiss. Oh, the others were obvious. Lionel of Antwerp had to die because he had bedded the woman you loved and was cruelly demeaning her by sleeping with a harlot. Father Clement because Violante had come to rely on him, telling him her innermost thoughts that she should have been sharing with only you. With them dead, the lady naturally sought comfort from her little brother. So, it was the hemlock for him.' Chaucer stopped. He saw Ferrante's stiletto tip pointing towards him in the half-light.

'But tonight, it all got away from you, didn't it? You hadn't reckoned with Richard Glanville's love for Violante – and, I suspect, her love for him.'

'*No!*' the Italian roared. 'She doesn't love him. She only has eyes for me!'

His dagger flashed, ripping Chaucer's lamb, wool and a glass eye flying in all directions. The seneschal jerked back, ready to try again.

'So,' Chaucer's hands were raised in supplication, more of Moderata's stitches ripping in protest. He'd struck lucky that time, but Ferrante knew about the padding now and he wouldn't miss again. 'There was no time for clever poison. You had to revert to simpler methods; older, probably. But tell me, Master Seneschal, what would have become of the girl if Giovanni had shared his special morsel with her?'

'She would have died,' the man said, without emotion. 'But that selfish child had never shared a thing in his life; he was spoiled by his father and then by his sister. He never left her side. He was a leech, a leech she could never remove. She should be glad he is dead. And I did it. But you are right, Master Chaucer, to assume I am an expert with a blade. I am good at everything I do. You should not have interfered, Comptroller; I had no quarrel with you.'

'Didn't you?' Chaucer was desperately playing for time. 'Didn't you know about Violante and me?'

'What?'

'God, yes.' The comptroller was trying to catch the man off guard. The Italian was younger, faster, *armed*. 'Did it never make you wonder, when Violante accompanied Lionel to the court, what she did with her time in London? It is a very simple answer – she was with me. You know what she likes, particularly?'

Ferrante screamed and lunged, the dagger driving through Chaucer's lamb and slicing his left forearm, blood pouring over the tatty smocking and the fleece. The Italian drew back for the *coup de grâce*, but a voice in the darkness stopped him.

'Signor Ferrante,' it said, '*ora tocca a te*. You've done enough.'

Chaucer turned, despite himself, to see Death himself standing on the stair below him. The black shadow he had sensed all night was in the open at last. His body was that of a skeleton, bones hanging on a black cloth like those damned souls of Chaucer's dreams, the people of the Pestilence dragging him to Hell. The skull gleamed a sickly ivory in the dying light, shadowed by the deep cowl of the cloak. There were bright eyes, though, peering out from the depths of Hell, blue, piercing and unmistakeable. They spoke of Purgatory for anyone who was trapped in their glare.

Death pointed at Ferrante, his skeleton hands encased in tightly fitting doeskin gloves. He beckoned him with the index finger of his right hand. From his left, a poignard hissed through the air, missing Chaucer by a lamb's whisker and embedding itself in the Italian's chest. The seneschal jerked backwards, dark blood bubbling from his nose and mouth, the stiletto clattering on the stone. He slid down the wall, his eyes crossing as they closed.

Death pulled off the skull and hood and breathed in gratefully. 'Thank God for that,' he said. 'I couldn't see a bloody thing with that hood on.'

Chaucer stood as well as he could on legs that had turned to jelly. His own blood was dripping onto the step, but that was no consequence. 'John Hawkwood,' he said. 'I owe you my life.'

Hawkwood crossed to the lifeless Italian and jerked the knife free. 'Death's dagger,' he said, wiping the blade on the dead man's sleeve. 'That's rather good, isn't it? I expect that phrase to be in one of your God-awful poems one day, Chaucer.'

'Count on it,' the comptroller said. Then he remembered the wounded man on the lower level and turned, wincing at the pain in his arm. 'Richard!'

'Glanville is safe,' Hawkwood said. 'He's also lucky. An inch or two to the left and young Hugh would be wearing the Glanville bear tomorrow. Any chance of a drink, Chaucer? Even the moat looks pretty inviting at the moment, if I'm honest.' And he smiled one of his rare smiles.

And Chaucer smiled too – nothing became a smiler quite like a knife.

# FIFTEEN

The morning of the day after May Day seemed to come all too soon for everyone in the town of Clare and its castle. The guildsmen were lucky – at one of their usually vituperative meetings more years ago than any could remember, someone had suggested the day after May Day should be a holiday for all guildsmen, and it was the only proposal which had ever gone through on the nod. However, the rider added the following year pointed out that this did not apply to anyone working for a guildsman; otherwise, what would they do for food, for shelter and for general care for a whole day more? May Day itself was difficult enough, having to lace your own points and find your own fodder; two days could prove fatal.

Even so, there were a lot of huddled sleepers-out in the inner bailey of Clare that morning. There was birdsong, to be sure, but only when it could be heard over the groans. Even the church bells had been a little unsteady. From certain dark corners, there were sounds of slapped cheeks and outraged shrieks; what was acceptable on May Day was certainly *not* acceptable the day after. Robert Whitlow was the first person to stagger into the centre of the bailey, both cheeks marked with the tattoo of the man who has gone too far, too often. He lurched out of the gate, heading home, calling a cheery good morrow to the guard at the wicket. He was a hard man to keep down, in almost every way.

In the kitchens of Clare, all was chaos. The fires were lit and ready to cook a breakfast fit for kings. The old cook, who had been at the castle since he was a lad, was standing dumbfounded, his ladle dropping glooping lumps of oatmeal onto the table in front of him. Bread, fresh from the ovens, was waiting on a long trestle table to be hacked into slices and taken in to the Great Hall, where a much smaller, quieter crowd than usual was waiting to break its fast. Something was wrong and it wasn't just because everyone was nursing a head still mazy with cuckoo-ale. The cook was uneasy, like a man tethered to a tall tree waiting for the lightning to strike. He turned to his under-cook, a stripling of sixty-five, who looked, if anything, more ill-at-ease than his superior. He usually had the job of stopping the cook from going for the Italian cook – who went by the title *Il Cuoco* – with a meat cleaver. It hadn't been too bad until the old man found out that this meant *The* Cook, and then the atmosphere in the kitchen was always that of a moment before the thunderhead breaks.

But today, nothing. Not an Italian to be seen. No silly little dishes of figs seethed in inferior Italian honey. No stinky loaves with herbs and olives in them. No pitchers of warm wine with yet more honey in it – fit for girls and lovesick boys only, as far as the old cook was concerned. Good English ale was good enough for Englishmen, in his opinion.

The scullions clustered, wide-eyed and silent, against one wall. A few of the smaller maids of all work were whimpering, some with regret at what they had allowed last night, some with fear for what might happen next and some with an uneasy mixture of both. All ears were cocked for the thud of many Florentine-leather-clad feet in the passageway, the raised voice of Niccolò Ferrante urging them on. But it never came.

Good English hobnails rang out instead and the door crashed back. One of the grooms stood there, straw still in his hair and his points unlaced. His eyes were wide with untold news and he took a deep breath. 'You'll never guess what!' he announced, and was immediately enveloped in a clamouring throng.

Sir Richard Glanville lay pale and still on his bed in his sunny solar in the castle of Clare. He had opened his eyes just the merest slit to check how many of his nearest and dearest were sitting in solemn vigil around him and was somewhat disheartened to find he was alone. Someone *had* been there, it was clear. Chairs had been gathered around and then pushed back and, by opening his eyes more widely, he could see who had been sitting where. A wisp of gauze, black as night and fine as a film of a tear, showed that the Lady Violante had sat near his head and if he cast his mind back, he could recall a soft hand in his and a warm voice muttering sweet nothings. He smiled to himself; whether he lived for another minute or another twenty years, he would never be happier than he was in that moment.

The chair on the other side had clearly held his only child, Hugh, squire of the castle. A hat, rakish with feathers and velvet though looking rather the worse for wear, was hanging from a carved protuberance on the chair's back. Richard Glanville smiled again as he remembered his boy saying, 'Pa? Pa?' over and over and then, in a voice full of tears, asking all and sundry whether his father would live. Glanville closed his eyes for a moment on his own tears – he loved that boy more than words could say and he made himself a promise to tell him so; it was easy to forget, sometimes, what needed to be said. A tear ran down from his closed eyes and ran into his ear – he reached up to wipe it away and was pleased that he seemed to be able to move at least one arm.

The third chair was further down the bed, almost at the foot and, for a moment, Richard Glanville thought he might actually have lost the use of his mind. A one-eyed lamb sat there, leaning on the bed. Its head was at a somewhat rakish angle and it really didn't look at all well. Then he remembered; Geoffrey Chaucer had spent a very long day wearing the creature across his stomach in his guise as the Shepherd and the Lost Sheep. Someone had obviously helped him out of his costume and Glanville, in his new-found role as Lover, hoped it was done discreetly, so as to not upset his Lady.

And that seemed to be all the chairs. Somewhere in the back of his mind, Glanville had a memory of a dark shape, leaning against the wall between the two tall windows which faced the bed. He seemed to be a man of few words but he did remember – memories were coming back to him randomly, piecemeal snippets coming and going, insubstantial as fog – Lady Violante going up to the figure and curtsying low, only to be pulled to her feet and enveloped in black arms. Richard Glanville's heart gave a sudden double beat and his stomach muscles twitched – he would kill the rogue; although perhaps he would leave that until the fire currently coursing through his body stopped burning.

He raised his head as much as he could and looked down at the coverlet of the bed. As far as he could judge, he seemed to have everything in the right place. He wiggled his toes and the covers moved. He knew his left arm worked and he tried to move the right, but it seemed tethered to his side. That was a worry, but as he explored with his left hand, he realized that it was because bandages encased him from chest to hip, his right arm swaddled close to his side. He was beginning to remember now. It was dark. There had been people . . . so many people. Then, no one, although he knew that ahead there had to be someone. Then a knife in the dark and . . . nothing, until now.

Richard Glanville cleared his throat and called.

Nothing.

He cleared his throat again and called. 'Hoo!'

Out in the passageway, scurrying feet. Then, a soft hand in his, soft lips on his. His eyes fluttered and he thought to himself – I love him like a brother, but I do hope this isn't Geoff Chaucer.

Chaucer and Hugh Glanville sat in the room opposite where Sir Richard Glanville lay. Lady Violante, they knew, had taken a hard chair into the passageway and sat there, still as a statue, waiting for signs of life. The apothecary, when first found and then roused from a cuckoo-ale stupor, had tended to the knight, with the help of Joyce and her soft linens and had told them that, were he to last the night, it would only be with the help of total peace and quiet. The Angel of Death would come for him whether they were there or not, but sleep would only come if he were left in the dark and total silence. So, reluctantly, they had filed out, John Hawkwood, Chaucer, Hugh and finally, with tears, Violante.

Hugh wouldn't sit still and Chaucer was coming to the point where he would have to snap at him or hit him upside the head. He knew the boy was worried, but the constantly jiggling knee, the sighing, the deep breath betokening a coming question but then nothing but another sigh, were all beginning to wear out his patience.

In the end, he could bear it no longer. 'Hugh,' he said, in his kindest voice, 'all this stress and strain will not make an iota of difference, you know. You heard what the apothecary said.'

'He was drunk,' Hugh snapped. 'I don't know why we listened to him.'

'Joyce wasn't drunk,' Chaucer reminded him. 'And she said the same.'

'What does she know about anything?' Hugh rounded on Chaucer. 'A trollop who all the castle could have if they were minded. She's well known for having no use for the word "No".' He looked at Chaucer suddenly, eyes wide. 'Oh. Geoffrey. I'm so sorry. I forgot you and she were . . . friends.' He bit his lip.

'We *are* friends,' Chaucer said, keeping his temper by a short margin. 'We *were* lovers and now we *are* friends and it would do you good, Hugh Glanville, to remember that love comes in many forms. So keep a civil tongue in your head!' It did him good to have a flash of temper. It would save him later having to go out and find a cat willing to allow a damn good kicking.

'But . . . Pa. He *will* be all right, won't he? You've seen people . . . you've seen people die.' He struggled to go on.

Chaucer sighed. 'I've seen people die,' he said. 'Two in the last twelve hours, to be sure. But I haven't seen your father die. I don't know what you're asking.'

Hugh bowed his head. He needed to ask the right question to get the answer he sought. 'Does my father . . . does my father have a look of death on him, Geoffrey? Is he going to die?'

Chaucer marshalled his thoughts. He was an honest man, but above all, a kind one. He didn't want to give the boy false hope, but, again, he didn't want to dash those hopes either. Before he could answer, the door opened and a black shape entered, silent as nightfall.

'Don't ask questions which have no answer, squire, and you'll have more breath for sensible things.' John Hawkwood was not known to mince his words. 'There is no look of death and those who tell you so are fools. Death comes when death comes, soon or late, and if he has you in his sights, you can be gambolling like a lamb or snatching your breaths as best you can, he will still take you. Master Chaucer and I have seen battlefields, we have seen Pestilence.' He turned to Chaucer and clicked his tongue. 'What about Milan, eh, Master Chaucer? We saw some sights there, didn't we?'

Chaucer nodded and dropped his head to hide his smile.

'So, lad,' Hawkwood said, 'stop worrying. What will be, will be. Or *que sera, sera*, as the wife often reminds me.' He squinted up through the window, assessing the sky. 'It's time I was off, Master Chaucer. My White Company are assembling on the other side of town and we need to run an errand before we head for London.'

'Errand?' Chaucer had never taken Hawkwood for anyone's lackey.

'Oh, a private one. A little visit to a man in Borley. It won't delay us long.'

'Borley . . .' the snarling, angry face of Peter Vickers flashed into his mind. 'Oh, not on my account!' Chaucer flexed his fingers, remembering his bruises, but carefully. His knife wound had been just a scratch, but it was not very comfortable, bandage or no.

'Oh, no, Master Chaucer, not on your account. Indeed, I don't think you could afford me.' And with that, John Hawkwood was gone.

Hugh watched him go and then turned to Chaucer. 'I should thank him. I should . . . join his Company. What he did last night . . . well . . .' He half-stood, to follow.

'You thanked him last night,' Chaucer said. 'And his Company would eat you alive.'

Hugh looked disdainful. 'I don't see why. They're just farm boys from round about and I have been in training for years.'

'Precisely,' Chaucer told him. 'And they have been brought up brawling in the furrows since before they could walk. I repeat – they would eat you alive and throw the bones to the pigs. He knows you're grateful – don't embarrass him with flowery thanks. He's not that kind of man.'

'He hugged Violante.' Hugh was still sulky.

'Well, of course he did. I didn't say he wasn't a man at all.'

Chaucer laughed and punched the boy lightly on his arm. 'Your father is a tough old devil – if anyone can make it to fight another day, it's him. And now, I refuse to speculate any more. Let's talk of something else.'

Hugh looked out of the window, fighting tears. He knew Chaucer was right, but that didn't mean he had to go along with it. After a few moments, he spoke. 'Did you think it was Ferrante?' he asked. 'I didn't have a clue.'

Chaucer was thoughtful. He didn't like to admit he was wrong at the best of times, but when he had been called in to solve a mystery, it was more difficult still. 'At first,' he said, 'I suspected literally everyone. There was hardly a soul in the castle who didn't have a motive, however slight.'

'My money was on Joyce,' Hugh reminded him.

'Yes, I know. Let's just say, once and for all, that Joyce is just a very pleasant woman who means harm to no one and let that be the end of it.'

'Yes, I know, but she and Lionel . . .'

Chaucer looked at him, his lips set.

'Sorry.' Hugh smiled and folded his hands in his lap and adopted an attitude of listening intently.

'You, for instance, had had your light o' love stolen by him, but it wasn't hard to find motives elsewhere. Your father, for example, clearly loved Violante.'

'I *know*!' Hugh's eyes were enormous. 'What about that? Will they get married? Will I have brothers and sisters?'

'You're not a child!' Chaucer snapped. 'Be quiet and listen. Clement was under pain of dismissal. But then, when *he* died, things were different. For a while – for a long while, as you know – I suspected Giovanni, but even before he died last night, I was becoming very doubtful. He just didn't behave like a murderer and, whilst not wishing to speak ill of the dead, he didn't have the brains. Then, I saw the look on Ferrante's face when Violante kissed your father.' He paused and looked up, waiting for another outburst, but Hugh simply looked back at him, blandly. 'And I realized that anyone who went near Violante would die. I would have been next after your father. Then Hawkwood. Then you . . . he would never have been able to stop. He was mad for love. Looking back,

I suppose I should have seen the signs. He was found at least once in the wrong part of the castle at dead of night – I expect he was spending all his hours pacing, checking, making sure no one went near his Lady. At the time, it just didn't occur to me. He was so . . . passionate about things. I didn't know how passionate, that was the trouble.'

Hugh looked down at his entwined hands, then looked up. 'That's an Italian for you, I suppose,' he said. 'They . . .'

But before he finished, they both heard it. From across the passageway, a faint 'Hoo!'

'The houppelande,' she spread her arms across the three robes spread on the bed. 'I thought the lime green, for the journey. Remind you of the spring when you get near to that old London. There was a darn under the armpit there, not very well done, but I unpicked it and did it again and you'd never know . . .'

Chaucer turned from his packing and went over to the woman standing beside the bed. He took her hands and kissed her, softly, on the lips.

'Joyce,' he said. 'It doesn't matter a jot what I wear on my journey. I am just going back to my life, my normal life, my old life. No one will notice when I get back and hardly anyone will have noticed I have been away. My table will be groaning with papers, sealed with seals as big as my hand but, at the end of the day, for all that paper and wax and ink, there will be nothing. Just some fleeces and some flagons and some bribes.'

Her eyebrows went up. That didn't sound like her Geoff.

'I don't say I take them, Joyce. I simply say there will be bribes. And I will take off my lime-green liripipe and will light my candle and add up and subtract and . . . well, I will be Comptroller of the King's Woollens again.' He gave her another kiss. 'Now, where's that lad of yours? Are you *sure* you want him to go to London? It's a long way from home.'

She shook her head. 'Of course I'm not sure, Geoff. But it was all I could do to stop him going with that White Company and I know at least in London you'll be there to stop him doing anything foolish.'

Chaucer wasn't so sure of that. He had done many foolish things in his life but tried to let them damage only himself. Once or twice . . . but he didn't need to burden Joyce with that. He smiled. 'Just one thing, Joyce . . .'

She tapped his nose. 'Another, Geoff?'

He shook his head. 'No, not that. I'm too old for another, these days, don't forget. No. I just need to know. Is the lad . . .?'

'Yours? Lord love you, Geoff. Of course he isn't yours. With that nose?'

Chaucer wasn't sure whether he was glad or sorry.

'I reckon he might be the blacksmith's lad's, but . . .' she laughed. 'I am what I am, Geoff, never forget that. Now, be off with you.' She gave his houppelande a final pat and brushed a stray hair from his shoulder. She leaned in and whispered, 'Even London's pretty at this time of year, I hear. Goodbye.'

The castle watched with its many eyes as the bright green dot disappeared into the trees. The mare tripped lightly; her rider was a little too portly to be totally comfortable in the saddle and there were many miles still to go. But he had company and that comforted the watchers. They didn't want to think of him, all by himself, with that long journey ahead. If the castle walls had ears as well as eyes, they would hear a voice on the breeze, dying as the trees engulfed the speaker.

'A knyght ther was, and that a worthy man, that fro the tyme that he first bigan to riden out, he loved chivalrie, trouthe and honour, fredom and curteisie . . .'